Don't Knock The Corners Off

Don't Knock The Corners Off

Caroline Glyn

Coward—McCann, Inc.
New York

c. 5

Copyright © 1963 by Caroline Glyn

FIRST AMERICAN EDITION, 1964

Second Impression

Manufactured in the United States of America

This is a work of fiction. Occasionally I have mixed together one or two characteristics of people I have known or who have been described to me, and combined them with invented ones, to form a completely imaginary portrait. The same applies to schools. But I want to make it quite clear that no character and no school in this novel has, or except by a series of coincidences could even seem to have, any actual existence at all.

The eleven-plus examination in England is taken by all children at government schools at the age of eleven. Four out of five always fail, and then have no hope of going on to a university later. Those who pass go to grammar schools, where they study for the G.C.E. examination. Unless they do well in this, they leave school at sixteen. Only the very ablest pupils can get into a university.

C.G.

PART ONE

Antonia Rutherford, precocious nine-year-old with an Artist father and a doting mother is sent to an English school. Her experiences in winning recognition from suspicious and reluctant teachers and students finally win a place for herself when "the corners of her personality are planed down."

1

"THIS WON'T DO, it isn't in the least shabby. I'll find you something from the pile I was going to send to the refugees," Mummy said.

"Look, here are the socks I never mended, and the blouse with red paint all over it!" I shouted triumphantly. I was going to be the worst dressed little girl in the school. Nobody would guess I had a bedroom to myself and went abroad in the summer. I could just sit at the back and be clever. No one need ever know I had never been to school before, nor that I didn't live in a Council flat. I wished that I could take the eleven-plus now, this very moment. I should of course do brilliantly, get full marks plus some extra for age. In my excitement I broke my shoe-lace. All the better, I thought, and didn't try to do it up.

In the yard I could still see the remains of the bonfire which we had made, one riotous evening about a month before, out of Snelling's *Arithmetical Exercises*, after I had finished it. For months—years—I had looked forward gleefully to consigning to the flames all those stupid children who could never count their pocket money and never stopped quarrelling over their marbles. Now at school, I should probably be going back to them, I reflected sadly.

The school was red-brick and dingy. I drifted into the custody of a girl called Sandra. She had been called in from the playground to show me over the school. I was amazed to see the number of dark stone staircases that had been crammed into the building. I didn't say so, though. She didn't talk either.

She led me up to our classroom. We stood in the doorway and surveyed it. A man in dungarees suddenly pushed his way rudely between us, without even glancing at us. Sandra stepped politely aside, but I stood my ground. Obviously some caretaker, who didn't know his way round the school. What right had he to barge in here, I thought indignantly.

9

"Antonia!" Sandra whispered, shocked. "You mustn't stand in a teacher's way!"

Some boys and girls, looking much better dressed than I had expected, began to come in and sit down at the desks. Sandra went and sat down too. I stood around miserably. I couldn't see anywhere to sit. I wished after all that someone did know that this was my first day at school, for then I might have been told what to do.

"I suppose you must be the new girl," said the teacher, scornfully I thought. "Antonia Rutherford."

I said, "Yes." He told me to sit down. I still couldn't see a place. I blundered about unhappily. He began to call our names out; everyone answered, "Yes, sir." I supposed this was the lunch register. I knew I was going to have lunch at home, and so when he called, "Rutherford," I answered promptly, "No, sir."

Everyone turned round and gazed at me in astonishment. Instead of going on, the teacher folded his arms and stared at me furiously.

"You're here, aren't you?" he bellowed.

"Why—yes," I stammered.

"Well, then!" he shouted. I cringed.

He made us recite all our arithmetical tables aloud. I began to cheer up. Here at least was something I could do.

I began to look at my classmates. They were all still looking at me, but I didn't care any more, they would all merely see how well I knew my tables. Suddenly I realized I wasn't attending, and stammered and forgot what table we had got to. Perhaps they weren't looking at me after all.

I thought how serious they were, how even the most ruffianly-looking of the boys was attending and being good. I was surprised. I had read so many school books in which everyone took everything in dead earnest, that I had imagined that in actual fact people would take school as a big joke. I had been quite prepared to do so myself, and felt all thrown out.

Everyone I knew had expected me to go to some expensive boarding-school. But Daddy said he wanted me to get to know all sorts and classes of people, not just the boarding-school type, and that anyway it was either boarding-school fees or holidays abroad, and not both. Why pay fees anyway when there was perfectly good education available for the asking, quite free?

10

Besides, he had heard that you learnt much more at a state school than at some play-way boarding-school where you never did anything except riding and ballet. "It's all right for debs, but not for our Totty." And so here I was at primary school. Daddy had chosen the best one near us, with the most eleven-plus passes.

"Sir, can I go to the cloakroom?"

"Please, sir, I haven't got a pen."

We had finished the tables. Everyone was talking. I leant across on to Sandra's desk and tried to join brightly in her conversation with another girl. They ignored me.

Sir was writing fractions on the board. Once again I felt a wave of pleasure. I knew fractions inside out. Mummy had always said that no one learns anything at school. You just have to know it all before you go. That was why I had had to suffer so much with Snelling.

I found I didn't know fractions as well as I thought. At least, I got several wrong. I was recovering from this, and wishing someone would let me join in one of the conversations that were going on incessantly behind the lesson books, when to my surprise one of the boys stood up and rang a large bell. Instantly hubbub broke out. Sir seemed to disappear. Everyone began to dash screaming towards the door. Panicking, I clutched at Sandra, and was dragged down some different flights, apparently endless, of dark stone stairs. There seemed to be hundreds of children in this wild stampede. Suddenly we emerged on to a large muddy stretch of asphalt. I felt giddy; I couldn't imagine where we could be. On we dashed recklessly, through a hole in the wall into a small enclosure with five or six doors along one wall. I thought it looked uncommonly like a public lavatory. Here we halted. There didn't seem to be any boys.

I let go of Sandra. She was chatting to some other girls as if nothing had happened. I tried to look bright and pretend I was chatting with them. They took no notice of me.

I said to one of them, "My name's Antonia. I'm new. Where is this, please?"

She didn't even turn her head.

In another corner there was a group of girls looking at a picture book. I went up and tried to look too. There wasn't room. I went away.

It was very crowded; it wasn't any bigger than my own bedroom, and there must have been dozens of girls. Most of them were bouncing balls against the row of doors. In desperation I went up to one and shook her.

"Please tell me! What's happened? Where are we? What are we doing?"

She gazed at me, and uttered the word, "Play." All was now clear. This was some form of recreation room. It seemed decidedly small, and muddy, and smelly. The noise was deafening. It was raining, and there wasn't even a roof. I leant against the wall and shivered.

"Hullo, Schoolgirl! Back already? What was it like? How did it go? What did you do?"

I said, "We did sums."

"What else? How did you get on?"

"Nothing else. I got on all right, thank you."

"What happened? Oh, tell us all about it!"

I considered. Now that I was home I couldn't remember anything about school. Not anything special to tell people, anyhow. I made a great effort and said, "All the boys wore shorts."

"All?"

"Yes. And all the girls wore pinafore dresses."

"All?"

"Yes. Like me."

"And?" said Daddy.

I racked my brains. "Nobody would talk to me."

"Ah, but did you talk to them?"

"Yes."

"Well, that's easy," Mummy said brightly. "You just take some chocolates to school and give them to everyone, and then they'll all be friendly. Just you see."

"Yes, why not try it?" said Daddy eagerly. Everyone was looking at me expectantly.

"Good idea," I said weakly. I tried to visualize myself handing a chocolate to Sandra. Her expression—no, she wouldn't have an expression, because she would have her back to me and wouldn't turn round. It seemed my only hope, however. I bought a pound of soft centred chocolates, covered in silver paper with different coloured patterns on each one, depending on the flavour. I wondered if I would get any. It seemed unlikely, as they would be sure to be snapped up straight away.

I was finally given a desk next to a girl called, I discovered, Felicity Dearchild. I don't know how I found out about the Felicity, everyone called her Dearchild, just as I was Rutherford. She was the bad girl of the class, but I, all unsuspecting, put a chocolate shaped like a strawberry furtively into her desk.

"Coo, you silly little thing!" she roared in my face when she found it. She was about twice my size; her hair was filthy and couldn't have been brushed for years—if at all. "Just shows you're new." She glanced at my super-shabby pinafore dress. "You little fright!" she screeched. "What sort of a mum have you got to let you go around like that?"

I cowered. I could very well have said exactly the same back, but I didn't; after all, she was bigger than me. She didn't eat the chocolate. Later I found it squashed on the floor.

I noticed how everybody avoided one tall boy who stood apart at the back of the classroom with a sneering expression on his face. Just what I want, I thought, pleased; I went up to him and dropped a chocolate covered with blue forget-me-nots in his breast pocket. He gaped at me and forgot to sneer. Suddenly I realized that the entire class was gaping at me too. I couldn't imagine why.

It seemed a good idea to win the friendship of a short, dark boy with a ferocious expression, who was engaged in slamming his desk lid, apparently absorbed. I gave him a truffle. He didn't take it and it dropped on to the floor. He gave a blood-curdling whoop and kicked it across the room. All the boys sprang after it, yelling, and began a violent game of football with it. The girls huddled in a corner in terror. The poor truffle flew to and fro, and presently hit the ceiling and stuck there. Sir gave it a resigned look when he came in and saw it. I took the rest of the chocolates home; they weren't very nice, after all.

I began to get things sorted out when we went down to play this time. As I crossed the corner of the wide asphalt stretch, ready to dive into the small enclosure, I was utterly baffled to see a group of girls chasing each other at the far end. I gazed in surprise, while the bigger girls continued to pour through the little doorway. Suddenly everything came into focus. This was a playground, and the place in there really was the lavatories. It

13

was much nicer out here, I thought. What a silly I had been yesterday!

Suddenly behind me I heard a scream of triumph. My skirt was flung up, exposing my long knickers. Mummy always bought me boys' pants, because they were thicker. All round me was a ring of tiny girls, jumping and dancing and shouting.

"Coo! Just look at 'er. She's got her father's pants on, and she's made messes in them! Pooh-pooh-pants! Pooh-pooh-pants!"

I tried to say sternly, "Shut up, you."

"Pooh-pooh-pants!" they shrieked back.

I held my dress tightly round my legs and wobbled sedately into the little enclosure to hide, feeling very hot in the face, and hoping nobody had noticed. Outside in the playground, the chant seemed to be still going on. I glanced out. Those merciless midgets had cornered another big girl, and were doing their war-dance round her. It was hard to remember how sweet they had looked in prayers. I realized at last why all the big girls stayed permanently in the lavatories.

A voice just outside suddenly said loudly, "True, Dare, Love, Kiss, Lick or Promise?" I peeped out; it was the ringleader of Pooh-Pooh-Pants. She was addressing some girls lined up in front of her. I listened, fascinated. One of them answered, "Lick."

"Go and lick that girl under the arms!"

Uncomfortable pause. "No."

"Give me your shoe as a forfeit."

"I'll have True," said another voice.

"Is it true that you've just kissed the ground?"

The girl did so; I saw her. "Yes!"

"Dare, please," said another.

"Dare!" said the girl who was It gloatingly. She came and looked through the doorway at me. She really did look just like a rat.

"I dare you to go up to that girl," pointing at me, "pull up her dress, and pull down her knickers." I screamed. To my intense relief the whistle went. The girl's face fell, but she made up for it by clinging on to the shoe.

"You can't have it back, you've got to win it back," she said to her victim. They were still quarrelling about it on the stairs as I turned into my classroom.

14

I was beginning to get the hang of some of the girls' names. There were King, Pope, Wilson, Page, Barker, Smith, Little and Tatley, and they were alternately Sandra and Valerie with a couple of Lindas. The Sandra I had first met was Sandra King. Most of them were prefects. They never stopped talking unless I spoke to them. On the other side of me sat Linda Tatley; she was obviously delighted to have me, new and helpless, next to her. She instructed me, warned me, shepherded me around, sometimes even dictated my work to me. I followed her about like a grateful dog, and considered her my good angel.

When I got home, there was a fat, brown envelope waiting for me, marked "Pioneer." My poems back, I thought as I opened it. It wasn't. It was two copies of the September issue. I glanced down the index; my hands were damp. There it was! *The Spirit of Day* by Antonia Rutherford, page 26.

"Whoopee! Wow!" I shouted, charging up the stairs, "Mummy! Daddy! I've done it! I'm in!" Everyone was round me, flushed and excited.

"Which poem?"

"Which magazine?"

"That's your sixth in print."

"Show us!"

"Triunfadora! Come and celebrate." Everybody was shouting, "Celebrate! Celebrate!"

> "Beautiful as a rose, she led me
> Through fields where the sun always shone.
> Where a silver-paper river lay motionless
> Where seed-knotted grass bent upon
> Dancing poppy-maidens, clothed in silk,
> Frivolous, laughing, tripping up on
> Nests of clover, wine and milk;
> So it seemed; and as I watched, the more
> I knew the fair Day Spirit guided me
> And taught me beauties that I never knew before."

I crooned it to myself. It certainly looked good in print. Was it really the sixth to be published? Six was my lucky number, I thought happily. I remembered that five had been, a few months ago, and before that, four. Perhaps it would be seven soon, now that I'd broken into *Pioneer*, which had been my ambition for years.

"Look what I've got for our little poet," called Mummy. She burst into the room. "I saw them on a stall as I was going to buy you some crème-de-menthe to celebrate in, and knew they were just your affair. There!" She unwrapped her parcel.

"Oh! Gladioli!" I gasped. They were beautiful. They almost inspired me . . . yes . . . "Cream and flame in a sheath of green," —no, not quite . . . "Mummy, have you got a pencil?" I asked.

2

THE FOURTEENTH OF September was my tenth birthday. Double figures, I thought, feeling awed. That really is as good as grown up.

There were boys behind me and in front of me. They were very friendly, much friendlier than the girls, I decided, except of course for Tatley. The one in front was called Matthews. He had freckles, and ink all over his handkerchief. Apparently he was very clever, and so I was pleased to find that he was fascinated by my family life and never ceased questioning me.

"What? Your father paints pictures? Really? That's his job? Coo!"

When I told him that I'd had six poems published he was deeply impressed. I think he spread it all over the class; anyhow I gradually began to find that I had stopped being "new." One day I remarked to Sandra that there didn't seem to be any school rules, and she replied. She said vaguely that there were, but they didn't really begin to work for the first week of term.

I began to learn how to walk with my dress held so tightly round my legs that I could only move them from my knees down, without falling over. All the girls in the top classes did this. I began to think it funny, rather than a hardship. Perhaps those little Class Four menaces weren't really so bad. After all, they didn't mean any harm. They were only joking.

There came a yell from behind me: "Look what I've found!" I looked round. There was one of them, hopping on one foot and brandishing my purse triumphantly in the air. My purse! With my precious front door key, the fourth I'd had; I'd already lost three. "Never again," I had promised Mummy. "I'll take care of this one." I must have dropped it. I could have kicked myself.

17

"My purse, thank you," I said nervously, approaching the girl.

"Hee-hee! Look what I've found!" she shouted to her accomplices, and darted away. This was going too far: I was frightened.

"Come here! That's my purse," I bellowed, and bounded after her. It was hopeless; she was as slippery as an eel, and clearly had no intention of relinquishing her find. In desperation I went to beg help from Pope, Wilson and Little. We chased her at length into a corner. She hadn't got the purse. Eventually we found it in the bottom of the lavatory, which no one ever flushed. Luckily, Little had no sense of disgust and she fished it out for me.

I ran upstairs to the classroom, feeling a bit shaken. As I passed a particularly dark nook on those dark stairs, someone—or something—suddenly reached out and grabbed hold of me, and pulled me back into the corner. I screamed, and fought, hitting and kicking into the blackness. Whatever it was held me like a vice. I pummelled and squirmed.

A voice said, "Oh, let her go, she's new." I was suddenly released; I reeled, and staggered on up, feeling dizzy. Another voice suddenly called, "Come here, you!" I ran faster than ever and collapsed gasping into my chair.

"Who were those people? Why did they jump out at me on the stairs like that?" I asked Linda Tatley, feeling as frightened and bewildered as I had on the first day. She was writing something; she looked at me coldly.

"Look, when a stair monitor tells you to come here, you come, see? You were running on the stairs just now. King told you to come out. You didn't come, and so I'm writing your name in the prefects' book." So it had been a prefect who collared me.

I gazed at her in consternation. Somehow I'd contrived to do something wrong. Was being written in the prefects' book a very grave matter, I wondered?

"But ... is running wrong?" I faltered. Were the school rules coming into operation, as Sandra had warned?

"Yes, it is," she snapped.

"Oh, leave off, Tatley," said the boy behind me. He was big and handsome and a prefect too. He suddenly snatched the book away from her and crossed my name out. She didn't protest. I thanked the boy warmly. He frowned.

18

Sir came in, in his dungarees. He had enormous teeth, like a horse. Arithmetic again, I thought sadly; I caught myself thinking it and deliberately made myself think : Oh good, arithmetic, today I really will master those fractions.

"Come out here, you, Johnson and Alcock," he called. They were two tiny boys who sat at the back and got all their sums right and answered Sir's trick questions when nobody else could, and sometimes even caught Sir out on them himself. They came out, positively radiating cleverness. Sir produced a six-foot ruler from somewhere and made Johnson hold it across the middle of Alcock.

"Now then, Alcock, you're five-eighths," said Sir. The class went into hysterics for several minutes. "And Johnson's a quarter."

"Quarter-pint size," said Matthews loudly. I thought no one would ever recover from the laughing-fit this sent us into.

"And we want to divide Alcock into Johnson", Sir went on ruthlessly. "What do we do?" Nobody answered, more because we couldn't speak for laughing than because we didn't know, I think. "We turn the divisor upside down and multiply!" And he seized Alcock round his waist and held him upside down. An enormous tangle of string fell out of his pocket, all tied up with an armoury of pen-knives. The class was in uproar. I saw Miss Lovely (that's the nearest I can get to what her name sounded like) appear, looking angry, on the other side of the glass partition between the classrooms.

"And anyone who forgets how to divide fractions will be boiled in oil!" roared Sir. And as a matter of fact, nobody ever did, not even me.

Then Miss Lovely came in and complained. Sir, rather sheepishly, told us to be quiet. We all found this quite impossible. He made us stand on our chairs with our hands on our heads until we were quiet. That sobered us down a little. Then he set us an exercise from Snelling. I don't know if anyone really did it. I began it, got stuck on the first one, and started laughing again. I was still laughing when I went home for lunch.

I had to walk through some hideous streets of villas on my way home. Their only quality was that they were lined with cherry trees. I noticed the leaves were beginning to fall, and I walked very slowly, gazing up into the trees in the hope of catching a leaf and getting a lucky month.

"Whatever are you looking at, Antonia?" I heard someone say in a surprised voice. I jumped, and looked round. It was the headmaster, this half legendary character of whom I had stood in awe ever since I first heard I was going to school.

"Oh, hullo, sir," I said idiotically, and smiled wanly. "Well, sir, I'm trying to catch falling leaves—happy months, you know," I explained lamely. He gave me a strange look and glanced up into the tree.

"Good idea; I'm glad you're having fun," he said. He was a kindly man; I hoped he didn't think me quite dotty. He had reason to, after that interview with Mummy when she had explained to him why I was going to school for the first time aged nearly ten. "We didn't think Antonia's temperament was really suited to school, and so we've tried to spare her as much as possible, sending her late," Mummy had said. I tried not to be cross with her; after all, she had meant well.

My pinafore dress was a little less shabby, after I had told Mummy about the disapproving glances the other girls had given the original one. I still had to wear my bright red coat, however. It looked so conspicuous in the cloakroom, and everyone looked at it so disgustedly, that, warm and jolly though it was, I longed for my raincoat to arrive. We had scoured the shops to find one with a proper tartan lining just like everyone else's. At all costs I had to be just like everyone else.

When we were set a composition to write later on "My Holiday" I wrote an inspired description of Lake Como, which we had visited the year before. Sir took a fancy to it, perhaps because he didn't find any mistakes, and read it out aloud to the class. I waited in suspense to see how they would take it. Most of them were mildly envious; some of them, including Matthews, appeared to be quite overawed—not by the fact that I had been abroad, but by the composition itself which, they declared, was "wonderful."

I felt relieved. My secret about my foreign holidays had come out, and everybody was still as friendly as ever. In fact they were becoming friendlier every day. All the girls seemed willing to chat with me in spite of the fact that I couldn't for the life of me play Two Balls against a wall, nor even, I discovered, One Ball. All the other girls performed feats of juggling, bouncing balls between their legs, over their legs, backwards and forwards. I just had to be an admiring spectator.

I had begun to know my way around the school, though it was a mystery to me how there was a large playground where there should have been the street. But Tatley continued to order me about as if it were still my first day. This rapidly changed from helpful to tiresome, and when she took it into her head to do my work for me she was a positive bore. As soon as I had got going on some exciting composition she would lean across, read it, and announce authoritatively:

"That's all wrong. Cross it out!"

As I very well knew that it was nothing of the sort, I would indignantly refuse. Then she would lean over, snatch my pen away, and cross it out herself by main force. I tried to think that she was trying to help me. I couldn't understand it though, because my work was always perfectly good. Sir even preferred it to hers and often used to read it out to the class, when he never even mentioned hers. In arithmetic, however, which I really did find difficult, she never helped me at all. I found her behaviour very baffling.

I came down late for play one morning, and had to cross the playground fully exposed to the Class Four girls. They were, as usual, standing in a long line. As I passed them, one girl suddenly shouted, "Watering-can!" and the whole line spat at me. I jumped several feet and ran for the lavatories.

I asked Tatley, "What was that for?"

She looked stonily at me and said, "Honestly, you can't take a joke, can you? It was only a game. We play who can spit farthest."

I glowered at her, and wiped the spit off my dress.

There came one happy day when a boy called Thompson, smiling all over his face, came up to me and whispered that Eric Stevens was in love with me.

I stared at him incredulously. "What—me? Which one's Stevens?" I asked Thompson.

"That one with the dark eyes," he answered. I picked him out; he had a mooning look on his face, just like a cow. I felt flattered. If it were true, it would be a compliment indeed.

"Now," said Thompson, producing a piece of paper folded so that I couldn't see what was written on it, "you just sign here."

I guessed what it was. I signed my name, "Penelope Gum-drop."

21

"Hey! Sign properly," said Thompson.

I caught at the paper and unfolded it, and got a glimpse of the words, "Darling Eric, I love you very much." Then Thompson with a shriek snatched it back. It tore across the middle. I heard a great sigh go up. I glanced up and saw half the boys watching us. So it was a conspiracy!

I began to concoct a similar note for Thompson, but, as usual, Sir came in at just the wrong moment and gave us a mental arithmetic test. I was incredibly bad at mental arithmetic. I was as quick as I could, but even so I only managed to do about every fifth question. Most of what I did I got hopelessly wrong. By the time this dreadful ordeal was over, the paper I was writing the message on had mysteriously disappeared from my desk.

A week or two later the headmaster made an announcement in prayers which set everyone talking.

"The boys and the girls are going to be put together in one playground in future, with classes One and Two in the back playground and classes Three and Four in the front one."

When I heard that I jumped for joy. I was going to get rid of those horrid little girls. Bliss! To be able to walk freely round the playground without being attacked and molested; what more could anyone desire? Eagerly I waited for playtime.

I was half killed on the stairs, as we poured down at a quarter to eleven. I hadn't realized that a couple of classes of boys could make such a stampede. I had thought that the crush was total chaos before, but it was nothing to this. At last, battered and breathless, I got through the bottleneck and into the playground. Rejoicing in my loosely swinging skirt, I ran out into the open, and promptly had the wind knocked out of me by a large and muddy football which landed hard in my middle. I collapsed in agony into a puddle. A gang of boys, yelling and screaming, dashed across the playground in pursuit of a couple of girls and gave me a few hefty kicks on their way. I tried to get up. The boys who were playing football suddenly saw where their ball had got to. They flung themselves upon me, kicking and fighting for the ball. Never mind what happened to that silly girl! I got a boot in my eye, a boot on my head, boots all over me, boys all over me. I tried to wriggle away. Another boy, leaping into the fray, landed square on my tummy. I couldn't breathe, I couldn't see, there was mud in my mouth; I thought I must die soon.

Suddenly all the boys were gone. I sat up. The ball was zooming to and fro like a torpedo at the other end of the playground. I was near tears. Then I saw that the ground was littered with boys who actually were in tears. I looked at them disdainfully, and decided that after all I'd never felt less like crying. The terrible football flew over my head. With a cry I leapt up and made for the haven of the lavatories. As I ran, little O'Brien, that same boy I had given the truffle to, flung himself upon me and dragged me towards a dark and gloomy nook under the fire-escape, at the farthest corner of the playground. I could hear shrieks coming from it. I fought and shouted. He almost twisted my arm off. We were in the shelter entrance. Dimly I saw the tall, sneering boy, Roberts, torturing Valerie Wilson in some way and making her cry, and a weedy but murderous boy, Skinner, bashing Sandra on the head with her shoe. With a last desperate effort, I broke away from O'Brien and ran for my life. I couldn't get into the lavatories because they were besieged by boys. I huddled in a recess in the wall, keeping an eye on the football, watching Roberts and O'Brien and Skinner, and taking care to hop out of the way when one of the constant wrestling bouts came dangerously close. I couldn't avoid getting bashed up once or twice, none the less. I couldn't understand what had happened to the boys in the playground. They were on the whole quiet, well-behaved, friendly and hardworking in class. Now they were monsters. Even Matthews and Alcock were fighting furiously. Half the boys were permanently crying. I decided that hell would be just like this when I arrived.

Playtime got worse and worse. I began to have nightmares that made me afraid to go to sleep again after I had woken up. A little later the school took us on a bus journey through an area which was smoky and grey and full of tall chimneys, to watch our team play netball against a school there. One night the next week, after a particularly horrible dream, I wrote another poem.

"Grey, grim, menacing, the factory walls rose high
Scowling over the slimy, grimy street,
Grey walls, grey cheerless slums, grey sky,
An oppressing, unceasing nightmare.

23

So often in my dreams I have been chased
Through pitch-black streets, by some disguised
Monster, as mad donkey, man or ghost,
Unknown fear weighing on my shoulders.

This haunted world beyond the factory I have found,
Where nothing happens, nothing changes; it is all the same.
Where Something clutches me, drags me, bound
Back to never-ceasing fear."

I felt awful the next morning. I looked at myself in the mirror and thought my eyes seemed queer. Washing didn't make any difference. Mummy took one look at me, stuck the thermometer in my mouth and kept me back from school. Daddy never got up before half past ten, and we all had breakfast together at eleven o'clock. As we sat down, I produced my poem, and waited, shivering with suspense, to see what they would say.

Mummy read it, looked at me in alarm, re-read it, put on a face of concentration, and said, "Well, you've never written anything like it before."

"But do you like it?" I asked anxiously.

"It's very queer," she said. She gave it to Daddy, and said, "I see now what's wrong with you. I hate to think that this is how you pass your nights."

"But the poem? Is it all right?" I begged.

"It's gorgeous!" Daddy said.

"I wonder whether we ought after all to have sent her to school, just see what it's done to her," worried Mummy. "She used to write such happy little poems."

Daddy meanwhile was appreciating it properly. I turned hopelessly from Mummy, and asked him, "What do you think of it?"

"I think it's your best yet. It's fascinating," said Daddy reassuringly. "I should send it to *Doorway*."

"*Doorway*! What, that highbrow thing?" I said, stupefied.

"Yes, why not?"

"But—I might as well try to get into *The Times Lit. Supp.*," I protested.

"Try them both," he said.

"It's a waste of postage. And don't forget who's going to have to type the copies," I grumbled.

Daddy crashed his fist down on the table. "Shut up! Get a piece of writing-paper and take down this letter to the editor of *Doorway*. 'Dear Sir'.... For goodness' sake don't start crying!"

"Run and get the thermometer, it's high time we took your temperature again," said Mummy.

3

I WAS ILL FOR a week after that. When I went back to school I had to give an absence note to Miss Lovely, according to some school rule. I showed it to Sir first.

He said, "You haven't put her name on the envelope."

"Er—oh," I said. "Um—well, sir. Please could you tell me how you spell it?"

"Good grief, don't you know your own teacher's name? Well, you ought to," he said and left me none the wiser. I thought this grossly unfair, as she didn't even teach our class. I had to ask Tatley, which was most annoying, as I was trying to become independent of her. I said to her, "Please, how do you spell Miss Lovely?"

"M-I-S-S," she said, and stopped.

"Go on," I said, thinking her the most boring and tiresome girl I had ever met.

She didn't answer. I decided she didn't know. I went round the class, asking all the girls, but none of them knew.

"Have none of you ever had to bring a note?" I asked exasperated.

In the end Matthews addressed the envelope for me.

"What an odd name," I remarked, wondering how he knew when nobody else did.

"Oh, not really," he answered airily, "All women teachers have silly names like that."

I went down warily to play. I let the boys go first and then dashed for the lavatories.

"Are we doomed to spend all our playtime in here for ever?" I asked Valerie Barker. It was specially smelly that day.

"Well, we all stay in here," she said, obviously thinking nothing of it.

The girls by the doorway suddenly screamed and came scuttling across to us, followed by an invasion of murderous-looking boys headed by Roberts, Skinner and O'Brien. I stood paralysed with horror. Boys! In here! Weren't we safe even in the girls' lavatories?

They seized on Barker, Little, and some Class One girls I didn't know, and dragged them out screaming. O'Brien was more ambitious, however. He advanced resolutely into our little refuge, with his eyes fixed on me. Without stopping our screeching, we threw ourselves on him and bundled him into one of the lavatories, and leant against the door, still shrieking non-stop. There seemed to be a great commotion going on inside, though I couldn't really hear much through our frantic yelling.

Suddenly the door burst open and O'Brien dashed out in headlong flight, pursued by a perfect Gorgon of a Dearchild, busily scrubbing his neck with the lavatory brush. We had shut her in with O'Brien, but she wasn't going to stand any nonsense. O'Brien never came back.

I peeped out of the doorway, feeling very bloodthirsty. There was a nice fierce tussle going on just outside. Just as things were getting interesting, one of the boys burst into tears and sat down nursing his arm. Instantly his enemy was all concern.

"Oh, David, have I hurt you? Oh, I'm really sorry. Here, have a pear drop."

I looked away in disgust. All the fights seemed to end like that. Now then, I told myself sternly, of course these boys cry all the time, it's perfectly natural. They've every reason. They aren't even safe in the boys' lavatory. And I'm glad to see that they're kind to their vanquished opponents.

Roberts, the tall boy, and little Thompson came into my field of vision, fighting. Roberts gave Thompson a kick in his stomach and banged his head ferociously against the wall. Thompson doubled up and started to cry. I waited for the pear drop. Roberts just gave a snarl and laughed scornfully, and to my disgust and amazement flung poor Thompson on to the ground and jumped on him.

"Ugh! Did you see that?" I exclaimed to Valerie Clark.

"Oh, Roberts you mean? Oh, he's just a bully," she said laconically. "He always fights like that."

A bully! So he was. I hadn't thought of it. And I had given him a chocolate. My face went all hot when I thought of it.

The first thing we all noticed when we came back from our

half-term holiday was that all our desks had been rearranged, and that all the girls were sitting next to their deadly enemy on one side and to the boy they "loved" on the other. I don't know what the boys thought of this. The deadly enemies were, near me, O'Brien, Skinner, Roberts and Dearchild. Sir wouldn't let us put ourselves straight, to everybody's fury. I was the unluckiest of all, for on one side I had Roberts, and on the other I only had Valerie Wilson. She giggled and chattered and was cleverer than me at sums, just like all the other girls.

"You don't want to sit close to that horrid boy," she said, looking at Roberts, who was busily breaking his ruler into little bits. "Pull your desk right up to mine and then we can talk during the broadcast."

I thought this an excellent idea. But Sir, who had an absolute genius for poking in at the wrong moments, came round and straightened all the rows of desks and put the prefects on to keep them straight. I was left uncomfortably close to Roberts, and hoped he wouldn't dominate me like Tatley.

During the broadcast he settled down to read a magazine behind his desk. Out of curiosity I peeped over his shoulder at it, and saw a large photograph of a woman with nothing on at all. I suppose he must have seen me recoiling, for he looked at me and said, with his usual sneer, holding up the photograph,

"Wonder what you'd look like dressed up like that?"

All the nearby boys looked at me and grinned.

"Not like that, anyway," I said firmly, and tried to listen to the broadcast. It was apparently Real Factory Sounds from a Real Factory. That faint background rumble was the commentary, I realized. The poor wireless wheezed and crackled and roared. After a specially ear-splitting squeak Matthews said loudly.

"What's this—birdsong?"

Once again we dissolved into laughter. In desperation Sir turned the wireless off and gave us some money sums to do.

I started to labour away at them. As I was trying to think what fifty-three pence was, I was interrupted by a cuff on the arm.

"Here, you, Buddersmud," said Roberts. "What's two twos?"

"How should I know?" I snapped. Twelve into fifty-three goes . . .

"Oi! How do you spell cat?"

"You don't when you're doing sums," I said, despising him. Five twelves are sixty, well four then. Four twelves. Four twelves.

"Oh, the old man went down the drain.
'E went round the corner and there was nobody there
So 'e hid in the dustbin and the little fishies ate him up
And when 'e came up he was dead, dead,
Dead in the dustbin—"

"Shut up!" I yelled. Four twelves are forty-eight. Forty-eight
from fifty-three.

"Serve 'im right, silly old man,
'E got his head stuck and couldn't get out
So they gave 'im one up the bum. . . ."

It was impossible to concentrate. I began to count on my
fingers : Forty-eight. Forty-nine, fifty, fifty-one. I lost count and
had to begin again. Roberts droned on and on. Drains, dustbins
and old men seemed to be his main sources of inspiration. I found
myself counting the number of times he mentioned each of
them, instead of the number of shillings in the column. It didn't
seem to worry him that he was supposed to be subtracting forty-
eight from fifty-three. I told him several times that only idiots
went on like this and therefore he was an idiot. It didn't make
any difference. I looked at him contemptuously.

In the end the bell went. As Sir disappeared, Roberts stood
up, his lip curled, the sneer back. He was transformed. As he
entered the playground, he became a different boy, the terror
of the school. His eyes were bright and I could see the vein on
his forehead standing out.

Suddenly he sprang on a tiny boy who was standing with his
back to him and threw him on to the ground. He fell at my
feet. Roberts looked up and saw me. I had been standing watching, out in the open, fascinated. I remembered where I was just
in time, and as Roberts leapt at me I fled in terror to the lavatories. I peeped out, and saw him jump hard on the boy he had
knocked down.

O'Brien ran past the door, dragging Valerie Wilson. Remembering her friendliness in class, I foolishly ran out to her rescue,
and found myself face to face with Skinner. He was smaller
than me, I thought, but then, so was O'Brien. His cheeks were
red and stringy. He had me cornered against a wall. I tried to
smile.

29

"Oh, hullo," I said nervously. I fumbled in my pocket. "Have some banana sherbet."

"Coo! Do you like them?" he said, and took some.

A great wave of hope went over me.

"Well, not so much as some sweets," I said very fast. "They cost a lot too. I like toffee bars, do you?"

"I like bubble gum," he said.

"I've never tried that. No, thank you," I added hastily, for he seemed to be offering me some that he had taken out of his mouth to eat the sherbet. "Mummy doesn't like me to eat it—Mum, I mean," I explained. I saw that wasn't going down well, and changed the subject. "What comic do you like best?" I asked.

"I like *Beano*," he answered. He was smiling, I noticed, and I felt relieved.

"Ooh, so do I," I said eagerly. No use telling him that Mummy didn't allow me to read comics either. "Don't you laugh at that cat thing on the first page?" I had seen that on booksellers' stalls.

"I think that's just silly," he said.

"Oh," I had an inspiration. "What's your Christian name?"

"Stephen. Horrible, isn't it?"

"Well—Do you know it's Etienne in French?"

That surprised him. "What? Really? Etienne? That's my name in French? Coo, it's worse than the English. You can't tell, can you?"

This revelation kept him happy until we were at length separated by the football, which suddenly flew between us, followed by a dozen or so yelling boys. I got borne away on the tide and somewhat to my relief was deposited in the lavatories. You just can't escape from here, can you, I thought, holding my nose and looking round at the five green doors and the grimy brickwork.

Outside I could see Roberts having a wonderful time. He had got hold of the toy gramophone that Sandra Thomas from Class I (very foolishly I thought) had brought to school, and was kicking it round the playground. It was split open and there were bits of it strewn all over the ground. Thomas was crying in a corner. I felt sorry for her, and went across and gave her the rest of my banana sherbet. I don't think she liked it much.

As usual it seemed an hour before our ten minutes were up

and the whistle went. When it did, and we poured upstairs, evading the monitor, I almost fell headlong over Skinner, who had stopped dead in front of me. He stooped down, scraped something off the floor, and put it in his mouth. He saw me and grinned.

"Someone's old bubble gum," he explained. "Sure you don't want any?"

Well, it's the thought that counts, I told myself. I was flattered to have won the friendship of this boy. Now I need never be frightened of him again, as I was of O'Brien and Roberts.

As I stepped on to the landing he pounced on me and dragged me across it, almost twisting my arm off and half breaking my neck. I wrestled feebly, completely caught off my guard. Luckily Sir came by and broke the fight up. I went into the classroom and complained to Valerie Wilson.

"But why should he suddenly go for me like that? I had just made friends with him," I said.

"Oh well, it's your own fault for trusting him. You can't trust boys like that," she said reassuringly.

Roberts came in and sat down, flushed and triumphant, and the bully turned into the idiot. He produced a long red sausage balloon, stuck it between his legs, jumped up on his chair and stuck his tummy out. The boys guffawed loudly, the girls blushed and hid modestly under their desk lids.

"You know what he's pretending that is, don't you?" they all whispered to each other, giggling.

Sir confiscated the balloon, and we settled in to another session of old men and dustbins. Just to make a change, every few minutes Roberts bashed me on the head and shouted,

"Conk! Wood!" or alternatively, "Dong! Iron!" I got the lowest marks for any work I had ever done for that money exercise.

4

"Looks like your poems back," said Mummy gloomily and gave me that familiar, suspiciously bulgy envelope. I opened it sadly, and pulled out the creased old copy of *Nightmare Street*. I blinked, and looked again. It was nothing of the sort. It was a cheque for a guinea, with a letter headed *Doorway*.

"Mummy—look," I gasped.

She looked. "Good gracious!" she exclaimed. Then her face went all bright and eager. "Our little poet's done it again! Your biggest success. *Doorway*! It's a miracle to get in that at all, but at your age, why, it's genius!"

She read the letter, and suddenly cooled off. "*Nightmare Street?* What, not that horrid one you wrote when you were ill? Well, fancy that doing so well." She sounded doubtful.

"Aren't you pleased?" I asked anxiously.

"Well, of course I am," she said. "Still, how queer they should like that funny one. Why not send them *Sky After Sunset?*" she asked, brightening.

"I did. And *The Death of a Shell*." That was another of her favourites. "But they've sent them back, and chosen *Nightmare Street*."

"Well!" Mummy said. She didn't seem to be celebrating, I noticed with disappointment.

"It was a better poem, anyway. The others I've written are so soppy," I said.

"But that's why I like them," she said, looking at me in surprise. Then she pulled herself together. "Well, it's wonderful news, anyway. I know! Run round to the dairy and get yourself a chocolate cake for tea, to celebrate." She didn't offer me any crème-de-menthe.

I thought the room looked a bit odd. It suddenly dawned on me what was different. On the side table was a huge new aquarium, instead of the bookcase. I blinked at it. Inside there were three queer-looking fish.

"What's that, Mummy?" I asked.

"Oh, that!" said Mummy, suddenly looking keen again. "That's my new bargain tank. Only twenty-five shillings. I couldn't miss it. It meant putting the books downstairs instead of the pink tank, and that's had to go in your bedroom, I'm afraid. But as you've got two already, I thought one more wouldn't make any difference."

"No, of course not, Mummy. Who have I got?"

"Lucinda and Trevor, the plain fantails, you know. You remember they spawned all fish with black markings, and we couldn't understand it because they're plain gold? But why I'm really so pleased with my new tank is that it means I can keep my new pearl-scales separate. I had to put Mabel in with them, but it's much better than being in the big tank in the kitchen. They're precious, you know. I wouldn't like them to feel crowded. But this is the only other aquarium I've got that's big enough. Do you think they look happy?"

"Oh yes, Mummy, they're quite skittish," I said. It wasn't quite the right word. They were as skittish as goldfish with fins that size can be, but still perhaps "lively" would have been more accurate.

Roberts didn't come to school until ten o'clock next day, apparently for no particular reason. For a whole lovely hour Little, on the other side of him, and I had been able to hope that he was ill and going to be away for days. We looked at each other sadly when he arrived.

Sir gave him half a page from an exercise book.

"Go outside and write down everything you know," he ordered him.

Linda Little and I smiled at each other again, inwardly blessing Sir for getting Roberts out of the way so easily.

After ten minutes or so there came a knock at the door, and he sauntered in, dropped the paper on Sir's desk, went to his own and upset his inkwell all over it. All the girls sitting nearby squealed and jumped up as the ink cascaded over their chairs. I sat still, absorbed in the paper on Sir's desk, which appeared only to have writing on one side. The ink dribbled on to my pinafore dress. I sprang to my feet in a fury, and was going to bash Roberts on the head with my dictionary when I saw he

33

was about to light a banger under his desk lid. I sat down again in the ink, paralysed with fear. I didn't hear Valerie Wilson shouting at me about my dress, only the deafening bang of the firework.

Roberts was sent outside again, but was allowed to join us for play. The rest of the day was sheer nightmare. In fact only two other bangers actually went off, but Roberts was fiddling with them the whole time, lighting the touchpapers and then snuffing them out, so that I was practically in tears with terror and suspense. And just as soon as I had managed to persuade myself that he was only playing, he would really let one go off, and reduce me almost to hysterics.

It gave me an idea, though, and on the way home, to cheer myself up, I went into a toy shop and asked to see their stock of fireworks.

"On the early side, aren't you?" the girl said.

"I don't want to get them mixed up with my Christmas shopping," I explained.

"Let alone your Easter eggs," she said, giggling. "Anyway, you're not fourteen."

I gave up and went home. At tea I said to Daddy,

"Isn't it a shame, they won't sell me any fireworks, and soon it will be Christmas."

"Christmas? Christmas! So it will!" he crowed happily. "Holly and bells and coaching scenes! 'Once in Royal David's city . . .'"

" 'Stood a lowly cattle shed'," I joined in, thinking of loggy fires and piles of tinselly presents.

After that it was nothing but carols and rustly parcels all through October and November. We had a tiny cottage in the country, seventy miles or so in the direction of London, where we could go at Christmas. It was specially snug, for, as the rooms were so small, they could be filled absolutely solid with decorations, so that you blundered through a forest of dangling silver corkscrews and paper chains. Daddy began to get quite sparkling with Christmassyness, as he called it, and went round chortling with glee and saying,

"Just think! It's almost Christmas!"

Christmas was one of Daddy's specialities. He began to look forward to it earlier and earlier each year. This year, it seemed, we were starting in October.

At the beginning of November the school started too. One morning, instead of tucking into our arithmetic and the children who could never count their pocket money, Sir said, fumbling with his hands and grinning shyly,

"Now, it's not Christmas yet but it soon will be, and I've just got an idea for it this year which we'll have to start working on soon if we're going to do it. I thought that perhaps we might put on a Christmas show for the parents, with a nativity play and afterwards maybe a school concert—"

We all shrieked with laughter. "A concert! Us!"

"Ever heard cats yowling, sir?" asked Matthews.

"Well, I don't see why not," said Sir. "I was rummaging in the downstairs cupboard the other day, and there were at least a dozen perfectly good mouth-organs, and a whole pile of books of unusual carols. I'm sure that if we worked hard we could make an excellent concert with those."

"But we can't play the mouth-organ, sir," Linda Tatley objected.

"All the more reason for starting rehearsals early, if I'm going to have to teach you," said Sir, who had stopped looking shy and was looking energetic instead. "I should imagine you'd make a very good player yourself, for example, Tatley."

She tossed her head, as she had a habit of doing when she was showing off, and said, "Perhaps you're right, sir."

"Well, now," said Sir, who was by this time shining with enthusiasm. His teeth looked even horsier than usual. "The first thing to do is to secure every dinner-hour, and at least two afternoons a week, to work in. I'll ask the headmaster about that to-day. Then we must cast the nativity play. We could do that now, couldn't we? And then we must just choose the carols and songs we'll have. I'll do that this very evening. Now, I think you, King, can be Mary, and Tatley, you be the Angel Gabriel. We'll have Philips as Joseph."

We went all down the list, the Wise Men, the shepherds, Herod, Elisabeth. I kept thinking he was going to give me a part, but he didn't, until at the end he said,

"And all the rest of you can be angels, and come in after Tatley's said her bit to the shepherds."

"That's us," Valerie Wilson said to me, tittering.

After that, we more or less gave up lessons. Most of the day you could hear sad squeaks going up from the room where Sir was trying to teach his new "music class' to play the mouth-organ. I wasn't one of them because Mummy wouldn't let me put "those filthy old things" in my mouth. "Goodness only knows what you might pick up!" I couldn't possibly say that to anyone, least of all Sir, and when I was asked to join the music class, as I was frequently, I had to make the most miserable excuses that left people looking at me strangely. Of course Mummy was right really. I had told her how the mouth-organs were passed from child to child without ever being wiped. Any mother might have objected.

Then, every other afternoon, we all trooped down to the hall and sang strange old carols about figgy pudding and wassails. On the afternoons in between we rehearsed our nativity play. Sir stormed around and shouted and raged because none of the cast would learn their lines, though it was hard to tell whether they had or not because they were giggling so much all the time that they could hardly speak. The boys thought the whole thing bonkers in any case, and just fooled about and never even tried to do their bit well.

"Act, will you? Act!" poor Sir used to shout at them. "If you play the fool just once more, Peters, I'll throw you out." He often did, too, but the new Herod, or whoever it was, was always even worse.

The first part of the play was greatly hampered by the crowds of angels who hung about in the wings ready to leap nippily on to the stage when Tatley had finished announcing that the babe would be wrapped in swathing-bands, lying in a manger. She didn't seem to notice the shepherds lying in a heap tickling each other on the floor. She had pages to recite, and enjoyed it tremendously. A pleased sort of smile appeared on Sir's face whenever she came on stage, and he could rest from his shouting and bullying. She was the only one in the play you could hear clearly in the wings. When all the angels were "off" and we had to sit at the back of the hall for the rest of the play, we couldn't even hear a faint mumble.

I felt sorry for Sir. He worked so hard, and had planned it as such an event, that I thought it was unkind of the class to make such a mess of it deliberately. They did the same with his carol concert too, until he was forced to have only his music class singing, and chucked everyone else out. The music class were all earnest girls like Tatley and King and they learnt all the songs and sang quite nicely, except that you couldn't hear them.

I sang all Sir's carols to Daddy at home, and he took a great fancy to them and kept singing them himself. It was Christmas all day at school and then Christmas all evening at home, and it was still only mid-November.

Soon, Daddy started hoping for Christmas cards. Mummy and I kept him going by sending them to him occasionally.

5

I WAS HUNTING ROUND Woolworth's one evening for a jolly present for Daddy, when I saw and fell in love with a beautiful Christmas stocking, ready packed with mysterious parcels, on the toy counter. It only cost a shilling, and I bought one for Daddy. As I was going out of the door I decided that it was Christmas for me too, and I went back and bought another for myself. That made me feel guilty, and so I spent the rest of my pocket money on an extra present for Daddy to make up. He couldn't object to that, he's got much the best of the bargain, I thought. And anyway I just wanted that stocking so much.

"Oh, it was lovely, all full of surprises," I said eagerly to Valerie Barker. "And worth double the money, too. There was a funny—"

"Shut up, don't tell me. I don't want to know. I'm going to buy one too, and I want it to be a surprise," she said.

"Good idea. It's at Woolworth's," I told her.

Her face fell. "Oh, I can't get there before tomorrow. Oh, Antonia!" Suddenly she was all over me. "Oh, please, do you think you could get it for me in the lunch hour (you do go home to dinner, don't you?) and bring it to me, if I gave you the money?" She put her arms round me. "Oh please, Antonia!"

"Why, of course, I'd love to," I said, overjoyed to think that at last I seemed to have made a friend.

"You will? Really? Ooh, I do love you, Antonia." She hugged me tightly and wouldn't let go. I hugged her back, feeling a bit uncomfortable, but determined to make friends with her. She gave me elevenpence and said did the other penny matter, and I said of course not, and paid it for her instead of buying my day's supply of sherbet. It was a bright, cold day. When I came back to school after lunch she was sitting on her

38

raincoat in the entrance to the lavatories. I had taken care to be back early so that she could have time to open the stocking.

"Oh, Antonia! Have you got it?" she called.

"Here it is," I said, handing it to her.

She tore it open and began to pull out the novelties, games and toys inside, gasping and sighing over each one, and kissing it before putting it reverently down on the raincoat. I noticed that there seemed to be a lot of boys hanging around outside, whispering and pointing at us idiotically. I gave them what was meant to be a withering look, and turned back to Valerie. She was carefully putting everything back into the stocking in the exact order it had been in originally. Something seemed to be wrong with the jack-in-the-box, which was to go on top, and she put the stocking down to attend to it.

O'Brien darted forward, snatched up the stocking and flung it to Grant. Valerie screamed. A ball fell out and split open, gushing sawdust. The boys were tossing the stocking to and fro, whooping and yelling. All the precious toys were rolling across the asphalt, torn and broken. The stocking itself seemed to be in two bits now. Poor Valerie burst into tears. I felt the same way myself, with anger. Roberts was waving the paper trumpet triumphantly aloft, hooting with laughter. In his other hand he held one half of the stocking. There still seemed to be something in it. I crept up behind him and grabbed it. It only tore again; the plastic sputnik inside fell on the ground and smashed. Roberts spun round. I dashed back to Valerie with my bit of torn muslin. There was a small piece of the snakes and ladders board inside it. I seemed to have made Roberts very angry. I saw him deliberately rip the paper trumpet to pieces just afterwards. Valerie cried all day, although I pointed out that she still had the jack-in-the-box and tried to cheer her up with it.

The performance of Sir's Christmas show was on December 18th, two days before the end of term. Mummy took me to the dentist on the day of the dress rehearsal, but by the temper Sir was in next day I guessed what it had been like.

"Got your dress ready?" Linda Tatley asked me.

"My dress?"

"Your angel's dress, silly."

"Oh, that," I said, going cold all over. I had forgotten all about it, but I wasn't going to let Tatley know.

"You'd forgotten, hadn't you?"

"None of your business," I said, hating her.

"Bet you don't even know what you've got to have."

"Wings."

"What else?"

I gave in. "I don't know," I admitted.

"You've got to have a long white dress, like a nightgown," she said, looking superior. I should have been grateful if any-one else had told me.

"You'd better have it tomorrow," she warned me.

I made up rhymes to remind me to remember all through the last sad afternoon, with Sir in despair with everything, even the mouth-organs, which had been his pride and joy, and that evening I said to Mummy :

"Please can I have a long white dress for the play tomorrow?"

"A long white dress?" she said, gaping at me. "But I don't possess such a thing."

"A petticoat would do."

"I never wear them. Gave all mine to the refugees."

"A nightdress, then."

"I wear pyjamas."

We looked at each other. Mummy flopped into a chair.

"Must you have it?"

"Well, yes."

"Tomorrow?"

"I'm afraid so."

"Well, I know what," she said brightly, getting up. "I'll con-coct you a dress with towels and sheets and pins. Wait a minute." Mummy never had been able to sew.

She found a white blouse for me. "That's half the battle won," she said. "Now, look, it's not very difficult. I'll try it out now and then you'll know what to do tomorrow. You pin this towel round your waist. Bother, it's too short. Well, you pin this one on the bottom of the other and twine it round you and pin it there—get someone to hold it for you and then just pin it—"

"It's beautiful," I said, "but it's awfully tight."

"Will that matter? It's loose enough to walk in."

It was, just.

"No, I don't think towels are very beautiful, especially not these ragged old things," said Mummy. "Look! Aren't I clever? Don't you think these are perfect for going on top?"

She produced an ancient pair of muslin curtains which had been on the bedroom windows when we moved in. We all hated such things and had torn them down immediately. I thought they had gone to the refugees long ago.

"Now, you just tuck them in here, and pin them round you. Yes, they just fit. That really looks nice, you know."

They made the towel contraption even tighter. I hobbled across to the mirror. I looked a mess.

"It's brilliant," I said, kissing Mummy. "Really angelic."

"Yes, it's a success," she agreed, surveying me.

"What about the wings, Mummy?" I asked, after a moment.

Poor Mummy gave me a look, and then went into the kitchen. I heard her burrowing in the old cardboard boxes in the corner. She came back brandishing triumphantly two great pieces of cardboard and a bottle of glue. It was very old glue, and was covered in fungus, but after we'd dug that away it stuck quite well. We worked hard all the evening and produced a beautiful pair of wings, with gold and silver feathers painted on by me, and an elaborate strap affair invented by Mummy.

"It had better be a good play," she groaned. "But you'll be a sweet little angel."

I wouldn't have dreamt of telling her what I secretly thought, that the play would be over before I'd managed to get dressed.

In fact, it was all right, because all the other angels slipped into their petticoats in a minute, and came and helped me to wrestle with my towels and wings, so that I was just ready in time.

We had the mouth-organs first. I thought they made the most horrible noise I had ever heard, with no apparent tune. In the last two songs Class One had to sing with them, but that only made it worse. The parents clapped them loudly, however, and Sir, who was conducting them, didn't look too miserable. They were the best item in the show. The carols might have been nice. It was impossible to tell, the singers were completely drowned by the piano.

Then we had the nativity play. King, acting Mary, looked suitably saintly, and I saw a satisfied look come over Sir's face. Then she forgot to look frightened when Tatley appeared, and just looked mildly amused, and I saw poor Sir writhe with misery in the wings. Tatley was quite impressive, but King made up for that by reciting the Magnificat very quietly into Little's lap with her back to the audience. However, I thought it was going very well, and made a mental note to tell Mummy to congratulate Sir afterwards.

The shepherds seemed to think they were acting circus clowns, and Tatley sounded very stern when she talked to them. All the angels were fluttering about by the edge of the stage in a fluster, ready to jump up on to it when Tatley said ". . . . in a manger."

". . . . In a manger," announced Tatley.

"Alleluia !" we cried, leaping up. Something happened to my legs and I found I hadn't leapt up. I tried again. My legs wouldn't move. It was my dress, my white angel's robe, that was too tight to let me jump on to the stage.

Valerie Clark, alleluia-ing on the stage, nudged Barker violently.

"Antonia can't get up !"

I don't know what the parents can have thought. Half the heavenly host suddenly turned round and started tugging and heaving at a little angel struggling to get on to the cloud at their feet. I saw Sir jumping up and down and shaking his fist at us, with his face all screwed up like an old raisin. At last some hefty angel got me round the waist and pulled me up. All the others seized me, and I rolled out into the middle of the stage. Then we discovered that we should have been away a long time ago, and piled off in disorder. Nobody had said "Alleluia" for a long time, and I don't think the "Glory to God in the highest" ever got said. Sir looked as if he were going to cry.

All the rest of the play was acted by boys, and none of them knew their lines, and they all missed their cues and had to be pushed and prompted, and the prompter, Sir, was the only one you could hear in any case. The Three Kings' pages, from Class Four, looked sweet, but invariably went in the opposite direction to their masters, so that they all kept getting lost, and Balthazar's cloak fell off. Then Matthews, operating the curtain, missed his cue and left everyone standing about uncomfortably at the end, thinking it was someone's turn to speak. Sir had to go across the back of the stage in full view of the audience and swear at Matthews.

As soon as it had finished I stumbled over to Sir, and said,

"It was wonderful, sir. Only a few unfortunate incidents. That song you wrote was tremendous. Didn't you see how impressed the parents were looking?"

He brightened for an instant at that, but then just shook his head, and didn't speak.

I dashed across as fast as I could in my towels, and caught Mummy going out.

"Quickly, go and say how wonderful it was to Sir!" I said, pushing her over. I went and got out of my white dress. It took ages. When I found her again Mummy said,

"I told him how impressive it was, but he just said, 'I'm so glad you think so.'" She seemed quite depressed herself. "I complimented him on his mouth-organs, and his choice of carols, and thought of all sorts of nice things to say about the play, but I don't think I cheered him up much. And in any case it was bad, wasn't it?"

"Poor Sir," I said. He hardly spoke at all the next day, but seemed sunk in gloom, until as we were going home he said,

"You'd better all bring games and things to do tomorrow, there won't be any lessons." It was the end of term.

There weren't either. The girls all settled in to make hundreds upon hundreds of Christmas cards, getting more and more bored, while the boys rampaged around, clockwork tanks crawled all over everything like great insects, and the air fairly buzzed with rubbers, bits of chalk, paper darts and so on. We never saw a teacher all day. I wondered why we had to come to school when the teachers didn't, and very nearly stayed at home after lunch. Daddy jumped at the idea when I told him what we were doing, but Mummy put her foot down, and made me go back.

I had had my pocket money that morning. It was one and six. On the way home from school I ran across to Woolworth's and bought another of the muslin novelty stockings for Valerie Barker. I'll give it to her on the first day of next term, and she'll be so pleased that we really will be best friends for ever, I thought. It was almost the last stocking left. There were girls in the window taking down the Christmas decorations, and putting up posters saying "Sale starts January 5th." That's a sign that Christmas really is beginning at last, I thought, and ran all the rest of the way home without stopping.

There was our little red bubble car outside the house, all

loaded up with piles and piles of tempting parcels, so that you could hardly see out of the back window.

"Nowell! Nowell!" I sang, running into the house, and collided with Daddy tottering out under a great armful of yet more gorgeously wrapped presents. He smiled at me happily over the top of them. I went into the kitchen. There was Mummy, in a fluster, trying to get everything cleaned and put away before we left. The whole room was littered with teacups full of sand and bits of chopped worm and stuff. I realized that Mummy wasn't making tea, as I had hoped, but putting out food for the goldfish.

"On January 2nd please give all the fish except the ones in the pink tank a pinch of dried water fleas, in the sideboard," said Mummy, writing frantically. "Oh, my goodness, Antonia, I only hope this baby-sitter I've hired to feed the fish comes all right, and obeys all my instructions. Just supposing she's stupid or forgets to come and we find all the fish dead when we come back. Now the minced lettuce for Mabel—if she doesn't have that regularly goodness knows what may happen, she's dreadfully constipated. I think I'd better label her tank, to make sure the woman doesn't forget her."

I decided there was no hope of tea, but I saw a piece of holly stuck in the roller towel.

"Do you want this?" I asked Mummy.

"Oh, please take it away! I keep getting caught on it, it's driving me mad, mad," said Mummy. "Now, what more? Oh yes, the egg yolk for the baby lionheads...."

I ran off with the holly and fixed it on Paydirt's roof with a bit of red ribbon. Paydirt was the name of the bubble car, so called because it had been bought with the profits of a picture Daddy had sold, as a calendar, in America.

When he saw the holly, Daddy jumped up in the air.

"Oh, isn't it Christmassy!" he shouted.

"And perhaps there'll be some Christmas cards waiting for us at the cottage," I said. There would be, I knew. Mummy had sent him some there, coaching scenes with people in red coats quaffing tankards of ale, and great dollops of snow in the foreground.

We squashed into Paydirt. The back window was now completely blocked, by a box of crackers and a whole Stilton that Daddy had put on at the last minute.

"Just think, in a couple of hours we'll be all cosy in our little cottage, with a great big yule log on the fire and carol-singers outside in the snow!" gloated Daddy.

"There really might be carol-singers," Mummy said. "The Salvation Army usually comes round about a week before Christmas."

"Let's sing some carols now," I suggested.

We did, as loudly as we could, all the way. Good King Wenceslas, God rest you merry, Ding dong, merrily on high, all the jolliest we could think of. People in the street turned and smiled at us in our sleigh full of presents.

It was dark when we arrived. The moment we had got the fire lit we started to put the decorations up and dress the Christmas tree.

"Now, remember," said Daddy as we started, "our object is to leave no tree showing and no room showing."

So we filled the room solid with the tinsel, and stopped up the gaps with presents and the Christmas cards. The window we covered with the tree, which we had managed to make into a great rustling parcel of glitter and lights with the tree part successfully hidden. In a few days there were dozens more Christmas cards, and we heaped them over all the flat surfaces, tables, bookcase, piano, and when those gave out we lined the walls with them. On Sunday we went to a carol service, and Daddy was happier than he had been since last Christmas.

Then there came the night in the year when I hardly slept at all. It's the same every year. With great ceremony everyone came and helped me to hang up my stocking, and tucked me down to sing carols to myself. When Mummy and Daddy went to the midnight communion, I could steal downstairs and look at the Christmas tree lights. Daddy always left them on all night on Christmas Eve, "to show Father Christmas where to come." Their light and the fire-light shone from different angles on the decorations, which shimmered and glinted until I began to feel quite poetic.

When I heard Mummy and Daddy coming up the path I knew I had to bolt back to bed and shut my eyes tight while Father Christmas came and bumbled round the room, making exciting rustlings and dropping mysterious heavy things on my feet. Sometimes he would groan and say,

"Oh, never have I made such a noise!"

Then it was back to the carols. I lay trying to imagine organ and choir as I sang them, until I decided that it was light enough to count as morning, and dared at last to look at my stocking. It was one of Daddy's biggest socks, stretched out of all recognition with "little nonsenses," as Mummy called them. I unpacked it in slow motion, relishing every moment, until my bed was a gorgeous mass of chocolate Father Christmasses, novelty pencil-sharpeners, paper dolls and Christmas-tree fairies. I couldn't help pitying my poor friends at school who all indignantly denied that they still had stockings. On the other hand, they all had Christmas puddings, not bought but properly made by their mothers, which everyone could help to stir and hide sixpences in. I wished mildly that Mummy didn't hate cooking quite so much. Then I discovered that I wasn't yet anywhere near the tangerine in the stocking toe, and forgot all about her.

The proper presents were all piled on the chairs. I'd put mine right on top of Mummy's pile. I had been on the lookout since September, and had found just the thing : a great big plastic pink elephant to go in her collection of pink elephants. She had six, and they stood on their heads on the mantelpiece. I couldn't wait to see her open her present and find another. I had tried it out in the shop to make sure it really could stand on its head. There were some other things too. And as for that great heap on my chair! I looked longingly at it. Lunch seemed to drag on for hours, while Mummy and Daddy discussed Roy who came to the pub, and wondered if he was married, methodically eating helping after helping of Stilton, and then deciding they'd like some tangerines. I fidgeted on my chair, wondering how they could be so unfeeling, when there were those glittering heaps of parcels just wanting to be unwrapped. In fact, as we all knew, they wouldn't really be very wonderful, at least not expensive. Daddy had always insisted on quantity instead of quality, and it had to be either or. But who wants quality anyway? Lots of jolly little things are far more fun, I thought, as I thought every Christmas, and looked appealingly at Mummy.

"Do have some cheese, Antonia, it's awfully good," she said.

6

"AND ANOTHER THING," Miss Lovely was saying. "I saw all you girls were wearing your coats in the playground. Well, you aren't to do that. Yes, I know it's cold, but you can easily keep warm running about. That's what I want you to do. No coats and run about."

"Ugh, beastly weather," Mummy had said, "Whatever you do, Antonia, don't get cold. Remember to wear your raincoat in the playground." It had just arrived, my specially ordinary raincoat with the tartan lining. I wanted to show it off.

I put up my hand. "Please, Miss Lovely, my mother says—"

"That's just what I don't want to hear, My mother says. If your mothers don't know the rules you must tell them. In future, girls must not wear their coats in play, and that's flat. Do you see that, Rutherford? If you're ill or something you shouldn't be at school."

Oh, well, if it was one of those mysterious school rules that cropped up from time to time—"Yes, Miss Lovely."

The girls were so cold that they couldn't play Two-Ball in the lavatory during break. We huddled in a corner, all the hairs on our legs sticking out. I thought I had gooseflesh all over me.

"Now run about and take exercise, girls," I said sarcastically. Everyone groaned. Outside I could see the boys tearing to and fro with the football. They were sweating and red in the face. One of them stripped off his jersey and flung it down just outside the entrance. He dashed away after his gang, hurriedly undoing his shirt. Felicity Dearchild leant out, grabbed the jersey and put it on. All the rest of us gasped at her daring, and then looked at the great boy's pullover enviously. The boy wasn't in our class.

"Look, Valerie!" I said to Barker when we got upstairs, "See what I've got for you. A late Christmas present," and I gave her the stocking full of toys that I had bought for her.

"Oh!" she gasped. "Oh, Antonia! Another stocking!" She flung her arms round my neck and waltzed me round the room. "Oh, I adore Antonia," she announced to all the girls we ran into. "She's a beautiful, kind, clever girl and she's my best friend." This last statement quite made up for my embarrassment, for really it was all a little embarrassing, and although I dutifully hugged her back I couldn't quite bring myself to tell Tatley that I adored Valerie Barker.

"Don't open it here!" I exclaimed, seeing her about to. "The boys'll see. Take it home and open it there."

"Can't I look at what's inside?" she said petulantly.

I felt like shaking her. "Not here! If you open it here I won't let you have it," I said. Already, I thought, O'Brien had seen it. "Quick, hide it!"

She put it away, sulking. Next moment, however, she was adoring me again. I was relieved, for I had really feared that I might have broken up our friendship.

"Oh, I do wish I sat next to you, Antonia," she said.

"Mmm, so do I," I answered. I was horrified to find myself adding secretly, "if I've got to choose between you and Roberts, that is."

When Sir had called the register, he said, "A lightning spelling test. I'm not going to wait for slowcoaches. Number one, Greatly. Number two, Through. Number three—"

"Oh, sir!" pleaded Peters, "I'm still trying to write the first one. My hands are too numb to hold the pen."

"Same here," murmured everyone else.

"It's all right for you, sir, you've been in a lovely warm staffroom while we were freezing out there," said Matthews.

"Well, what about you, tearing around playing football?" retorted Dearchild. "We just had to stand growing icicles."

"You're no one to talk," Tatley pointed out. Dearchild was still wearing her stolen jersey. I felt sorry for the boy it belonged to, shivering somewhere in his shirt sleeves.

Sir pulled at his cheeks. "Alcock," he said, "how many of those big inkpots were there, that you counted this morning?"

"There were thirty-one and a half, sir," Alcock answered. "One was broken, I mean, sir."

"Well," said Sir, "I think you can all have some more ink. Thompson and Johnson, there's a tin of ink powder in the cupboard. Go down to the cloakroom and make a big can of ink with

48

it. Use the hottest water you can find." He was a nice man really.

Everyone cheered. The two boys went, grinning, and brought back a great jug steaming like a soup tureen. The inkpots were really big, big like tumblers, and you could hold them in your hands. We all stroked them and patted them and said how gorgeous they were and our hands began to go red instead of pale blue.

Roberts touched his.

"Ow!" he screeched, "It's hot!" He swiped at it with the back of his hand so that it flew off his desk without spilling a drop on him, and landed upside down in my lap. It was hot, too. I yelled, and jumped up trying to shake the inkpot off. As it rolled down me it contrived to empty itself completely right down my front. I gazed at it, remembering how I had spent half the evening before trying to get the school ink off my other dress and how in the end Mummy had had to send it to those unfortunate refugees.

"Getting quite an expert at this, aren't you?" I said crossly to Roberts.

"Good old Sir! My hands aren't a bit cold now," announced Matthews, waggling his fingers in the air.

"Splendid," said Sir with a grin. "Well, now you can take down number three, Bottle."

We all booed Matthews and wrote down number three, Bottel, Botal, Bottol. When we came to number nine, Square, I saw that Roberts was ticking all his work as he did it. Linda Little on the other side was watching him too. When Sir said, "Now we'll go over it," she said:

"Please, sir, Roberts has ticked all his already."

"Oh, never mind Roberts, he's just a nutcase," Sir said.

"He's a dangerous lunatic," I said, looking at my wet dress. Roberts seemed quite unaware that we were talking about him.

I went apprehensively downstairs for afternoon play, trying to persuade myself that it had got warmer since this morning and that the sun might be out. I stepped outside, gazing at the sky to see if it was. Suddenly a row of boys bore down on me, yelling and looking ferocious. I tried to dodge between them, but they seemed to be a solid wall of trampling feet. I stumbled away. They were coming after me, they were driving me into a corner. They were in a long chain so that I couldn't get round them. I saw them looming over me, intent on crushing me underfoot. Then, in the corner, they got me. I lay screaming in the mud, while the stampede of boys went over me, kicking and jumping on me. One of them, as a farewell gift, gave me a kick on the head that made me feel dizzy. Then dimly I saw them, in a great line across the playground, chasing little Johnson. They were holding hands, sweeping over all obstacles. They wheeled in an arc across the body of Johnson and began to close in on me again. I raced to the lavatory entrance before they did. I was almost cut off. I flung myself at it and staggered inside just as the chain of boys rushed past it.

"Those horrid boys—they were chasing me," I gasped to Sandra King, as I collapsed on the ground in the corner.

"It's a game they sometimes play, they run across the playground holding hands and try to catch people," she told me, making it sound as if it were a nice, gentle game like "Oranges and Lemons" instead of a miniature battle charge. "Only the boys here play that you mustn't let go hands whatever you come to, so it gets a bit rough."

"I should think it does," I said, still feeling faint from the fright I had had, and bruised and smarting all over.

When I came home, Mummy exclaimed :

"Good gracious, whatever do they do to you at school! At lunch time you were soused in ink and now you're smothered in mud, and look at your poor legs, they're all grazed and tattered, and what an awful great bruise on your face, however did that happen?"

I explained wearily, "It's a game the boys were playing, a sort of 'Chain-He' I think. They all rush round the playground in a line holding hands, and try to catch people and knock them down and tread on them, and I just happened to get caught, that's all."

"How perfectly awful!" said Mummy. "I don't know what the headmaster's about to allow such things. I think it's too bad. I feel like writing to him and complaining about what's happened to you."

I thought she was joking, and joked back. "Well, while you're about it, I wish you'd complain about Roberts. Get him expelled for me!"

"Roberts?"

"He's the boy who's spilt ink down me twice, and won't let me work in peace," I said, knowing that that would win her sympathy. "I have the good fortune to be sitting next to him."

"Well, that's something I really might do, get him moved," said Mummy.

I looked at her in alarm. "But Mummy—not really—I was only joking—I mean to say—you can't do things like that!"

"Why not? I think it's a very good idea. I'll write to the headmaster tonight."

It occurred to me that it would be sheer bliss to have Roberts dumped on someone else for a change, and so I only said,

"Oh, very well, Mummy."

She said that I looked tired, and sent me to bed extra early, but I couldn't sleep, and when I did I dreamt violently. All through those streets of tall dark houses they were coming at me, mobs of people with knives, hemming me in, mowing me down. Whichever way I ran, down alleys and across gas-lit bombed sites, they were always there, crowds with horrible faces chasing me, more of them at every corner. Even the houses, patched with blind windows, were closing in.

At breakfast Mummy said,

"You really do look awful, Antonia. All sort of pale and hardly there. Are you tired?"

"Yes, very. I didn't sleep well," I said, As I put on my raincoat, ready to leave, she said :

"Well, I hope you're all right. Do keep warm. Is your raincoat thick enough, or should you go back to wearing your red coat?"

"I'm not allowed to wear either in the playground," I said.

"Not allowed? Who won't allow you?" said Mummy.

"It's Miss Lovely. She said it's a school rule that we mustn't wear coats in the playground, so I've just got to put up with it."

"You shan't do anything of the kind. Whoever heard of anything so ridiculous as to go out in January without a coat? Just tell them that your mother says you are to wear your coat, and that's flat."

"I told her that, and she just said that you obviously don't know the rule, and she said that's flat, too."

"I shouldn't pay any attention to her and her silly old-fashioned notions," said Mummy. "Just put on your coat."

"But Mummy, I mustn't. It's against the school rule," I argued.

"Well, I say you must. I'm not having you catching your death of cold for a stupid rule like that. Don't look so miserable. Anyone would think you didn't want to wear it!"

"Oh, I do, Mummy," I said, "I simply froze yesterday. I'm just frightened of Miss Lovely."

"Just tell her that I'm writing to the headmaster about it. I'll put it in with the letter I wrote last night. Why do you look so dismayed? It's only sense. Oh dear, you're looking iller and iller. Perhaps you had better stay at home. Run and take your temperature. I bet you've got one."

It was just under ninety-six but Mummy still decided to keep me in bed.

"Would you like me to look for a book for you?" asked Mummy.

"That's awfully kind of you, but I think I'd rather just have a pen and piece of paper," I said. As she turned to go I added:

"And please don't be cross with me about my coat, of course I'll wear it and be really glad of it. It was just that, you see, I'm frightened of the school and Miss Lovely—"

"Well, I think it's absolutely crazy. The woman must be mad," said Mummy fiercely. "I really will write to the headmaster. Here's your paper. Don't wear yourself out. We value you."

When she came up with my lunch, three hours later, I had finished the poem and only needed the title. I felt quite guilty because I had, in fact, worn myself out, and felt much worse. When Mummy came in I quickly hid the poem under the bed-clothes.

"I saw you! What can you have written?" said Mummy. "You haven't been working all this time, have you?"

"Well, yes, I have, and made myself much worse," I confessed. "Not that that would matter if it were any good." It came over me in a wave that the poem was a total failure. "Look, Mummy, isn't it ordinary and boring and ghastly?"

"Oh goodness, it's another of these weirdies," exclaimed Mummy the instant she saw it. "I might have known what was coming, when you were ill." She read it all through. Her eyebrows went up and down as if they were itching, and she looked utterly miserable.

"Well, well, well," she said, "Well, it's certainly peculiar. It . . . I think I'll take your temperature again," she finished lamely, and hurried out to get the thermometer.

"The darkness whirls around me with staring eyes,
Thousands on thousands; whichever way I turn
The eyes surround me, lidless; paralyse
Their victim, me. They close in for the kill.

I try to run, but there is no escape.
Eyes everywhere, hypnotizing me with hate.
They mill round, each alight with blood-red spark.
I would scream, but do not dare;
Only the darkness can hear.
I am alone with that murderer, the Dark."

"Don't you really like it, Mummy?" I asked her when she came back.

"Well, it's very queer," she said. "But I think it would be better if you worked on your rhyme-scheme. I mean, you've got two different forms for the two verses. Do you see what I mean?"

"Oh, but," I said, wriggling uncomfortably in the bed, "that's part of the poem. What else could I possibly write? I mean, nothing else would be the same, would it?"

"And then you wreck it with that line, 'Eyes everywhere, hypnotizing me with hate.' It's all wrong, somehow."

"Hullo, everyone, how's poor Antonelia-Pamelia?" asked Daddy, coming in. He had only just got up, and still looked all warm and sleepy and like a boiled egg.

"Hullo, Daddy, I'm improving, thank you," I said, talking through the thermometer. "But, Mummy, I simply must have that line in somewhere, I simply must."

"But it ruins the rhythm of the poem, " Mummy objected. "Hullo, Man, how did you sleep?"

"Moderately well, Man," answered Daddy, "Let me see this poem you're all talking about."

"If I were you, Antonia, I'd put it like this : 'Eyes everywhere, which, hating, hypnotize.' How's that?"

"Oh, no, no, no, Mummy, that's awful," I said, feeling near tears. "Oh, Mummy, I couldn't possibly write that. You might, but it just isn't me."

"Well, at least it scans, that's the main thing. Rhymes, too. How did your new pill work?" she asked Daddy.

"It made no difference at all. I think I'll take two tonight," he said. "This is a wow of a poem. It's true though, that line doesn't fit. I should take it out altogether."

"But I just can't. I just can't, it's the best line in the whole poem," I said writhing.

"Don't get in such a frenzy with the thermometer in your mouth! Here, it must be cooked by now, let me see it," said Mummy, rescuing the thermometer, which was in great danger.

Daddy was reading and re-reading the poem, obviously with great relish.

"Dig this," he said. "Just how I passed last night."

"Don't!" said Mummy, wincing. "What between the two of you, it's a wonder this place hasn't been made an asylum."

"I know! I've got it!" I shouted. " 'Eyes everywhere, they hypnotize with hate.' "

"Yes, that's splendid," said Daddy enthusiastically.

"Mmm," said Mummy.

"No," I said gloomily, "it's not really any good."

To my astonishment I found myself crying.

"Well, no wonder," said Mummy, "now she's got a temperature of over a hundred and she was ninety-six at breakfast. Besides, just look at what she's written. I'm afraid she must have flu."

I did have flu for the next fortnight, and mooched round the house for days after that making a perfect misery of myself, which made me cross with myself, which made me even more of a misery. At last, however, Mummy decided that I could go back to school, at least until I wrote another poem and got measles, as she put it.

"And for heaven's sake, Antonia, don't let that lunatic send you out without a coat! It should be all right, though. The headmaster promised to talk to her."

Obviously he had, for all the girls were wearing coats when I came to school the next morning and joined them in the playground. Miss Lovely passed through it twice and glared at us, but she didn't say anything.

We went into the classroom, Valerie Barker hanging round my neck and talking hard. I noticed that Roberts was mucking about with her desk.

"Hey! Look what Roberts is doing to your desk," I said.

"Oh, don't you know?" she said, fiddling with my hair. "It's the most gorgeous thing, Antonia. Sir made him change desks with me and now I'm sitting next to you."

"How perfectly wonderful," I said.

My desk was in total chaos. I had forgotten how bad it was. Valerie's was a model of neatness and orderliness. I looked at it enviously and wondered what she did with all the bits of paper covered with half-finished pictures and exercises, which we were always told to keep "and we'll go back to them later." I couldn't find my pen anywhere. I searched my whole desk, a tremendous undertaking, but I only succeeded in finding half a broken nib.

"Oh, Antonia!" gasped Valerie when I told her, as if I had done something scandalous, "you'll have to ask for a new pen."

"Oh, how awful!" I said sympathetically.

Miss Lovely came in and said, "Good morning."

"Good morning, Miss Lovely," we said. She began to call the register.

"Where's Sir? Is he ill?" I asked Valerie.

"Oh, no, but you see Class One will soon be taking their eleven-plus and he's teaching them now, coaching them, you know. In fact I expect he'll probably stay with them for the rest of the term."

"So we've got landed with Miss Lovely for a term," I said sadly.

After the register I went up to her and asked for a new pen.

"Where's your other?" she asked.

"It's broken, Miss Lovely," I told her.

"You mean you broke it," she said.

"Well, I suppose I must have," I admitted.

"You've broken school property! I ought really to charge you for it, but I won't. I most certainly will not give you another, however," she said sternly, to my dismay.

I went back to Valerie and wailed at her that I had nothing to write with.

"Oh, you're just a nuisance," she said crossly. "If you bothered to keep your desk tidy you wouldn't have lost your pen."

"Oh—dear—I am sorry," I stuttered, taken aback at her attitude. "I'll tidy it in play—"

"For goodness' sake take this and be quiet," she said, tossing a pen on to my desk, and then turned her back to me and began to talk to Linda Little.

I stared at her, wondering what had come over her, and trying to decide whether she was just having me on, or whether I had really annoyed her. Should I try making a little joke to make her turn round and giggle? Her back looked somehow hostile. I sighed, opened her pen, and looked round. Peters was giving out the poetry books. That's good, I thought, copying out poems is almost my favourite lesson.

"Today we'll write out *Silver* on page seven, in italic writing. I've put the alphabet on the board. Now do it as nicely as you can, because I'm going to give you marks for this, and the best ones will get stars," said Miss Lovely.

We gasped. Stars were the highest honour that could be had, and involved being congratulated by the headmaster. Sir gave out about one a year.

I studied Miss Lovely's "S" and began to copy it. The pen Valerie had lent me refused to write. I turned towards her, meaning to ask her whether it was a fountain pen and did she mind if I filled it with school ink, but her back still looked so hostile that I didn't dare. I dipped it gingerly in the inkwell and tried again to write the "S".

The pen seemed to leap in my hand, and rivers of ink cascaded over the paper. Everything was spattered with blue. I could even feel some on my face. I mopped it up with my hand-kerchief, reflecting sadly that the school ink had proved itself before to be totally indelible, and examined Valerie's horrible pen. The nib was splayed out and bent and it was oozing ink all over itself.

"Er—um—Valerie, does your pen usually do this? I mean, is it all right?" I said to her back.

She looked up and gave a screech of horror.

"You've broken it! My best pen! Oh, Antonia, you are too bad. I'll never lend you anything again."

"Oh, I'm sorry. I'm sorry!" I said, almost in tears. "I just don't know what happened, it wouldn't write and then it flooded —have I really broken it? Oh dear. How much did it cost?" I asked, desperate to make amends. "I'll buy you another."

"Oh no, you won't," she said, with her back to me, "I know you. Oh, you just break everything you get your hands on! It cost eight and six."

"Oh, my goodness," I said. "Well, I'll save up. I got one and six this week and then—it'll take about six weeks."

"I hate you. I wish I'd never come to sit next to you," she said into her handkerchief.

"Oh, don't say that! Really, I'm sorry. I'll buy you another in six weeks." My voice tailed off as I remembered that I could do nothing of the sort, as I had of course to buy one for myself too.

"Stop talking, Rutherford. I'm going to take the poems in now, and if you haven't finished I'll know just why," said Miss Lovely.

I hadn't written anything at all, but there was the most fascinating pattern of ink blots on the page. I scribbled away frantically with my own bit of broken nib, and tried to make it look as if I had tried terribly hard but had found the new italic writing difficult. Peters, collecting up the papers, had almost reached me, and I had only done two lines in a sort of illegible shorthand. He was taking in Valerie Wilson's. I wrote "A. Rutherford" underneath. It looked more like a motif of birds' footprints. Peters put his hand on the wet ink and smeared it all over the fascinating blot design.

"Ugh!" he said, wiping his hand on his jersey. "What a mess! Can't you write, Buddersmud?"

"Obviously not," I said. Valerie was still talking hard to Little with her back to me.

7

Oɴᴄᴇ ᴀɢᴀɪɴ ᴛʜᴇ lavatories were besieged, and I had to huddle in a little recess in the wall and try to look inconspicuous. Matthews, dodging the football, came up to me and said, "You do stay away from school a long time, Rutherford. What've you been doing—writing poetry?"

"As a matter of fact, I have," I said, delighted to think that he had remembered about that. "Yes, Mummy—Mum I mean—says that I'm always ill when I write poems and it must be them that do it."

"Is it difficult, then?" he asked.

"Well, rather," I said, flattered at his interest.

"Bring what you've just written to school and show me," he suggested.

"Well, all right, I will," I said, feeling as happy as I ever had on getting a poem in print.

As I came in, Mummy asked me, "Has that Roberts boy been moved?"

"Yes, Mummy, isn't it wonderful? He's right the other side of the room, and can't get at anyone but boys, who can stand it. You really did a good thing there," I flumped into a chair. "Wow! I'm exhausted. Sometimes I think the school is a hundred miles away."

"The headmaster is wonderfully obedient. I only asked him once, just casually, if you could sit next to someone else. Yes, it's a pity, isn't it, that there isn't a bus to school," said Mummy. "Come down and have lunch. You're a bit late."

"What a lot of bother it would save if she had lunch at school," said Daddy from downstairs.

"Perhaps, but of course it's quite out of the question," said Mummy firmly. "Oh, come on, Antonia."

I dragged myself up from the chair.

"Oh, Mummy, I know what I must do." I suddenly remembered. "I must copy out my new poem for Matthews. He asked to see it." I began to write it out on a piece of the best writing-paper. "I must find a title for it."

"Oh, must you do that now?" said Mummy, looking wildly at the clock. I went reluctantly downstairs, and ate with one hand while writing with the other.

"I think it would be an excellent thing for her to eat at school," said Daddy. "It'll be an experience."

"But, oh poor Antonia! She's bullied all day. Must she be bullied while she's eating too? Goodness knows what poems it might make her write."

"I've got it! I know what I'll call my new poem," I said excitedly. "It shall be *Insomnia*."

Mummy waved her hands at me. "Don't stop eating," she said.

"Mmm!" said Daddy. "It's a wonderful title. *Insomnia*. I'm sorry you spend your nights like that too. It's a perfect description, though."

"I think I'd better give you one of my new extra strong sleeping-pills tonight," said Mummy. "How can I persuade you to continue eating?"

"All you do is, on Monday, you say to the teacher that you'll be having school lunches now and here's the money, and that'll save you having to come all the way home," said Daddy.

"It's a shame. School's doing awful things to her as it is, without making it worse than we need," groaned Mummy. "Still, if they can make her eat, I won't say another word."

"And you all agree with me about that line: 'Eyes everywhere; they hypnotize with hate'?" I asked, wondering why Mummy was trying to make me look at the clock.

Matthews read *Insomnia* all through, very slowly and carefully, mouthing the words.

"Why, it's marvellous," he said, "Isn't it, Andrews?" he asked, giving it to the big, handsome prefect who had once stood up for me against Tatley.

"Cor!" said Andrews. "Was it you wrote this then, Rutherford?"

"Yes, that's right, I wrote it," I said.

"What, you mean you wrote it?"

I nodded.

"You wrote this poem? Coo, aren't you clever!" he said, staring at me. "Thompson, look at this. It's what Rutherford wrote —isn't it?" he asked. I admitted that it was.

Thompson read it, and then gazed at me in admiration. "What, Rutherford wrote this? But it's wonderful!"

"Well, so's she," said Matthews.

This was sheer bliss. What more could any poet possibly desire than crowds of young men admiring her? I thought, mentally preening myself.

The poem was going round the girls now. Clark, Wilson, Little, King, even Valerie Barker, all read it with their mouths open and looked at me incredulously.

"But it's brilliant!"

"You're a real poet, Antonia, and you're my best friend," declared Barker.

"You'll be tremendously famous and I'll be rich just because I knew you once," said Wilson.

I asked her, "What do you think of that line about eyes everywhere that hypnotize with hate? I wasn't sure about it."

"It's wonderful," she said, and added, "I don't know what it means, though."

"Well, you know what hypnotizing is," I said. She looked at me blankly. "And eyes everywhere, that was a sort of a nightmare idea I had—like in a dream, you know, eyes all looking at me with hate."

"I don't understand it, though," she said encouragingly.

"Well," I felt hopeless. "Did you understand any of the poem?"

"Well, not really, no. But it's ever so good," she said.

I said to King, who was so clever at sums,

"Sometimes I'm afraid it's too lurid, with the horror laid on too thickly. Do you think I ought to water it down a bit?"

She looked at me in consternation. "Water it down? What do you mean?"

"Well, is it a bit overdone? Is it over-gruesome?"

"Oh, no." She shook her head emphatically. "It's not horrible at all. Don't you worry about that, it's not a bit disgusting."

"Well, I didn't mean disgusting so much," I explained, "as sort of—well, too frightening."

60

"Oh, no, that's all right," she said reassuringly. "I wasn't in the least bit frightened by it."

An awful idea struck me. "Did you really understand it?" I asked.

"Er—well, no, I didn't altogether," she admitted.

"Here y'are, Buddersmud," said Thompson, giving the poem back to me. "It's ever so good. I don't get what it's about, though."

"Oh, yes, it is good. I wish I could write poems like that," said Valerie Smith. I decided that on the whole the poem had been a success.

"I've marked your copies of *Silver*," said Miss Lovely, "they weren't too bad on the whole. Most of you have got stars. Alcock, give them out, please." I felt vaguely dismayed. Of course this would have had to happen some time, but I had been hoping not yet. She had made my copy look even worse than it need by covering it with crosses and slashes and illegible things that looked like swear-words, in red ink. I hadn't got a star.

"Now, here is yours, Derek," she said to Roberts. Even from the other side of the room I could see that his poem was worse than mine. He seemed to have torn a lot of holes in it with his pen. I could see the light through it in some places. "It was very well done, very well done indeed. I have given you two stars for it."

The class rustled uncomfortably.

She gave Roberts the paper. "Now, you see, isn't it nice to be good? Don't you think it is? Now, you keep on like this. Perhaps you will get some more stars. Wouldn't that be nice?"

She gave him a sickly smile. I had never seen her smile before, and hadn't thought she could.

Roberts said something that sounded like "Yah." As she turned away from him he screwed up his paper and threw it at her. It hit her in the middle of her back. She pretended not to notice.

Valerie Barker had made a perfectly beautiful copy in italic that looked even neater than Miss Lovely's had. She had got a star.

"That really is beautiful, Valerie," I said to her, trying to guess whether she would fly into a temper or tell me I was her best friend.

61

"Yes, it is nice, isn't it?" she agreed, examining it. "Yours was good, too, Antonia," she added.

"Mine? Oh, no. I didn't even get a star," I said.

"Well, stars are special. You don't get them unles you've done something really wonderful, so don't worry," she said, crayoning in hers as she talked.

8

THE MONDAY AFTER that was the day of the eleven-plus for Class One. Sir wandered around before it started, looking almost ill with anxiety. In prayers the headmaster had told us to be very quiet all day, very quiet indeed. Miss Lovely made Valerie spend the morning writing out "Silence Please during the Examination" on all the spare blackboards in the school, in italic. The rest of us had to prop them up in conspicuous places all over the school. We crashed round with them, shouting and fooling. Poor Sir came out and yelled at us in a whisper, but nobody except me took any notice of him.

The rest of the school, too, took care to be even noisier than usual, and the boys spent half playtime on the landing outside the room where the exam was going on, smashing milk bottles. Sir came out in a fury and caned half of them on the spot, which gave them a good excuse to howl the place down.

I was just setting out to go home at lunchtime when I remembered that I was to eat at school in future. I joined on to the end of a queue of Class Fourers who looked as if they might be going to have some lunch. I was feeling as lost and helpless as I had on my first day. We trailed down to the basement.

"Look at 'er—she's got lost!" shouted a voice, with a scream of laughter. I recognized it with a start. It was the leader of Pooh-Pooh-Pants. I turned and bolted back up the stairs. I didn't care if I didn't have any lunch, I wasn't hungry anyway, but I was not going to eat with those little harpies of Class Fourers.

I arrived at the top of the stairs again and cannoned into Tatley.

"Where on earth are you going?" she said loudly.

"I'm having school dinner today," I said, trying to look superior, as she did.

"Well, whatever were you doing there?" she said in a voice that echoed all over the school and made everyone look at me.

"You ought to be at the end of the line, over there. Go on, silly." She gave me a push that almost knocked me downstairs again.

We went into a room that I never knew existed. I had begun to think I had got the school straight, but I couldn't find a place for this anywhere. There were lots of oilcloth-topped tables and low chairs from the kindergarten. A strange woman in a white dressing-gown was arranging us at the tables. She stood me at a table beside Skinner. There were more women dressed like her dishing up brown stuff from a great cauldron through a hatchway. Some villainous-looking boys I didn't know came and stood next to Skinner, shepherded by the woman. The din was quite incredible. We were all screaming at the top of our voices. I found myself shouting too, for no reason. At the end of the room stood Miss Lovely on a wooden platform. She was shouting as well, quite inaudibly. The cooks were fussing round like nannies. They stood a boy I recognized from Class One beside me on the other side, and then Felicity Dearchild, and then O'Brien. They were all yelling hard. I looked at them in apprehension, and wished I were on the table with all the Valeries and Sandras.

Suddenly Miss Lovely rang a bell. Screaming more loudly than ever, everyone ran across the room and stood against the wall opposite the hatch. I followed, and was almost squashed to a pulp between Dearchild and one of the ruffianly looking boys. They had all got plates from somewhere. I looked wildly round. All I could see was a pile of broken vegetable dishes beside one of the hatches. When my part of the queue arrived there I snatched a bit of one and held that through the hatch. The cook didn't notice. She put a bit of pastry on it that might or might not have meat underneath, and then to my horror half emptied a bottle of ketchup over it. I grabbed it away. The ketchup ran off the broken edge of the dish all over my dress. I went back to my place next to Skinner hating Daddy for making me have school lunches, and thinking what I would say to him at home.

Miss Lovely blew a whistle. That seemed to be the signal for us to scream a shade less loudly. At least, by looking very hard at her mouth I could make out what she was saying.

"Benedictus benedicat per Jesum Christum dominum nostrum," said Miss Lovely very slowly, "Amen."

I looked at my plate. The pastry had disappeared, and there was only a bit of meat and some unattractive gristle. As I looked Dearchild leant across, yelling, speared the meat with her fork and put it on her own plate. I looked at my plate disbelievingly. One of the boys flicked a large lump of fat across the table on to it. I sat down on the tiny chair, thinking it was as well that I wasn't hungry. My head came just above the table. O'Brien and Skinner, who I had always thought were no bigger than me, didn't seem to have any trouble.

"Whee! Smash!" shouted one of the boys, rushing his mug of water across the table and spilling it into my ketchup. "Watch out! It's the Ferrari 216. Whoo!"

I said to the boy from Class One next to me,

"I suppose you've just been taking your eleven-plus. What did you think of it?"

He punched me in the face.

Miss Lovely rang a bell. All the children in the room jumped on to their chairs and put their hands on their heads.

"Now, silence, please!" she said. She checked us on the lunch register. "All right, get on."

We all screamed, and got down again. Instead of sitting down and finishing, however, we took our plates and rushed to queue at the hatches, still eating. I followed. We queued for ages. By the time they reached the hatch the others had finished and were served out some more, but I had had no intention of eating their leftovers that they had dumped on my plate, and was sent back in disgrace.

"Go on! You haven't finished. You can't have anything more till you do," said the cook. I went back to my place and waited till the rest of my table had eaten their second and third helpings. It took a long time because they kept taking things off each others' plates and fighting and playing cars with the water mugs. Twice more Miss Lovely rang a bell for silence, and we all jumped on to our chairs and put our hands on our heads. At last they finished, and the cook came to clear away the plates. Inside the hatches I could see piles of some steaming pudding which the cooks were dousing with treacle. It really didn't look too bad. I began to feel almost hungry.

"Just look at that! You haven't eaten a mouthful," said the cook, poking at my cold gristle. "Now you're just going to sit

65

there till you finish it, if it takes you all night." She stood beside me and made me do it while the rest ate the pudding.

I tried, unsuccessfully, to be sick down her.

In the afternoon, Miss Lovely made us strip to our vest and knickers and go outside in the back playground to play relay races. We stood in lines shuddering with cold and cheering feebly, while a few of us ran around with rounders pins. I looked at all the other girls wearing aertex underclothes, and compared theirs with my extra long and thick vest and knickers, and thought that I wouldn't be them for the world. It was January 23rd, I remembered, and might be going to snow tonight.

"Oh, come on, Buddersmud! Oh, you, get a move on," someone was shouting. "Quick, run!"

I ran, but had not got a notion what to do and got lost and had to round the course twice. Everybody shrieked at me.

"Oh, Buddersmud, you great idiot, now we're miles behind."

I said I was sorry, and shivered, and missed my second turn. Everyone booed me and despised me. I concentrated very hard and remembered the course and came in on time on my third turn. Unfortunately, Miss Lovely had changed the race while I wasn't looking, and although I was most conscientious about running round the chair and changing over rounders sticks I still had to go round again and lost my team the second race too. It really did begin to snow after a while, but Miss Lovely said it wouldn't hurt us and made us play ball games instead of going in. We stayed out the whole afternoon.

"In future we will have outdoor P.E. twice a week," said Miss Lovely afterwards, "and I'm not having anyone crying off. Is that understood? Not even those of us whose parents seem to think we're too soft to go out," she said, looking hard at me. "Do you all a world of good."

"It's absolutely lunatic! Lunatic!" said Mummy in a frenzy afterwards. "She might have given you pneumonia. It's enough to kill the lot of you. Better take your temperature at once."

I put the thermometer in my mouth, and said, "We're going to do it twice a week."

"It's wicked! I won't have it," said Mummy. "I don't think the thermometer would taste very nice crunched up, Antonia, I shouldn't try it. Now do you hear, you're not to do it. You are not to go out without a coat and that's that. Ninety-five! Oh,

66

it's a shame! Out in the snow with nothing on and a temperature of ninety-five! Next time just say 'Mummy says I'm to do games with my clothes on,' and if she bullies you again she ought to be sacked."

"I thought your parents would say something of the sort," said Miss Lovely glaring at me. "Have you got a medical certificate? Of course not. Right, out you come, then."

I wondered whether to warn her that she was now going to be sacked, but thought on the whole better not.

"Last night my temperature was only ninety-five and Mummy said I wasn't to go out without my coat," I said bravely.

She stared at me until I was practically not there any more, and then said, "Very well. Today I'll let it go. You can bring me a medical certificate tomorrow, and now instead of P.E. you can start on this." She rummaged in her drawer and brought out a big card covered with italic writing. "I was going to make you do it while the others did arithmetic anyway, as you're so bad at italic. Copy this out neatly until you know it."

I ventured to say, "Please, I haven't got a pen."

She flared up at me. "No, you never have anything, do you, you lazy, careless child! Well, here's one, but it's the last you'll ever have off me, mind. Now go and get on and stop making a nuisance of yourself."

I went and sat down and looked miserably at the card she had given me. I had only written out about half of it when she came back with the others from P.E. It was all spotted and smudged with tears. She said it was a horrible mess and made me start again.

I spent the whole day slaving over that italic, while the others wrote compositions and did arithmetic. Tatley's composition was read aloud and given a star. That nearly set me crying again, because I knew I could have written an even better composition and perhaps got two stars.

At the end of the day Miss Lovely looked at my italic and said it was shocking.

"You ought to be ashamed of yourself. I think you'll have to work on it again tomorrow," she said, and tore it up.

"Mummy, if I have to spend another minute writing out italic I shall run away from school," I said.

"It's so pointless. You say you didn't do any lessons all day, just spent the time learning to write?" said Mummy. "Why, you could write perfectly when you were five. Well, of all the stupid women your Miss Lovely must be the worst. Look, give me a bit of paper. I'll write to the headmaster about it now and he'll get it tomorrow and see you do some proper lessons. Really, what does that woman think I sent you to school for?"

Miss Lovely didn't make me write out that card again next day after all. Instead she said,

"Now, I've noticed that all your handwritings are perfectly disgusting, and so now you are all to write italic for all your work, and it will gradually replace your ordinary writing for good, I hope."

I decided that the headmaster couldn't have spoken to her yet.

She set us a composition to write. It was on "The Happiest Day of My Life." I had dozens of wonderful ideas and couldn't wait to begin.

"Now, don't forget. Your best italic," she said.

My dozens of ideas went down like a punctured balloon. I knew very well that I would hardly get half a line down in italic. I had cherished hopes of making up for yesterday with a brilliant essay that would beat Tatley's. I felt rebellious. Which mattered more, what I wrote or how I wrote?

"Hurry up," said Miss Lovely.

All right, I will, I thought, and wrote my brilliant composition in a sort of ungainly print that hardly even pretended to be italic. Valerie Barker next to me was writing perfect italic without a single mistake. She had written, "The hapest day of my life was my cosan Gorgy came too stay." Nothing more. Hurrah! I thought. My turn for the star.

After lunch, Miss Lovely said,

"I've marked your compositions. Most of you did very well. I don't know what happened to yours, Rutherford, it was appalling. Barker got a star for hers. Give them out, please, Johnson."

I stared at her, dumbfounded.

"However, I've been having a talk with the headmaster, and he says that after all he would rather that you didn't write italic all the time just yet." She was looking very hard at me as she spoke, just like the eyes in my poem. She really is hypnotizing me with hate, I thought, mentally congratulating Mummy.

All the same, Miss Lovely made me stay in during the lunch hour to re-write my composition. I didn't know whether I was pleased at escaping half an hour in the playground, or miserable at having to write out pages of italic.

"Valentine's Day," said Mummy on the doorstep, "I expect there'll be some high jinks at school."

"Oh, I wonder," I said doubtfully. "Still, you can't tell."

"Just supposing a boy sent you a valentine!"

"More likely a black eye," I said. "School's not a place for romance. I'm so sorry, Mummy." She looked quite crestfallen.

Just as I had expected, nobody even knew that it was Valentine's Day. "And Leap Year too," I said to Valerie Barker. "That's when the girls do the proposing, isn't it? You ought to propose to someone."

"Ooh, I know who," she said, and put her arms round my neck. "I'll marry you."

"Oh," I said, wriggling uncomfortably and wishing I'd never brought the subject up.

At the end of the afternoon I went into the cloakroom to get my raincoat. I heard a great trampling of feet behind me. Usually I waited for my raincoat until the boys had gone.

"Look out—here comes the rush hour," I tried to say to someone, but before I had finished speaking I was swallowed up in a wave of stamping boys. I lost my balance and fell over, and tried to wriggle away. Skinner, charging through, gave me such a kick in the face that I was knocked backwards again, feeling dizzy, under the boys' feet. I tried to clutch at the coat hook for support.

The boys rushed out again, treading on me as they went. I really did feel a bit peculiar from the kick Skinner had given me. My head was buzzing, my face was stinging, I felt sick and giddy, and I could hardly see. I sat down on the floor again.

"Oh, hullo, Antonia," said Valerie Smith falling over me. "What are you doing down there? Are you all right?"

"Yes, I'm all right, thank you," I said, getting up. "A boy kicked me in the face. No matter. It's not as if it were the first time. See you tomorrow!"

I aimed at the door, and lurched out, very cross with myself for forgetting to wait until the boys had gone before getting my coat, and even more cross because I felt so ill over nothing at all. At the end of the street a group of strange boys came past, staring at me.

69

"One—lovely—black eye!" sang one of them. They all laughed. Quite batty, I thought. Then it occurred to me that perhaps they were referring to me.

"What, back already?" called Mummy from the kitchen as I came in. "We're just finishing lunch. Well, how did you get on? Get any valentines? Come on down and talk to us."

I didn't think I could face the stairs just yet. I called down,

"Everything happened just as I said. No valentines, but I got a whacking great black eye. I'll come down in a minute."

"What's that? A black eye?" cried Mummy, and came running up. "Wow! So you have! Eeh, you poor child, the things they do to you at this awful school!"

"A black eye? Someone's given our Totty a black eye?" said Daddy, coming up. "A knockout!"

Wrestling was one of Daddy's hobbies. He watched it avidly every Saturday on television, and sometimes threatened to try out some of the holds on me.

"Yes. A knockout decided the winner," I said weakly. "It happened just now."

"It's too awful to think of. Come and lie down on the sofa. What brute did it?" said Mummy, tucking me down.

"Oh, I only got Skinner's foot in my face. It's my own fault for being where his foot wanted to go. Anyway, it's always happening. I'm getting quite used to the taste of boys' boots," I said.

"I don't see that that's any consolation at all," said Mummy. "Do you feel all right? No, you don't look it, either. By the way, I wrote to Dr. Harvey for your medical certificate. He said that after all your flu, he would willingly send one. Your poor eye does look awful."

"Why not complain about it to the headmaster?" suggested Daddy.

"Oh, not again!" I said, involuntarily.

"Good idea. I don't believe he has any idea what goes on behind his back. Skinner, you say it was? I'll ring him up now."

When she came back she said,

"The headmaster was horrified and promised to 'put the fear of God into him,' so I hope he'll be more careful in future."

"Will the headmaster cane him?" I asked anxiously.

"I sincerely hope so. Yes, sure to," she answered.

"Oh," I said miserably. "Oh, I wish you hadn't!"

"You wish we hadn't? Why I hope it'll teach him to leave you alone in future," Mummy said.

"But he didn't kick me on purpose. Now he really will want to get at me," I said, thinking of that dark place under the fire-escape in the playground where the boys dragged the girls and made them scream.

The medical certificate that Mummy had written for arrived the next morning. It said that on no account was I to go outside without warm clothes and a coat. I showed it triumphantly to Miss Lovely. She looked at it as if it were a rattlesnake and opened and shut her mouth without saying anything.

Finally she managed to say, "Very well. I suppose this doctor knows what he's doing, although I'm sure it wouldn't hurt you to get a little air to your body. You may do P.E. fully dressed." She said it as if she were granting a great honour. "Though mind you I asked for it several days ago." She looked in disgust at my black eye. "Your face is a disgrace. I suppose you've been fighting," she snorted, and stalked out of the room to go to prayers.

After prayers she told Skinner that the headmaster would like to see him. I felt a pang of remorse. The poor boy got into trouble often enough without my interfering. It wasn't as if he'd deliberately set on me. He came back presently looking none the worse for wear, but that didn't mean anything. I dreaded play-time.

When it came I crept downstairs behind the others, and peeped round the door into the playground. I couldn't see him, and stepped outside. Skinner was standing behind the door, and I found myself facing him. I prepared to fight for my life. He grinned at me, and stepped back to let me pass. As I went by I looked at him anxiously. He just grinned again. I ran to the lavatories, not knowing what to think; I wondered whether anything the headmaster could say would stop him bashing me up if he wanted to.

After play, as I was going upstairs, he put out his foot just in front of me in one of the dark corners. I fell over it, and tumbled down two flights of stone stairs, and was only saved by Tatley, standing duty as stair monitor from going further. I decided not to say anything at home. After all, it might have been an accident.

On the door of the classroom there hung a great chart with

71

everyone's points marked on it. I used to get quite a lot when Sir took our class, but now that we had Miss Lovely, I noticed sadly, I hadn't had a single one all term.

"Good gracious!" I said to Valerie Barker standing beside me, "look at all the marks Roberts has got! Six! Now how on earth did Roberts get six points? You can see, he got nothing but minuses last term."

"Didn't you know?" said Valerie, looking at me in surprise. "Miss Lovely's just made him House captain for Green and he gets all the points for sport. Anyway, he's one of her favourites."

"Funny. I wouldn't have thought he was at all the type to make a good House captain," I said, putting things mildly.

"Perhaps that's why Green came bottom last week," giggled Valerie.

While the others were still changing after P.E. Miss Lovely and Roberts came up together. I was there already, not having to change.

"Now, don't you think it's fun, being in a responsible position? Don't you get a wonderful feeling when you think that other people are relying on you?" she was saying.

"No, I don't," said Roberts, scowling.

"Oh, really now, Derek, try not to look at things like that. Of course, when one is put in authority life isn't so comfortable for oneself afterwards. But I'm sure you'll find that the pleasure of being able to make other people comfortable quite makes up for that. Now, your team isn't getting on very well at the moment, but you'll soon settle down and then if you really work hard it might come top at the end of term. Yes, it really might, if you work hard, as I'm sure you will. And wouldn't that be a lovely surprise for your form master to come back to? To see that you've improved so much that you can help your House to be top? Now then, you try really hard, and let everyone see how good you can be," said Miss Lovely, talking very gently and putting on an encouraging smile.

Roberts snarled in her face. She smiled more sweetly than ever. Roberts looked as if he would like to be sick down her. I found myself sympathizing with him.

"Now, Derek. I should very much like you to bring my tea to me in playtime, instead of Linda, in future," she said. "I know you aren't yet a prefect, but I'm sure nobody will mind."

"Oh, blast you, you old bag," growled Roberts into his shirt.

72

Everyone else suddenly finished changing and charged into the room, interrupting Miss Lovely before she could look shocked.

Miss Lovely broke the news to Tatley that she had been deprived of her special privilege of bringing her form teacher's tea. Tatley had a wonderful time being offended, and then saying in a hurt way that of course it was perfectly all right, although she didn't really see why Roberts. . . . But Miss Lovely wouldn't give in, and Tatley just had to go and sit down in a sulk.

Roberts didn't take Miss Lovely's tea up at playtime the next day. I had had a suspicion he wouldn't, and wondered whether I would have either. She had a little talk with him afterwards. I couldn't help admiring her patience and determination, or was it bone-headedness? Roberts played the fool with such energy throughout the next lesson that we didn't get any work done at all. Miss Lovely didn't say anything to him, and blamed everything on me instead, because I had leant across to ask Valerie the page.

"If you won't sit still and work, Rutherford, there are plenty of people who have to go to less good schools who would be only too glad to take your place at this one!" she roared. I shut my eyes and held on to my chair while the blast of words went over me.

Sandra King, at the front of the class, suddenly screamed and tucked her feet up under her chair. All the other girls did the same, giggling and squealing. The boys kept their feet resolutely on the floor, watching the girls in amusement.

"Now what's the matter?" snapped Miss Lovely.

"There's a spider, Miss Lovely," squeaked Sandra Pope.

"A spider? What a lot of fuss for nothing!" said Miss Lovely, moving nervously across to the other side of the class-room.

"You scared of spiders then, Miss Lovely?" called Mason.

"Of course not. Don't be rude," said Miss Lovely, coming back again.

The girls in front began to scream extra loudly, and the spider ran past them to the front of the room, almost to Miss Lovely's feet. It certainly was the biggest, blackest spider I had ever seen, even bigger than the ones that came out of the walls in our country cottage. Miss Lovely squeaked and retreated again. The spider ran on a bit further, as if it were chasing her. She marched all the way over to the door, pretending to be looking for the board rubber, and the spider followed. The whole class began to giggle. I felt really sorry for her.

Roberts got up with a matchbox, caught the spider and put it in the box. Miss Lovely shuddered all the way down when he picked it up in his hand.

"Oh, Roberts, you old spoil-sport," shouted the class, who had been enjoying seeing Miss Lovely in torment.

"Oh, thank you, Derek," gasped Miss Lovely. "Now throw the nasty thing away, and let's have no more of this nonsense."

Roberts didn't throw the spider away. He put it, in its box, in his pocket. He was as good as gold all the rest of the lesson, which made me suspicious anyway, and when next day he actually took up a cup of tea at playtime, I should have thought that even Miss Lovely might have guessed what was coming. She didn't, however. As we all tore down the stairs to the playground, we heard a hysterical scream come from inside the staff room. Everyone stopped instantly, absolutely still, listening. I saw that the others all had an expression of great glee on their faces, and I suspected I had the same.

"Look, it's all right now, I've thrown it away. I'll get you some more tea," said Sir's voice, sounding most embarrassed. Someone was gasping, almost sobbing. Sir came out, pink in the face.

"Go on. Get out," he said, waving us downstairs. We had to go.

Later I noticed that Andrews was wearing the Green House captain badge instead of Roberts. The rumour went round that the headmaster had been caning someone in the lunch hour, and Roberts certainly looked peculiarly pink and snarled extra defiantly all the afternoon. Tatley took up Miss Lovely's tea next day.

9

"THE HEADMASTER HAS decided to change the library system. There are lots of new books, and now we need two people to sort them, probably just in playtime. Who would like to do that?" said Miss Lovely.

To be able to spend playtime, the worst moment of the day, safely in the library! I shot up my arm.

"I think you were first, Rutherford. We'll have you. And you, Page, you were next, I think. Will you two come up to me at dinner time and I'll tell you what to do."

"It will be lovely, won't it?" I said to Lynda Page as we sat playing Jacks in the lavatories at playtime. "To spend play sorting books indoors, instead of hanging about here freezing, looking at that row of green doors."

"Yes, that's just why I volunteered," she said. "Anyway, I like books. I read an awful lot."

"Do you really? I do too," I said eagerly. "Just at the moment I'm reading *David Copperfield*. I'm about halfway through. Daddy gave it to me." I didn't bother to correct myself to "Dad."

"That's pretty long, isn't it? I read an abridged edition of it years ago, and that was six hundred pages."

"I suppose it is long," I said. It hadn't struck me before. Daddy produced these epics from time to time and I always read them avidly, without really noticing their length. "I've just finished reading *The Three Musketeers*, only that was abridged, and there's *The Man in the Iron Mask* waiting for me."

"I'm reading a book of Greek legends," said Lynda.

"I like them too. The King Arthur stories are my favourites though," I said. "I've got knights in armour all over my bedroom walls."

"Could you read when you were eight?"

"Of course. I could read when I was five," I told her.

"So could I," she said.

I noticed Valerie Barker hanging around, listening aghast to our conversation. I asked her, "What books do you like?"

"Oh, I like school stories, Antonia," she said, "though I don't read much. I don't really like books."

She was looking miserable. I could have kicked myself. I remembered now, too late, that I had decided long ago that she couldn't read. Not enough to count, anyway.

"What a pretty poodle brooch that is," I said hastily. "Simply sweet!"

"My aunt bought it for me at Christmas," she said, brightening. "And you'll never guess what I gave her, Antonia. The cutest little doggy calendar...."

Lynda Page drifted away. Valerie chattered on and on. I kept telling myself how lucky I was to be her special confidential friend, and how kind it was of her to befriend me.

In class I suddenly remembered the letter that had come the day before. *Pioneer* had decided to print *The Death of a Shell* and had accordingly sent me ten shillings. Mummy was wild with excitement because someone at last had condescended to publish her favourite poem, but, after *Doorway*, *Pioneer* had somewhat lost its glamour for me, and in any case I had always loathed *The Death of a Shell*. Still, ten shillings was ten shillings.

"Valerie," I said excitedly, interrupting her account of the umbrella her mother wanted, "do you know what, I've got enough money now to buy your new pen, instead of the one I broke. Where do I buy it, please?"

"Oh, that! Oh, forget about that. You needn't bother to get me another because you're my best friend, and anyway it was broken already and wouldn't fill," she said, forgivingly. "It's got a sort of small pattern, just like the border of my new handkerchiefs. Not the pen, silly. Don't keep on about that."

I felt pleased and grateful at her generosity, though I did think she might have told me before I saved up for so long.

After lunch, Lynda Page and I went to the staff room and asked for Miss Lovely. She came out with piles of books and led us to a sort of little cubby-hole behind the big cupboard in our classroom. It was solid with books just heaped anyhow, almost up to the ceiling. Lynda and I gaped at it, while Miss Lovely showed us a few small shelves hidden in strange places like under the table. There was hardly room for the three of us, even though we were standing on the piles of books as if they were perfectly good floor.

"What a sweet little library," I said.

Miss Lovely glared at me. "Yes, I suppose you want to bring your dollies to tea here, Rutherford," she said. I wasn't sure whether she was joking or not, and didn't know whether to smile (and be half-witted) or to look rebuked (and sulk).

"Now, I want you to arrange the books on these shelves in alphabetical order, under authors," she explained. "And label the shelves. And enter the books in this catalogue, one book on each card. Now then, I think you can start at once. You'll have to put in quite a bit of work to get this straight."

"Oh, but we'll enjoy it, Miss Lovely," said Lynda. Miss Lovely looked at her (I had never seen her smile at anyone except Roberts) and left us sitting on top of a mountain of books, like fairy-tale princesses about to spend the night separating peas from beans.

"This is going to be fun," I said, climbing down on to the bit of floor that Miss Lovely had been standing on.

"Oh yes, it is," said Lynda. "You take this half of the pile and I'll stay over this side. Let's have the A books here."

"And the B books next to them. *Man and his Occupations* by P. L. Bond, that's B. Can I have the catalogue, please?"

"*The History of Sugar.* No author."

"List it under the publisher," I suggested.

"The publisher?"

"Yes, that's the publisher there on the back, look," I said, pleased at knowing something she didn't. "After you with the catalogue."

"You sort out the books. I'll write them down," she suggested after a while. That worked much better. Miss Lovely came in presently, said we weren't getting on as fast as she had hoped we would, and perhaps we had better go on all the afternoon instead of doing lessons. Lynda and I tried swopping jobs every ten minutes. We were still bored. The books were all most unappetising, and had lengthy titles that took a long time to write down. We amused each other by making little jokes, but still we couldn't help listening longingly to the class reciting their tables on the other side of the cupboard.

"Swing high! Swing low!" sang Lynda, doing a little dance on top of the books.

"What's that?" I asked, laughing.

"It's the name of a book of exercises in musical rhythm."

I wrote it down.

By the following Wednesday we had reduced the pile to only a sort of carpeting of books on the floor. Miss Lovely kept bringing in more, but even so it really looked as if we had almost finished. There were little rows of books on every flat ridge and surface in the room. The catalogue was almost full. When we went in on Thursday in the dinner-hour we felt almost keen again to think that this would be the last afternoon we would have to spend listing books.

"About time too," I said, when we were gloating over this. "I was just about getting fed up with stewing over these books in here."

"Me too," said Lynda, "I feel as if I'd been breathing books for the last week. *Clothes of the Old Testament* by Rosalind Peters."

Miss Lovely came in and said,

"Oh, you've nearly finished. Too bad, I'd hoped to save you work. Now I'm afraid we're scrapping this system and you have sorted all the books into the wrong categories. Still, a bit of honest work won't hurt you, and the catalogue may be useful. Now, I want you to sort the books into Fiction, History, Music, Geography and so on, and put a card inside each cover with the title and author written on it. Now, here are the cards. I want you to make a really good job of this, do you understand?"

I heard Lynda mutter, "That's what you said last time." I hoped Miss Lovely had heard too.

"And finish the catalogue, of course. Now, you're so far behind after wasting such a lot of time that I think you had better work all this afternoon again. Not that you really wasted that time, of course. It will have helped to teach you to be neat and methodical over a piece of work, however boring it may be. And that will have done you more good than I can say. You're flighty, that's what you are, can't apply yourselves to a job without moaning and groaning and wanting a change the whole time," said Miss Lovely, looking at me as if she thought that she could turn me into stone.

78

"Yes, Miss Lovely," we said, hoping she would go away soon.

At the door, just as we were thinking that she had, she turned and said,

"And I'm not putting up with messy cards. Do you hear, not a single mistake. And there are only just enough cards for the books. There are some more books arriving tomorrow, fifty I think."

"Yes, Miss Lovely," we growled.

She was actually outside the door when she turned and came in again, and said,

"Oh yes. And it's your duty as library monitors to see that the library is kept attractive and interesting. It's up to you to provide pictures."

Then she really did go.

Lynda and I sat sulking, with our elbows on the table. Presently I said,

"In medieval times she would have been ducked in a pond."

"Or perhaps had her tongue cut out, so that she couldn't speak," suggested Lynda. We considered that for a bit. Then we got up heavily and began to throw all our neatly sorted books back into the pile on the floor, and said things like, "Let's have the A to C shelf for Fiction, it's the smallest, and I don't suppose there's a single Fiction book there."

We found, in fact, two Fiction books. One was *Fables and Proverbs from Many Lands* and the other was Lamb's *Tales from Shakespeare*.

Towards the end of the afternoon play we began to write out the cards. After a while I said to Lynda,

"Isn't it funny, that after all that about our awful writing and that business with the italic Miss Lovely should choose us to write out these cards."

"Oh, well, you see," Lynda said, "we're the only ones in the class who could do them accurately, and she knows that jolly well. So she just has to put up with our scrawls."

"I think both our writings are very nice," I said.

Lynda was drawing something on the back of her card. She put it in its place in the catalogue and took out another, and drew something on the back of that too. I looked over her shoulder. It was an excellent likeness of Miss Lovely, with her frizzed-up hair and long nose and disapproving scowl. She was carrying a huge pile of books and there was one lying on the ground in front of her. Lynda was smiling and looking almost mischievous as she drew. She always looked so good at other times that it was quite a surprise to see her looking mischievous. She put her card back in the box and took out another. She drew on the back the same caricature of Miss Lovely, but with her foot slightly raised and leaning forward a little.

In the next Miss Lovely had put her foot down on the edge of the book in front of her. Then Lynda drew her toppling over, picture by picture, with more and more of the books in her arms tumbling over the room and with a horrified expression on her face. On the back of the last card she was lying flat on her face on the ground looking positively diabolic, and all her books were lying round her.

Lynda looked at me and grinned, took out all the cards she had drawn on and flicked them quickly down on the table. The pictures of Miss Lovely went by so fast that you really saw her tripping and falling with all her beastly books.

"Bravo!" I shouted without thinking. Lynda shushed me and flicked the cards again. We collapsed on to the table, laughing silently. I took the cards and flicked them again. They were unmistakably Miss Lovely.

"Gosh!" I said suddenly, "you've done them in ink."

We stared at each other for a minute, and then Lynda burst out laughing again. She put the cards back in the catalogue, still with their caricatures. We could hear Miss Lovely's voice raised crossly in the classroom, through the cupboard. Lynda put out her tongue in that direction.

"I almost hope she does find the pictures," she said. We both laughed.

"*Dear Doctor*, what on earth is that?" I said, flicking through it.

The new system was much harder and it took far longer to sort each book. It had been quite easy to find the author, or editor, or publisher, but often we had to read great chunks of dull prose to decide whether a book was Geography, or Nature (Miss Lovely had told us to have that one), or General Knowledge.

"It seems to be about Albert Schweitzer in Africa. Oh dear, we'll have to open a new section for Biographies."

"Couldn't it possibly be Geography?" asked Lynda.

"No, not really. Well, I'll call it Nature and she'll just have to lump it."

"After all, no one's ever going to look at it."

"No, I don't suppose anyone will ever look at any of them. Who's going to look through hundreds of cards?"

We thought of our picture sequences. "Just as well," Lynda said. We both giggled.

10

Valerie Barker was in a huff. I tried to chat with her, but she only sulked and turned her back. I felt a bit guilty at deserting her for Lynda, for it had gradually dawned on me that far from being her privileged friend I was her only friend. Still, it wasn't my fault, I thought.

"Oh, look here, Valerie, I'm sorry that I don't spend as much time as I used with you, but it's Miss Lovely's fault, you know, for making me spend all day in the library. I didn't ask her to put me on to do afternoons in there as well. I don't just play truant, you know," I said very fast, wringing my hands.

"You volunteered. And I know why, because that girl Page did. It's all your own fault and you don't care. You just leave me all alone, after all I've done for you, and you used to be my best friend," she said in a muffled voice, with her back to me.

"You know I put up my hand before Lynda did, you know that perfectly, so I couldn't have done it because of her," I said in exasperation. "And you know that Miss Lovely said it would only be for playtime. How could I know she'd keep me in there for hours on end, like a prisoner?" I hoped Valerie would giggle. She didn't, and so I went on, "Bother Miss Lovely, she's a great big cheat. Isn't she?" Valerie still didn't giggle, and so I gave her a lead by giggling myself.

But she only said, "You broke my best pen, Antonia, and you never bought me another."

I could have screamed. I took her by her hostile shoulders and I shook her. I shouted in her ear, "You little worm! Do you remember what you said, when I had the money and was going to buy it? You said 'Forget about the pen. You needn't buy me another because it was broken anyway.' Yes, you said that. And then you have the nerve to say what you did just now. Just because you're jealous. Well, you didn't have any reason to be jealous before, but you can go ahead now, because I like Lynda

Page a great deal better than I like you, you whining selfish thing!"

She collapsed on to her desk and burst into tears, sobbing and sniffing, and said through her handkerchief, "You're a horrible, cruel girl, Antonia, and I shall never love you again."

Oh, dear, yes, so I am, I thought, suddenly sorry for my bad temper. I wondered whether to apologize, but then I knew I couldn't, and even if I did it wouldn't make any difference.

Little went up to her, put her arm round her and said sympathetically, "Oh, poor Valerie! What's the matter? Don't cry!"

Valerie looked up at her like a little innocent girl that never did anything to deserve such treatment, and began to cry again. Little pulled up her chair and began to stroke her hair and soothe her. Valerie flung herself on Little's shoulder, buried her face in it and sobbed and sobbed. I turned away in relief, feeling that I had handed over a responsibility.

After that we sat with our desks pulled as far apart as possible. After a while Miss Lovely noticed and made us put them together again, but then she sent me back to work in the library, and so that didn't matter.

Lynda and I seemed to spend most of our time in the library. We hardly did any lessons. We always spent play and the dinner-hour and usually some of the afternoon sorting books and writing out cards. That day Miss Lovely made us stay in the library all the time between morning play and dinner as well. Lynda and I grumbled to each other about this, and hardly did any work. The heap of books was still enormous, and didn't get any less no matter how energetically we worked, and so we soon decided that there wasn't any point in working energetically.

In the evening I told Mummy and Daddy about my scene with Valerie Barker.

"I just lost my temper. It had been bottling up inside me for a long time, and then when she said that about the pen I boiled over. I was sorry afterwards, but she wasn't and so I didn't say so. Anyway, she's so maddening that I couldn't stand another minute of her," I explained.

"She must have been bad to make you say all that, certainly," said Mummy doubtfully.

"I can imagine her perfectly. I'd have done just the same," said Daddy, chuckling.

"Yes, so you would," said Mummy, looking at him.

"Oh yes, I meant to say, Miss Lovely wants some pictures to hang in the library," I said, suddenly remembering. "Lynda brought a newspaper cutting, but I haven't brought anything."

"Well, we must think of something you can have. I suppose it's got to be earnest and worthy? Otherwise that picture you did of Lake Como would be perfect. You remember, Antonia, the one where you got sand in the oil paint and it gave it such a wonderful texture," Mummy said, brightening.

"Oh, no! Oh, dear, no, nothing like that," I said aghast.

"There are lots of things of yours that anyone ought to be glad to be able to hang," she went on, "like that one of the sun on the water, the near-abstract."

"Now, steady on, steady on, this is a school, remember, full of dull teachers," said Daddy, laughing and patting her.

Mummy hung her head and looked downcast, and said, "Oh, very well, I suppose not, although if I were the teacher I'd hang everything Antonia's ever done."

"I'm sure you would, Mummy," I said hugging her, "but really, Mummy, not at school, not my pictures, really not."

"Well, I'll think of something schooly," she said. "Oh, no, that isn't really the time? Oh, my goodness, fly to bed!"

"*Three Men in a Jeep*. What on earth could that be?" I said, and began to read the first page. "Wow, it's dull."

Lynda groaned and flopped over the table. "Ooh, my foot really hurts. I didn't want to come this morning, but my mother said that there's always something wrong with me and called me an old moaner."

I sat down and flopped over the table too, next to her. "What's wrong with your foot, have you sprained it?" I asked.

"I think I must have. I can't walk on it properly."

"You shouldn't be at school, then," I said.

"I thought that, but Mum said, 'It was toothache yesterday and now it's your foot and tomorrow it'll be something else, and so you can just go.'"

"I've got a bit of a headache myself. These books aren't helping it," I said. We sat looking glumly at each other for a minute.

"Well, I suppose we'd better get on," said Lynda with a sigh. I picked up *Three Men in a Jeep* and looked hopelessly at it.

"It seems to be about photographing antelope. I suppose that's Nature?" I said.

"In Africa. Yes, I suppose it is," Lynda said, looking over my shoulder. "But people go hunting in Africa too, don't they? I mean, it would be Nature if they only photograph the antelope, but if they shoot them it'll have to be Geography or General or something."

"Well, I'm not going to read the whole book just in case they go shooting," I said. "It can just be Nature and like it."

"Anyway, nobody's going to catch you out. Nobody's going to look at the cards, or read the book either," said Lynda, beginning to sketch a caricature on the back of her card.

I made a picture sequence after that on the back of the cards in the catalogue, of Miss Lovely sitting on a drawing-pin. Then we used the cards that were to go inside the books, and drew caricatures of the teachers on the back of every one we did. We made quite long and complicated sequences. We laughed together over them, and it did cheer us up a bit.

We made them in class too, on the edges of our rough books, instead of getting on with our sewing or handwriting or modelling, and flicked them over to each other under our desks. After a while we could hardly see a book without exchanging significant glances and laughing to ourselves.

When I came home in the evening Mummy called out from the kitchen,

"I had such a brainwave about the pictures for your library! Come downstairs and have some tea, and I'll tell you what I've done."

I went down, feeling slightly apprehensive.

"I rang up all the embassies and asked them to send posters of their countries round to your school," announced Mummy, "Wasn't I brilliant?"

"Brilliant. Posters, did you say?" I said weakly.

"Yes, you know, big wall posters," said Mummy. "They were only too glad to send them. I rang up the French and German and Belgian and Norwegian embassies and they're all sending big posters that you can put up in your library."

She looked like a dog wanting to be patted, and I patted her. I said what a splendid idea and how pleased Miss Lovely would be. All the same, I couldn't help visualizing the library, a tiny little hidey-hole behind a cupboard, and the walls so criss-crossed with bookshelves that Lynda had only just managed to squeeze in her newspaper cutting between two of them.

After lunch, as we were settling in to another afternoon in the library, Miss Lovely came in looking harassed, and said,

"Some posters have just arrived from the German Embassy, and the man says they're for the library and that Mrs. Rutherford sent for them, that's your mother, isn't it? Well, it's very kind of her, but I really don't think there's room here for all three—"

"Three? Posters?" gasped Lynda.

"Yes, just so, Page. We might get one there, and of course there's always the ceiling," said Miss Lovely, looking miserable. "I don't think you can have explained to your mother the size of the library, Rutherford?"

"Well, no, but how could I know she'd send for posters?" I said. "I mean to say, I asked for pictures."

Miss Lovely glared at me. "Well, they're outside in the passage," she said. "I'll leave it to you to put them up."

We had got one up, draping it over the history shelf and totally blocking the window, when she came in again, red in the face.

"Rutherford, would you come outside for a moment," she said. I went out, guessing what had happened.

"Now then, what's all this about the posters?" she said sternly. She looked as if she wasn't being as angry as she would like. "Some more have come from the Norwegian and French Embassies for the library. The men said Mrs. Rutherford sent for them. Now, your mother surely..." She hesitated and glared at me.

"She did really send for them, it's nothing to do with me," I said hastily before she could accuse me. "I'm very sorry, Miss Lovely, but I never told her about the size of the library, and she was only trying to help. She sent for them without telling me, and thought they would be so suitable." Miss Lovely still looked suspicious. "If she realized about the library, I'm sure she wouldn't mind if we didn't hang all the posters there. They might look quite nice somewhere else," I added to soothe her.

"Well, if your mother really made a mistake...of course, we're delighted to have the posters...they'll be most useful... it was very kind of her." She kept pausing, looking at me sideways all the time, distrustfully.

"Oh good, I'll tell her you like them," I said. "By the way, I think there are more posters to come, from Belgium." I thought it was best to warn her.

She turned on me. "What? More posters? Now, this is a bit too much," she said, up in arms again.

"Perhaps Mummy thought each embassy would only send one poster. Four posters in any library except ours..." I began.

"Well, I suppose she meant well," she said, relaxing again.

In the library, Lynda asked, "What did she want?"

"Some more posters had come. She thought I had sent for them as a practical joke. It's all right, I hadn't," I said quickly. "It's funny though, that she should be so suspicious when it's me and I've done nothing, and yet she never guessed a thing when it was Roberts."

"You're certainly taking your time over this book sorting," said Miss Lovely coming in and scowling at the mountain of books on the floor. "I think you'd better work at it all tomorrow afternoon too." She looked at me as if she hated me and stamped out.

"Did your Miss Lovely like the posters?" asked Mummy eagerly when I came home.

"Er—yes—they were beautiful posters," I mumbled. "Oh Mummy, what a wonderful goldfish! Why, it's black. When did you get it? Tell me about it."

As I had hoped, Mummy forgot about the posters. "Oh yes, that's my new Black Moor goldfish. I'm really bucked about getting hold of it. It's very rare, you see, and I was afraid I wouldn't get it. I thought this aquarium was the only one worthy of it. This is really quite a showpiece now, isn't it, what with the pearl-scales and now this? Oh, do you think I'll be able to breed the pearl-scales? I would love to. Just supposing it came off, and I managed to rear a whole school of little pearl-scales!"

"Do you know, Lynda, that since I began this ghastly library job I haven't been able to bring myself to open a book at home. I'm no further on with *David Copperfield*," I complained.

"Well, cheer up, there can't be more than another two hundred books to go," said Lynda. "And only a few weeks to go to the end of term. And then you needn't look at a book for three solid weeks."

In fact the pile of unsorted books was at last beginning to disappear, like a melting iceberg. You could step over it at one stride now, instead of having to climb and clamber. We were on the last box of cards, and we had been telling each other for a long time that when those were finished we would have to stop, because we couldn't write out cards when there weren't any, could we?

"Give them to me and I'll chuck them down the lavatory in playtime," I had suggested. There didn't seem to be any need for that now, for they were going fast anyway.

We began to brighten up and put on a last sprint of hard work. The pile on the floor was really quite insignificant now beside all the shelves and shelves full, lining the wall. The big cupboard had been turned round for us to fill with books, and we had. And every book had its beautiful little card tucked inside, and every card had its beautiful little caricature.

"We'll be finished by the end of term, I really think we will," said Lynda a bit later. "That's in a fortnight."

"Oh, we'll have finished ages and ages before that," I said gaily. "Oh, here's our old friend *Swing High, Swing Low*." I danced across the library to the Music shelf.

The door opened, and Miss Lovely staggered in loaded with dozens of long white boxes, just like the ones our cards had been in.

"Here, help me, will you, take some of this," she snapped. We dutifully took an armful each. I could see the label on the top box of my armful. It said, "Folder Type Cards, Pink." I had an unpleasant feeling in the pit of my stomach.

"Now, I'm sorry about this, but the headmaster has just decided that the original idea of putting the cards in loose won't do. He has decided to adopt the system used in most schools where these new cards are stuck inside the books, with the name and so on of the book written on this bit here, and the old cards put inside, like this. You have a different colour for each category : green for Nature, and so on. I'm afraid it'll mean starting all over again, and of course it will take you longer this way." She smiled brightly at us. "But I'm sure you agree that the new plan is much better than the other. Don't you?"

"Well, don't you?" she said menacingly.

"I suppose so," muttered Lynda.

"Well, yes," I said. "It's just that—well, we seem to be wasting so much of our lesson time in here—"

"Wasting! Wasting! I like that! That's just the sort of stupid, short-sighted remark you would make, Rutherford," Miss Lovely shouted. "You're doing some really useful work in this library, for a change—useful to someone besides yourself, that is. Now for goodness' sake just stop grumbling and complaining, if you can do such a thing, and make a start. Glue? There's paste powder in the cupboard. No initiative, have you?"

She stamped out. Lynda and I sat with our heads on our arms at the table.

After a while I shook myself, and reached down a book. "Old beast," I grumbled, "I don't believe she wants us to finish this library job. *Setting Up a Miniature Rockery*. Can I have a green card, please?"

11

"Help! Oh, no! Don't say that's Daddy!" exclaimed Mummy. "Gosh, and we've only just finished breakfast. He oughtn't to wake up for hours and hours yet."

It was Daddy. He slammed open the door and came in, scowling, and didn't say good morning.

"Oh Man, don't say I woke you?" I asked, horrified.

"It was the dustman, or someone. Crashing round the street at eight in the morning. And then there were hyenas banging car doors all night, and a brute of a dog barked non-stop from three till five. Oh, what's the use of trying to live in a place like this?"

"Oh, dear, I'm so sorry, it must be misery," said Mummy. "Didn't you get any sleep at all?"

"I dozed between seven and eight. Oh, it's all hell." He put his elbows all over the table and looked black. "Why can't we go away and live somewhere quiet? This is as bad as London."

"Oh, poor, poor Man, how you suffer. But it's a pretty street, though, isn't it?" said Mummy, trying to cheer him up.

"Oh, no, it isn't! Oh, no, it isn't!" roared Daddy, banging his fist on the table. "How can it be pretty when it rains all day? Anyway, people bang car doors all night and keep watch-dogs and that's enough for me. I'm supposed to be painting. How can I paint if I don't sleep? Let's go away somewhere where I can."

"Time you left, Antonia," whispered Mummy. I squeezed past Daddy, who had pushed his chair back so that I could hardly get by, and slunk out. He really looked terrifying, and I was glad to get away.

In the evening, when I came home from school, I tiptoed in, not knowing what to expect, but feeling a bit apprehensive.

"Is that our little Antonina-Serena, creeping in?" came the happy voice of Daddy from the drawing-room. I went in, feeling relieved. He and Mummy were on the sofa in a nest of holiday brochures. He was reading one with a big picture of a veiled woman and a bottle of wine and a big yellow sun with a great happy grin on it, on the cover.

"You'd better start packing, we're leaving tomorrow for Ibiza."

"We're what?" I gasped.

"Getting out of this place as fast as we can," explained Daddy.

"We're both fed up with not sleeping and with the horrible weather and we're off to the sun. Yippee!" said Mummy.

"You mean to say we're going abroad somewhere—in the middle of term—just like that?" It seemed too good to be true.

"Tomorrow," said Daddy. I stared at him. His face looked just like the one on the big sun on his brochure cover.

"Whoopee! Oh, Man!" I shouted, diving into the nest of travel catalogues and trying to hug Mummy and Daddy both together. "Say that again? Tomorrow? Where? How? When? Wow!"

"Ibiza. By air. In a few hours' time," said Daddy, looking almost as happy as he had at Christmas. "All ready and packed and everything? We've left!"

"Help! Panic!" I jumped up and ran upstairs to pack my china flying horses, my paper flying horses, my plasticine flying horses, my toy knights in armour, my cardboard castle and all its extra pieces, like the Moat of Fire and the Wishing Well.

"Don't forget your pyjamas," Mummy called up. I had.

We packed all night. Mummy and Daddy kept drinking champagne, and we laughed and sang and covered the drawing-room with clothes. Most of mine had to go in Mummy's case, because I didn't want to squash the cardboard castle.

In the aeroplane I tried to write a poem about the clouds, but I was too excited to concentrate.

As we climbed out at the end of the journey Daddy suddenly turned to me and said, "Down on your knees and kiss the soil of Ibiza!"

"Why, it really is soil. We've landed in a field," I said as I began to obey.

"Don't! Man, the things you think of," said Mummy, hauling me up. "What a pretty little white cottage that is."

"That's the airport terminal, Mummy, don't you see that it says 'IBIZA' on it?" I pointed out, dancing round her.

We got into a bus and careered across the island. "Hurrah! We're here! What a darling little house! What a beautiful windmill! What a sweet little place!" I kept shouting.

We reached Ibiza city in time for dinner, and we ate at a restaurant on the waterfront. I ran up and down it afterwards, looking at the boats and the lights across the water.

"Oh Man, I'm so glad to be here!" we said to each other, again and again.

"Hullo, Antonetta-Janetta," said Daddy next morning, coming in. "How's thee?"

"I'm terribly happy, it's a beautiful day, how did you sleep?" I said, hugging him.

"It's getting on for one o'clock. I must have had nearly twelve hours' sleep. Don't let's ever go home," he said.

"Isn't this wonderful?" said Mummy sleepily.

"I don't suppose we'll get any breakfast now. Let's go and have some snails in the town," suggested Daddy.

"I'll get my paints," I said.

"Hullo! I've finished. I found such a sweet little street in the old town to paint. That's my eighth picture and we've only been here a fortnight. Gosh, Daddy, what are you eating?"

He was sitting outside a café, and his mouth and tongue were quite black.

"It's squid cooked in its own ink," he said gleefully. "Yum yum!"

"Tell her about what we've been discussing," said Mummy, putting on a mysterious smile.

"Discussing? Fear! Terror! Is it nice?" I asked anxiously.

"Very," Daddy said. "How would you like to be Bird instead of Rutherford?"

"Look at her, quivering like a frightened rabbit," said Mummy. "He means that we're thinking of changing our surname to Bird."

"Antonoria-Gloria Bird," said Daddy.

"I thought I was supposed to be the lunatic in this family," I laughed. "Would I like to be called Bird? Do you know, Man, I think I would."

"That's just as well, because that's what you're going to be," chuckled Daddy.

"What, really? But can you just change your name like that?"

"Why not?"

"Man, this is simply wonderful!" I cried. "No more of that stupid cumbersome Rutherford! Bird. Antonia Bird." I imagined it in print. *Insomnia* by Antonia Rutherford. *Insomnia* by Antonia Bird. "Oh Man, why didn't we do this before I got into *Doorway*?"

"I found all the bills I'd brought to pay, in the bottom of the suitcase, this morning, and I suddenly thought that if I had to sign one more cheque 'Georgina Rutherford' I should go mad, mad, and there are dozens that need doing. So there was only one thing to be done," Mummy explained.

She came and squeezed in on the side of the table where Daddy and I were sitting.

"Oh, hullo," we said.

"I can't sit over there any longer, I was right over an open drain," she said. "I must see your picture. Oh, I like it. You've really captured the sun."

"You haven't signed it," Daddy pointed out. They both grinned at me. Daddy's grin was black with squid ink.

I signed it in big letters, "Antonia Bird."

"Have you noticed," said Mummy, "that all the women here have long black pigtails with pink bows on the end?"

I looked round. There was a woman in long black robes arm-in-arm with a girl in red jeans. They both had pigtails and pink bows. Another old woman came by with an armful of something. She was the same. Farther up the street there was another woman in an orange dress. Her pink bow stuck out most conspicuously.

"Shall I go Ibicenco?" asked Mummy, patting her bun. "Let down my hair and tie a pink bow on the end?"

"You'd look gorgeous," said Daddy.

"Whatever did you ask for? You've got long hair, and it's dark, and you're in Ibiza—what more do you want?" I said. "Now for the difficult bit, the black. It's got to look like shadows across the yellow."

I was trying to paint a semi-abstract. All the cafés we had been in had had wild abstract paintings all over the walls and I had decided it was time I tried my hand at one too.

"I suppose I couldn't put in a flying horse anywhere? You don't think the picture's crying out for one just here?" I asked hopefully.

"Oh no, not another," Daddy said, laughing. "You've painted three flying horse pictures already."

"I won't stop you. It's your picture," said Mummy.

"Oh well, if you feel so strongly about it." I knew she meant no. "You're right really."

"Look, there's someone typing, in the café opposite. What piles of manuscript he's got," Mummy remarked.

"I expect he's writing a book," said Daddy. "Man! Shall I bring my easel out and paint sitting here in this café tomorrow, like him, instead of on the hotel balcony?"

"What a good idea. You'd be much more inspired, painting in a jolly street in this romantic place and getting 'with it'," said Mummy.

"He's got a beard. He's a real beatnik. Oh Man, shall I grow a beard and paint in a café and be a beatnik too?"

"Why not? Where do you suppose I can get a pink bow?" Mummy took out her hairpins and let down her bun into a plait. "Man, here we are in a beautiful place and all because of Mr. Most Popular Man," she sang, waving her plait at him.

"Mr. Most Popular Man! Mr. Most Popular Man!" I joined in. "Oh Daddy, look what you've done to Bannani. He's all covered in wine." Bannani was my latest paper flying horse and he had flown right across the terrace that morning.

"Well, what could be more romantic?" Daddy asked. "Besides, he was pink anyway."

"Miss Lovely will have a fit when I tell her why I missed the last week of term, and specially when she hears about changing our name," I said. "It'll be something to make up for being back at school."

"I expect she'll be jealous," said Mummy, tickling the back of my neck with her plait.

Daddy took his paints down to the café the next day and finished his picture there. It was a huge picture of a wonderful fiery Ibicenco plant. I sat at the next table setting up my cardboard castle, called Spinazzolala, and arranging the knights. It was windy and the castle kept blowing down, but the winged horses flew beautifully. Mummy sat at another table reading *On the Road*.

The beatnik we had seen the day before came into the café with his typewriter and to our horror sat down at Daddy's table. Daddy looked up crossly, but seeing who it was only put on his dark glasses and let the man be. His typewriter made an awful noise.

I decided that it was too windy here for Spinazzolala and it might be better to set it up on the sheltered hotel terrace, and left Daddy with the beatnik clacking away. At lunch I asked Daddy,

"How did you get on with your beatnik?"

"Oh, it was all a big niddle," he answered. "I was willing to put up with him when I thought he was a genuine beatnik writing *On the Road*, but then I found out the title of his book and moved tables. It was called *How to Set Up a Tortoise Observation Cage*."

"Oh, no! Not here! What, him?" I exclaimed. "I see what you mean. I'll look out for that in the school library."

It was almost Easter. Daddy's beard was really looking quite beard-like. I drew him with it, beside Mummy with her plait and pink bow. I wasn't going to be out of it, and so I made myself a paper pink-bowed pigtail. Daddy photographed us both together. I photographed him afterwards with squid-ink in his beard. He looked really happy. He spent several hours a day sunbathing on the hotel terrace and had the brownest tummy in Ibiza.

"As brown as bitter chocolate," I said to Lynda Page at school. "His beard looks so funny in England, but he looked funny without it in Ibiza."

"Was your dad as brown as the Indian girl?" asked Carter, leaning across his desk.

"Indian girl?"

"Yes, over there, sitting next to Roberts. She's new."

I looked. The girl was sitting hunched up over her desk. I wasn't sure that she wasn't crying.

"It's hard to tell. Dad's a different shade of brown," I said. "Poor little girl, fancy putting her next to Roberts."

"Milk-chocolate girl! Milk-chocolate girl!" the rest of the class were shouting at her.

"Do you know, after you ran away Miss Lovely made me work extra in the library. I hope you've got something to show for it," Lynda said.

"Something to show for it? What do you mean?"

"I mean, have you written any more poetry?"

"No, I didn't write. I painted pictures instead," I said.

"Painted? You must bring all your pictures to school and show me. And all your poetry too. I want to see everything you've done," she commanded.

"Why, of course," I said, thrilled. I had a sudden idea. "Please tell me. In *Insomnia*—that was the poem you read—do you think I exaggerated the horror, made it too gruesome?"

She considered. "Well, it was a poem about horror, wasn't it? I don't see that you could have done any different without spoiling the point of the poem."

"Oh, good. Oh, thank you," I said. "Do you know, you're the first person who's ever given me a sensible answer about that. Even Mummy just hummed and hawed and didn't like to say what she really thought. Oh bother, where could my hymn book be?"

Sir strode into the room and said, "Good morning."

"Good morning, sir!" we all shouted.

"Welcome back, sir!" said Matthews. We all cheered and stamped and thumped our desks. I remembered that this, at last, was *next term* when we were to have Sir back instead of Miss Lovely, and thumped and cheered as loudly as I could. Sir grinned at us shyly.

He began to call the register.

"Powell—absent—Rutherford?"

"Yes, sir. Please, sir, I'm not Rutherford," I said.

"Eh? What's that?" shouted the others.

"What's the old cow on about now?" Roberts said loudly.

"We've changed our name, sir," I explained. "We've stopped being Rutherford and now we're Bird."

The class roared with laughter. Sir pulled at his chin in a puzzled way and looked at me queerly.

"It's quite true, sir. We've done it by deed poll. Changed our name to Bird. B-I-R-D," I said.

"Old Buddersmud's gone off the rail," said Matthews.

"Oh, well, they're all dotty in that family," Andrews said.

"You could put it that way," I admitted.

"But why, Antonia? What for? You aren't serious?" asked Sandra King.

"Yes, I am. It's because Rutherford's a stupid name." I despaired of explaining about Mummy's cheques.

"Bird's stupider," said Felicity Dearchild.

"At least it's short," I retorted.

"All right! Shut up!" said Sir. "Stevens? Is he absent too?"

After prayers he said:

"Now, first we'll have a quick test to find out how much Miss Lovely has managed to teach you. Number one, express three-quarters as a decimal, and number two, express it as a percentage."

"Eh? What?" we gasped.

"We haven't done that sir," Thompson said.

"You haven't done decimals and percentages?" said Sir, looking flabbergasted.

"No, sir!" we shouted.

"Good heavens! What did you do, then? Problems?"

"No, sir. Addition and subtraction of money."

"But you did that in Class Three."

"Well, Miss Lovely usually teaches Class Three," Matthews said.

"We didn't do much arithmetic anyway. We did mostly handwork," Tatley said.

"Yes, sir. She put all the girls on to making embroidered traycloths," said Andrews disgustedly. "And we had to weave baskets."

Poor Sir ran his hands through his hair and looked distracted. "All right," he said, pulling himself together. "Decimals. To begin with, what's a fraction? Smith? Ruther-Bird? Yes, Johnson?"

He gave us a brilliant arithmetic lesson all the morning, at the end of which everyone but me understood perfectly the intricacies of decimals. It was all above my head. In the middle I suddenly remembered that Mummy had taught me all about decimals ages ago, before I came to school, and that I had thought I understood them. It didn't help at all. Sir kept saying something about the numbers on one side of the point being the opposite to the ones on the other side, or something like that. Then a figure next to another figure was worth ten times as much, he said, even if they were both the same figure. At least,

I think it was ten times as much. I couldn't make sense of that at all. He said it was just the same with ordinary numbers, but that was news to me too. Everyone else thought it was as clear as could be, however.

Sir dashed to and fro sweating, his eyes bright. He shouted, scribbled and drew as if he were inspired. He stood a row of boys on one side of the table and a row of girls on the other, with short boys and tall girls next to it, to illustrate his point. I didn't see why the girls next to the table had to be tall when the boys were short. He explained and explained, but I didn't see it. That wasn't his fault though : the rest of the class understood perfectly.

He went through it with us again after lunch. In the middle Miss Lovely came in and said,

"Could I have Antonia Rutherford and Lynda Page, please, to work in the library?"

"Work in the library?" said Sir. "But they're doing lessons at the moment."

"Yes, I know," said Miss Lovely impatiently. "But they've been accustomed to spend some time sorting books. They're doing a most useful job. So if I could have them, please—"

"Well, I'm sorry, Miss Lovely," Sir said, "but I really don't think I can spare them. I've found that they're a long way behind with their work and I'm afraid that they can't afford to miss any more lesson-time. Perhaps they could sort books in the dinner-hour tomorrow?"

She went out of the room without answering, and slammed the door. She didn't send for us at lunchtime next day. I went to the staff room with Lynda, but she only said something cross about coming there without permission and slammed the door on us. She never asked for us again, and we didn't volunteer.

Sir was obviously worried because the class had wasted so much time. We were to take our own eleven-plus in January. He made us work extra hard all through the summer. He never let us waste precious time playing games or practising our handwriting. He even forsook the Japanese paper-folding that he liked us to do. We weren't officially meant to do homework but he set it "for the keen ones." I always did it.

12

In the summer half-term Mummy said, "It's such a beautiful day, Antonia, why don't you go out to the Gardens or somewhere?"

"Oh, no thank you, Mummy," I said quickly, "I'm going up to Felias."

"Felias?"

"Oh, yes, you know, my country on the roof," I said. I had invented and made a special new bubble liquid that morning, shampoo and glycerine, which was supposed to make extra big, long-lasting bubbles, and I wanted to try it out. Besides, I had some new paper flying horses that I had been meaning to fly down into the street for a long time.

Felias was a beautiful country. There were two great mountains of slates, with a magnificent skyline of chimney-pots at the summits. In the valley between the mountains was a gutter, which was the bed of the River Flowfast. Sometimes, when it was raining, I could sail fleets of toy boats all the way along this.

I could climb out through my bedroom window. The roof of my room made a lovely plateau, high up on the mountain, which I could just climb on to. Here, of course, was the royal castle of Spinazzolala. The cardboard castle was a model of it. There were also rows and rows of gladiolus bulbs in flower-pots. They always came up and flowered when we were abroad in the summer holidays, but I found the leaves afterwards.

The slates, I thought, were very dull plain grey, and so I had covered them with beautiful pictures. I found that wax crayon was waterproof, and had used it to draw all the adventures of the knights, winged horses, unicorns, and so on, that inhabited Felias. The best was an enormous picture of two knights in armour, charging a dragon. It covered almost the whole of Mount Snowleft. Mount Snowright was mainly concerned with

99

portraits of Golden Shoes, Queen Antonia's royal flying horse, and views of Spinazzolala.

At the far end was a wall, overlooking the street. I climbed out with my bubble liquid and went and looked over. Here, there was the most beautiful view in the town. Across forests of chimneys I could see the spire of our church, looking tremendously imposing. Away in the distance there was a mysterious flag, which always flew. It was the flag of a secret, enchanted country, even more beautiful than Felias. The Promised Land, I called it, for, of course, it was nameless.

I blew a bubble, very carefully, and launched it over the wall into the street. It was huge. It shimmered pink and blue and gold. It wobbled, and then floated down, right across the road. It sailed past two ladies who were walking by.

One of them said, "Where's that come from?" She looked round, but didn't see me. In Felias, as I had found, I was always invisible. People might stare straight at me and never notice me.

The woman reached up to burst the bubble, but just in time it was caught by the breeze and flew away up over the houses. I cheered it out loud, but she still didn't notice me. The bubble went up and up. I could just see it against the sky. It was going quite fast with the wind, and the wind was blowing towards the flag of the Promised Land. I followed it with my eyes until I began to see imaginary bubbles, and then I blinked and lost it. I haven't seen it burst, I thought, and therefore it probably hasn't. Perhaps it will get to the Promised Land.

I sent fleets of bubbles to the Promised Land, every one huge and beautiful, and only a few burst in the street. Mostly they floated straight up above the chimneys, out of danger. I sent several paper flying horses after them too. They glided gracefully round the street and surprised a lot of people. One or two went over the houses on the opposite side of the street, where I couldn't see them, and undoubtedly got to the Promised Land, but they weren't really designed to fly so far and mostly went down into other people's areas. I found two of the ones that did this in our letterbox afterwards. Mummy thought someone had put them there but I knew that they didn't have my address on them, only a magic charm, "Keep Breezing Along," and that they must have flown there themselves.

I went out again to Felias when it was almost dark. In the travel brochures I had written for it I had always urged visitors,

"Above all, do not miss twilight in Felias! At this wonderful time, when all is cool and dim and calm, and the sky a wonderful shade of soft blue, what could be nicer than to spread your wings and soar away like a puff of smoke, and really appreciate the Feliasian evening?"

I sat down in the bed of the River Flowfast and imagined a great flying horse doing this, swooping and wheeling, almost invisible in the twilight.

"A flounce of luminous cloud
Sprang out of the silhouetted chimney-pot
Glided across the soft pale sky.
The great sweeping wings unfolded,
Proud head lifted, tail flowing behind,
The flying horse soared, gleaming grey,
Wheeled, rose and turned, leaping in sheer joy,
Glowing in the glowing night,
Shining lullabies over the world.
The starlight ran through it, never seeing
How the horse curvetted:
How the wings rose, majestic, and the eyes
Shone black in ecstasy.
The horse faltered;
Faded transparent, a shadow, melting away,
Dissolved into mist whence it came
And slowly returned into nothingness."

It was really dark now. I went inside with my poem.

"Half-past ten! It can't be! Oh Child, and this was to be your early night. I was reading such an interesting article, and it was longer than I thought," I heard Mummy's voice say downstairs. She came panting up. "Jump into bed! I'm beating my breast. Now you've probably lost your sleepy feeling, and it's all my fault."

"I don't know why you keep on with this tucking her up. It always ends like this," Daddy called up.

"But it's so nice. Anyway, I don't suppose she'd go to bed at all if I didn't. Though it couldn't really be much worse than this," said Mummy miserably.

"Look, I've written a poem. Do you like it?" I said to console her.

"Ooh! Another poem? Heroine!" Mummy said eagerly. She

read it all through. I watched her face. Her eyebrows didn't go up once. She had her appreciating expression on.

"Why, it's sweet! Lovely!" she said. "Really poetic, just the sort I like. Not like those queer ones. Why not send it to *Doorway*?"

I stared at her. Just the sort of poem she liked! So it was! I ran over it in my mind. Yes, one of my real soppies.

"Well, you know, Mummy, I'm not really sure that it's the sort for *Doorway*," I said unhappily.

"I can't think why not. They accepted that nightmare one, so just think how they'd snap up this one! It's so sweet and charming."

Overwritten and sentimental, I thought. "Oh, no, please, I'd much rather not. Really, I don't want to a bit." I writhed under the bedclothes. "Look, Mummy, you keep it as a present, a souvenir. I'd much rather you had it than *Doorway*."

"Do you really mean that? I'd love to have it, it's so typically you," said Mummy, brightening. I writhed again. "But it does seem a shame to throw away such a good poem. It's such a long time since you wrote one."

"Oh, no, Mummy, it's hardly any time since I wrote *Insomnia*," I protested. Mummy smiled and put on her well-I-don't-agree-with-you-but-don't-let's-argue face.

"Is that child never going to bed?" shouted Daddy crossly from downstairs.

"What do you think of that, Lynda?" I asked, giving her the poem.

She read it and said, "Well, you had an original idea, certainly."

"But I wrote it badly."

"Well, not exactly badly," she said, hesitating. "But perhaps a bit sort of over-well-written, if you see what I mean. Too much flowery language. I don't think it's bad, though, I didn't mean that."

"No, I want to know what you really think," I said glumly, remembering how it had seemed my masterpiece while I was writing it.

"Well, it's not like that other one. Perhaps that was a bit flowery too, but there wasn't really anything that wasn't important in it as I remember," Lynda said, putting her head on one side and staring attentively at the patch of sky above the lavatories, and talking very quietly. "But in this—I don't know, but it seems to me that you say what you have to say and that all that gushy stuff is extra. I know! Your *Insomnia* was written in a much more economical style. That's the word, economical."

"And you think that's better," I said, thinking how clever and good Lynda was looking, even now, out of class, when she didn't have to. She wasn't pretty, but she had cheerful freckles and radiated cleverness and enthusiasm. I bet nobody else but us in the whole school knows what "economical" means, I thought, admiring her seriousness, and comparing her most favourably with Valerie Barker.

"Well, yes. Perhaps it's just me, but it seems a much better style. It makes more impact on you without the beautiful words. That line for instance, 'Shining lullabies over the world,' that's what I mean by gush. It doesn't really add anything to your theme, only spoils the impression it makes." She had a funny grown-up way of talking, but I thought it sounded intelligent and wonderful. "I'd leave it out altogether. I'd like to take out everything that's 'extra.' I think you shouldn't put anything into a poem except the bare theme, because if you start embroidering it, as you did here, it's almost certain to end up overwritten," she added, putting her hands behind her back and looking thoughtful, and tilting her head even higher.

"Yes, I see what you mean. Yes, I agree with all that," I said, trying to copy her. "It's perfectly true. I used to write all my poems in the style of *Smoke-Horse,* the style you don't like, and they only ever got printed in children's magazines, or things like that. And then as soon as I wrote *Nightmare Street,* you haven't seen that, well it's a bit like *Insomnia,* it was taken straight away by an important grown-up magazine." I was talking very fast, not a bit like Lynda, who always talked deliberately and slowly.

She really is a friend, I thought, she understands me perfectly and talks sensibly about poetry and sees eye to eye with me about everything. Hurrah! Here at last is someone I can go about with, without having to put on an act. Or can go about with at all, I thought sadly. Most people had dozens of best friends. I'd only had one, the rest of the class's cast-off. I didn't count Tatley. I'd never been her friend, only her subject. She is my only enemy, though, I thought to console myself, I'm

103

on very good terms with all the other girls and most of the boys. And anyway, I've got a best friend too now.

A few days afterwards Lynda said to me, "Would you like to come with me and see the St. Rhadigond's School concert on the twentieth?"

"Why, I'd love to," I said eagerly. "What's St. Rhadigond's School?"

"Don't you know it? It's a grammar school, founded in the nineteenth century, I think, where I'm hoping to go," explained Lynda. "And every year the girls perform a concert, with a bit of stuff thrown in showing off how wonderful the school is now and what a fascinating history it's had. Publicity, you know. But it does give you an idea of the school, even if it's only the idea the headmistress wants you to have. And the concert part's always awfully good."

"Ooh, I'll come," I said. "Did you say you're going there?"

"Hoping to. Everyone wants to, so it's not easy to get in. You have to be the brainy sort, like you."

"Me? I'm not half as brainy as you. Why, I couldn't even see why my new poem was worse than the last until you told me," I assured her.

After he had blown the whistle at the end of play, and we had all lined up, Sir said, looking uncomfortable,

"Now, Class Two, Miss Lovely has—er—persuaded me—"
We all laughed.

"Well, all right," said Sir sheepishly, "she has at last bullied me into wasting half a precious morning and giving you a lesson in P.E. I mean, letting you do some P.E."

"Not proper games, sir?" called Andrews.

"No, she said—I mean, I say—that you ought to have some proper exercise that no one can get out of and some gym in the play ground is really urgent and—well, I won't tell you what else she said. She really gave me the rocket," he said, grinning and blushing.

We laughed and cheered the idea of P.E. and booed Miss Lovely for not making it games and for being horrid to Sir.

"All right, off you go," he said.

It wasn't really very cold. The school thermometer had reached "Temperate" and some of the class were half dead with the heat, and so for the sake of peace I undressed with the rest. When I emerged from wrestling with my pinafore dress I saw that the rest of the class was clustered in a crowd round the teacher's desk. I went over to investigate. The little Indian girl, new that term, was huddling by the blackboard, crying silently and fully dressed. The others were laughing and jeering at her.

"She doesn't want to take her dress off. What's she got under there?" shouted Roberts, snatching at her skirt. The girl crouched over her dress, glowering at them.

"She don't want to show us her precious milk-chocolate skin," shrieked King, and the whole class began to chant: "Milk-chocolate girl! Milk-chocolate girl!"

"We'll take it off for yer, then," O'Brien called out. Everyone dashed at her. She broke away and ran across the room, clutching her skirt. The others ran after her.

"Leave her be! Just because she's Indian you..." I began. Nobody paid any attention to me. "When I wouldn't undress you left me alone, but you bully this girl just because she's brown. Leave her be!" I shouted. Only Lynda, who was sitting apart looking disgusted, heard me, and smiled at me. I flushed.

The girl was sheltering behind a desk at the back of the room. The others were round her again, shouting abuse.

"Get the air to you, perhaps you'll go white!"

"She's shy of taking off her clothes! That's why she never washes."

"She thinks we don't know she's a dirty great nigger."

A thought struck me. I shouted out, "You silly idiots, she isn't allowed by her religion to take off her clothes in front of boys."

They heard that, and turned to face me. I was glad that I, at least, had undressed. They were roaring with laughter at me.

"Hear what Buddersmud said?"

"Old Bird talking through her hat again."

Tatley stood out with her arms folded. "Just where does the Bible say that?" she demanded.

"Well, she isn't a Christian. She doesn't come in to prayers," I began.

"Well, then!" Tatley cried triumphantly. They turned back to the girl again.

"She isn't a Christian, so how can she not be allowed by her religion to undress? That old Bird just doesn't know what she's talking about."

"She's not a Christian, she belongs to another religion," I yelled. Nobody heard me. Tatley was fighting with the girl to get her dress off, and, being bigger, was succeeding. I ran out of the room. Sir was chatting to Mason, the Red House captain, in the passage.

"Please, sir," I began breathlessly.

"You're all ready, are you? You sound as if you've been running races already, Bird," said Sir good-humouredly, and went into the classroom. "All undressed? Out you come!"

Everyone forgot the milk-chocolate girl and poured out of the room and down the stairs to the playground. The girl came out last, still dressed, though with her zip undone and her blouse pulled out. She was trying to tuck it in and do herself up again. Sir looked at her for a moment, and then said,

"Oh yes, of course, I know about you. You're excused undressing. The headmaster told me. Come on, then."

13

LYNDA AND I went to the concert. The school had an imposing red brick façade, with little turrety things and arrow slits and mysterious patterns on the walls in red tiles. Runes, I thought, gazing at it awestruck.

We were ushered into an enormous entrance hall by girls wearing a wonderful purple uniform. There we were allowed to admire for a while a great stained glass window of the original founder, a woman called Agnes Winthrop. She was wearing a long white robe and a wreath, and was holding out an enormous book. We were suitably impressed. Lynda looked quite rapturous. She glowed with enthusiasm. I felt pretty rapturous too.

The girls in the purple uniform led us into a vast hall with a stage at one end. The ceiling was high and vaulted and made me feel as if I were in church. We tiptoed in and sat down on a bench next to the wall, under a great white figure in glazed tiling called Peace. She had a soppy face and lots of plaits round her head, and seemed to be wearing a toga. The red brick walls were tiled about half-way up, and all round the room were these draped figures : Justice, Duty, Charity, Honesty. I didn't see Mercy. They stood out against the olive green tiling. Perhaps after all it looked more like a bathroom than a church.

I thought it was the most fascinating room I had ever seen. How lovely it would be to go to school here! I thought. Suddenly an idea came into my mind : perhaps ... "You have to be the brainy sort, like you," Lynda had said. I imagined myself in the front entrance hall, in a purple tunic, standing against the stained glass window, wearing, of course, Lynda's expression of goodness and enthusiasm. Yes, I could visualize myself perfectly. Well, why not, I thought. All I need to do is to pass this eleven-plus. In my eagerness I began to recite my weights table to

myself, sitting in the magnificent great hall of St. Rhadigond's
School.

I thought the concert was wonderful, too. The girls sang and
played so beautifully, and real proper music too, by people like
Handel and Brahms. The school orchestra played some little
pieces by Bizet and someone else. It seemed a very big orchestra.

One of the items was a long epic poem of the history of St.
Rhadigond's, recited by a few girls. The school had had an
ignominious history—the girls had been starved, they had run
away, one, in her hatred, had tried to murder her headmistress—
but it was recited as if everything had been a deed of heroism
and valour. I, at least, took it that way, and merely longed more
than ever to go to the school. What brilliant teachers, what clever
girls they must be, and how keen, to be able to put on a show
like this, I thought, mentally comparing it with Sir's Christmas
concert.

The poem was illustrating how learned the mistresses were,
and all so kind and understanding, and how all the headmistresses were wise and motherly. The worth and good characters of the girls the school turned out were proved by their noble
behaviour in 1923, when there was a fire at the school. Arriving
one morning to find one of the main classroom blocks completely
gutted, the girls continued to come every day, and classes were
held in the open on the site, until rebuilding began. I couldn't
help wondering why they hadn't used the passages in the other
blocks, or that great stage, or just sat on the desks in the classrooms that hadn't been burnt, rather than stay outside and get
wet.

But I sternly controlled my thoughts, and concentrated instead
on the heroic girls and the headmistress, beloved by all, who
was the prop and stay of the school during this trying time.
Indeed, the school came to love and rely on her so much that
when she retired the girls found they could not manage without
her, and kept in personal contact with her until her death. I
listened enthralled.

At the end there was a scene about present-day St. Rhadigond's. We saw the girls in class. They were learning the most
amazingly difficult things. I'm going to learn them too, I'm
going to, I am, I told myself, wriggling in my seat. We saw
them playing games, organized games, and quite seriously. There
wasn't any fooling about at all. Bliss! I thought, remembering

the havoc of games in the back playground, with several games of netball going on simultaneously, and everyone fighting and scuffling.

Then the present head girl made a little speech, saying she was sure the girls of St. Rhadigond's today, like herself, loved and admired their own headmistress just as much as the girls of the previous generations had loved theirs. We all clapped, a little restrainedly.

When the concert was over we sang the school song. It was about the traditions of St. Rhadigond's being the foundation for the fortunate girls of today to build their lives on, and there was quite a lot about willing hands and meek souls. The words were in our programmes. Lynda and I sang as if it were the National Anthem.

"Have you—er—thought of a school you would like me to go to if I get through the eleven-plus?" I asked.

"Not yet. Why, have you?" Daddy answered.

"Well, yes, as a matter of fact I have," I said.

"What? Really? You've heard of a school you'd like? Tell us!" cried Mummy, her face lighting up.

"Yes, I have, really. You know Lynda Page took me to St. Rhadigond's School to see their concert, well, it's very grand and academic, you know, and old, nearly a hundred years, and with masses of traditions, and it's such a beautiful school, and Lynda's going there, and probably I won't get in but I've set my heart on it," I said.

"Well, you could try at least. It sounds perfect, don't you think, Man?"

"It does indeed, Man," Daddy agreed.

"Tell us all about it," Mummy said. I described enthusiastically everything I'd seen. Mummy put on the face she used when she was appreciating one of my poems, and kept nodding. Daddy chewed at his pipe. Both of them kept saying, "Mmm. Yes. Mmm." I was glad to see that they were so impressed. I couldn't sit still and kept dancing round the room as I talked about the wonderful school.

I found that I remembered the historical poem almost word for word, and gave Mummy and Daddy a repeat performance. They listened as if it were an epic of golden deeds too, and continued staring with rapt attention at the ceiling, even when I came to the bit where, in 1890, the girls had a bet on who could go longest without ever washing before being found out, and one of them kept it up for three years. Nobody had laughed at this bit in the actual performance, and neither did Mummy and Daddy, but just kept saying, "Mmm. Yes. Mmm."

When I had finished Mummy said, "Tell me again about the uniform the girls were wearing?"

I described it to her again.

"You'll look very smart in that," she said.

"Yes, most of the girls looked nice in it," I agreed, and then suddenly what she had said sank in. "Mummy! You mean—you really mean that you'd like me to go there, you'll put me down for it if I pass the eleven-plus?"

"Well, why not? It sounds an excellent school," Mummy said, glancing at Daddy.

"It is. I've heard of it. I think it's just what she'd like," he said.

"It is! It is! Oh, I will try!" I shouted, bouncing all over the sofa.

"Anyway, I think it would be a good thing to keep with your friend, this Lynda. You must ask her home to tea some time," Mummy said.

"I'll invite her tomorrow," I said firmly. "Would Thursday be all right?"

I did ask her, and our mothers wrote to each other, and she actually remembered and came. Before I went to school Mummy had always been finding girls for me to be friends with, and we would play together in the Public Gardens quite happily and everything would go beautifully until Mummy told me to ask the girl to tea. And then I'd forget, and she'd forget, and she would come without telling her mother on a night when her mother wanted to take her out, and there'd be a row and I would never see her again. Or she would tell her mother and forget to come, or somebody would forget something and everything would go wrong. In every single case these tea-parties broke up the friendship, and Mummy was always having to find me new friends. But with Lynda nothing went wrong. For the first time ever, both our mothers were fully informed, and she actually arrived. This made me even surer that she was fated to be my best friend for ever and ever.

She talked to Daddy over tea about art just as she had talked to me about my poetry. When she arrived I had noticed Daddy peering over the banisters, with a look of horror on his face. He hated visitors. By the end of tea he was looking at her with admiration. She had been reading Sir Kenneth Clark's latest book and Daddy hadn't yet read it. This shot her up miles in his estimation, I could see.

I took her upstairs, registering vaguely that a new goldfish had appeared on my bedtable, and wondered whether to tell her about Felias. She decided for me by staring out of the window for a minute and then saying, "Where is that, out there?"

"That's the roof," I said, not understanding.

"Yes, I know. But *where* is it?"

I looked out of the window beside her and saw what she meant. From the window you looked out on to Felias, and could see a bit of Mount Snowright. Lynda was looking at one of the best portraits of Golden Shoes, and below that, a wonderful picture of Spinazzolala, drawn on the slates in red and orange wax crayon.

"Oh!" I said. "I see! You mean my magic country. How did you guess?"

"Obvious," she said, laughing. "Tell me about it."

I saw now that there was also visible most of the verse written on one of the slates :

"Felias! Glorious Country!
Where everything is Lovely,
Where nothing happens Nasty,
And everyone is Happy."

So I told her all about it. She listened sympathetically. After a while I asked, "And what about you?"

"Me?" she said. "Oh, dear. That's difficult." She sat on the edge of the bed, folded her hands and looked at the ceiling. "You see, I'm not the creative type like you. I haven't got a world of my own. I make do with other people's worlds—I read instead of making up stories, I mean. And after I've read a book I live in the world of that book for a while, if you see what I mean. Not like you, you're the sort who would write the book in the first place. Oh, don't look so worried," She suddenly laughed. "Perhaps I do think up a bit of my own too. But while you might go out on to Felias and go into a daydream by yourself, I'd go out with a good book and go into a daydream through that. I'm the admiring public. It would be pretty discouraging writing books and poetry without me."

"Oh, no," I said instantly. "When I write I never think : now, who's going to read this? Who's going to print this? Nobody? Then I may as well give up. If I had an idea for a poem, and was the only person in the world, I'd still write it."

"Yes, I see that. All right, call me a by-product. Anyway, I feed on books."

"As a matter of fact, so do I," I said. I wondered whether she would like to pour water down the bed of the River Flowfast and sail boats on it. Then it occurred to me that she had wormed everything out of me concerning my family, and I didn't know a thing about hers. I asked hurriedly, "What does your father do?"

"He's a schoolteacher. He works in a big boys' grammar school. He's classics—Latin and Greek."

"He sounds brainy. What about your mother?"

"Oh, well, she used to go to St. Rhadigond's (that's why she wants me to go there) and now she's our local librarian. Most useful for me," Lynda said, laughing.

"Oh, well, if that's what she likes," I said. "I've had just about enough of being a librarian to last me quite a while."

"I know. I can't imagine how she stands it. I used to think it would suit me, but after my spell in the school library I'm quite sure that I'd just end up in a loony-bin." We both laughed and agreed that it would be a fate worse than death.

I did take her out to play ships on Felias. She bore it meekly. I wasn't sure that she was really liking it, though, and after a while we went indoors and played word games.

"How are you getting on with *David Copperfield*?" she asked presently.

"I've nearly finished, though I don't seem to read so much lately. Are you doing the school homework?" I asked.

"Yes, it's good practice and it doesn't really take long, does it?"

"The arithmetic does. I don't have any trouble with the English and intelligence tests, but I hardly ever get a sum right, only those mechanical ones, money and weights and fractions and so on. The problems absolutely finish me. I do try, but they're all different and I can't get the hang of them at all. I think the last time I got one right was ages back in last term," I said miserably.

"Isn't that odd?" said Lynda. "You'd have thought they would have come quite easily to you. Surely, they're only common sense. Anyway, you can't really be in any difficulty with the eleven-plus. You're sure to pass."

"Oh, I don't know. Still, I keep trying. Perhaps I can scrape a pass in arithmetic and make up the marks in the other papers. I tell myself that it's only till next January, I can put on a sprint till then and then relax."

Lynda was staring at me with a slightly ironical smile. When she saw I was looking at her she shook herself and said, "Well, never mind."

I kept up my sprint all through the rest of the term. At the end of it I could do simple decimals and quite complicated fractions (Mummy coaching me hard whenever possible. I began to dread train journeys). However, I was still totally baffled by problems. They were always irregular, they always had a catch (and I always fell for it). They were always out of the common run. There were no two the same; I might master one in an exercise and then find that the others were completely different. Still, I had definitely begun to get the hang of the ordinary sums. Sir once told me that if I got most of those right in the exam and attempted the problems (you got marks for trying) I might get through.

So I sprinted and sprinted and obediently let Mummy coach me. Only till January, I said to myself. If once I can pass the eleven-plus everything will be all right. And if I can get into St. Rhadigond's, I always added as an afterthought.

In December, shortly before we broke up at the end of the autumn term, when I went into the little lavatory for playtime, I found some girls skipping with a long rope, two girls turning the ends. They didn't seem to think that the fact that the place was solid with girls was any obstacle. The crush didn't in fact, hinder them at all.

When I came in Valerie Wilson had just been skipping. They had just finished their ditty, and she jumped out.

"Hullo, Antonia! Come and have a go," called Little, who was turning the rope.

"Well, all right, I will," I said, laughing, and jumped in and began skipping.

The girls sang as I skipped :

> "On the mountain stands a lady,
> Who she is I do not know,
> All she wants is gold and silver,
> All she wants is a nice young man.
>   So come in, my—Eric Stevens dear,"

They could hardly sing for giggling.

"Eric Stevens—dear—Eric—Stevens dear—"

"Come in, my Eric Stevens dear," I sang lustily.

"Come in and kiss her!" we finished, and collapsed, silly with laughter, on to the rope and into the puddles. All the girls there joined in.

"Why him?" I asked, when I could talk again.

"Well, there was that note last year, in Class Two."

"Oh, that!" I remembered Thompson's joke letter. "Do you really still remember that?" I was about to say, "Well, that was just a trick of Thompson's," but changed my mind. Instead, I put on a pose and said in a very high voice, "Oh! I've lost my heart!"

We went into another laughing fit. Everyone was willing to laugh at me and with me. They were all jolly and friendly towards me. Even while I joked and giggled, I was thinking : They like me! They're all my friends! They're actually talking to me! I'm popular! Hurrah!

We broke up on the twentieth of December. The year before, we had wasted the day playing games and making Christmas cards, but this year we did lessons hard all day.

In the afternoon Sir took us over all our tables and gave us quick arithmetic tests. To my chagrin I got less than half marks in three of them, but in the others I didn't do too badly. One or two of the stupider boys and girls complained to Sir that "we've never done lessons on the last day of term, sir, it isn't fair." Sir always answered, "Well, you're doing them now." The rest of us accepted them meekly.

When Alcock rang the bell for the end of afternoon school, Sir held up his hand to stop us going.

"Well, have a good Christmas," he said.

"Same to you, sir!" we shouted.

"Wait a minute! There's something I'd like to say. You've got your eleven-plus less than three weeks after you come back next term."

There was an absolute silence. We stared glumly at him.

"You've got three weeks of holidays now, enough to forget all you know in. And three weeks of next term isn't enough to learn it in again."

"I know, sir," said Matthews gloomily, "you're going to set us homework." We tittered faintly. Nobody felt like laughing.

"Not exactly," said Sir, smiling. "But what you can do is to say all your tables over to yourself every morning when you get up. Pence tables—weights and measures—fractions of a pound—the lot. It won't hurt you. Yes, even Christmas morning, before you open your stockings. That'll keep your arithmetic from going rusty. It won't kill you. Just repeat them to yourself every morning."

We groaned. Nobody objected out loud.

"Goodbye, enjoy yourselves," Sir finished, and strode out of the room.

I did begin by doing as he had said, but it took me so long to get through all my tables that I was always late for breakfast, and after a while I gave it up. When I told Mummy about saying my tables before I opened my stocking she just said, "If you do that I'll box your ears." So I didn't.

They were still selling the muslin stockings full of toys in Woolworth's, but I didn't seem to feel so attracted towards them as I had the previous year. They were just the same, but I didn't feel interested. I had bought it as a present for Daddy last Christmas, I remembered astonished. How could I even have thought he would want that?

Instead, I bought him an enormous shining glass Christmas-tree decoration, pink and gold, with great spirals and whorls. It reminded me of the pointed, twisted towers and turrets of Spinazzolala.

14

ON THE FIRST day of the spring term, after the Christmas holidays, I didn't get to school until five to nine. We had fallen out of the habit of waking up early and neither Mummy nor I had been able to hurry the slightest little bit. I dashed in, terrified of having missed the register, but luckily Sir was late too.

Valerie Barker, Valerie Wilson and Sandra Pope were sitting on their desks, huddled together in a corner. When I came in they called out, "Antonia, come here!"

I went over. Pope said, "Valerie likes . . ."

"She likes Thompson, and she . . ." broke in Barker.

"She sent him a Christmas present anonymously!" said Pope, almost whispering in my ear.

"Why anonymously?" I said, and then realized that that was the wrong thing to say. I tried to make up by giggling with my hand over my mouth, like the others, and not saying anything.

"You mustn't tell! You won't, will you, Antonia?" said Wilson anxiously. "Don't tell anyone."

"No, of course not," I said. I wanted to add, "But if it's such a secret, why tell me?" but realized in time that they were going to tell all the girls and it was the boys I mustn't say anything to.

Suddenly Pope noticed Andrews stealing up behind. She screamed, and the rest of us followed her example, and we fled across the classroom. I took the opportunity to escape and go and talk to Lynda.

In playtime, as I was making the dash across the open from the door to the entrance to the lavatories, Andrews jumped on me from behind and grabbed at my arms. I screamed and fought, but it was no good, he was far stronger than me and I knew no one would come to my help. Most of the other girls were in the same predicament anyway. Andrews twisted both my arms behind my back and hauled me away towards the dreadful dark corner at the far end of the playground. I shouted from pain and fear and dug my heels into the ground, but he gave a great tug at my poor arms and I lurched into the corner.

All round me there were boys hitting and mauling screaming girls. One boy threw a small girl on the ground at my feet and I tripped over her and would have fallen, except that Andrews wrenched me back. He gripped my arms tighter and twisted the right hard against the elbow joint. I found myself thinking about Daddy's wrestling, about wrist locks and arm levers, and how they usually produced submissions. I'll submit in a minute, I was thinking, idiotically.

"What did those girls tell you this morning?" Andrews hissed into my ear.

I said, "I submit."

He wrung my arm harder. I yelled. He said, "Tell me!" I didn't say anything. I was wishing for an umpire. "Go on, tell me! What did that Barker tell you this morning?"

"You're a stupid nit," I gasped out.

"Was that what she said?" he said surprised, relaxing his hold a little. "No, it wasn't. Go on, she didn't say that, did she?"

"No, I'm saying it," I said.

"What did she say, then?" He wrenched at my arm. Why don't I tell, I wondered. If I don't another girl will.

"Go on, Buddersmud! What did she say?"

That was easier. "I'm not Rutherford."

"No, you won't be in a minute if you don't say," said Andrews.

Suddenly the place was filled with a stampede of boys and screeching girls. It was one of the scavenging expeditions that were always roaming round the playground, catching girls to torture. They dashed in, knocking me and Andrews apart. I butted my way through them and ran for the lavatories.

"What did Andrews want?" Valerie Wilson asked me anxiously as I staggered in, nursing my arm.

"He wanted to know what you told me this morning," I said.

"What did you say?"

"I didn't say anything," I said, and turned away, not feeling very kindly disposed towards her.

"Oh, thank you, Antonia," she said. "Though, actually, Thompson got hold of me and made me tell. . . ." I sighed.

When we came back after play we wrote compositions. The subject was "A Tree." I wrote fast and excitedly.

117

"In the paddock there stood a huge blasted tree. It was withered and white, and leaned over, deformed and distorted. There were no branches all down one side. It seemed like a blight, a curse, on the paddock. Nothing but stinging-nettles grew within sight of that tree.

"Then came the storm. It finished the work of the other storm, killing where it had crippled. All night long the wind blew with incredible force, bending the tree nearer and nearer to the ground. In the morning, the wind had died down a little. It was fine, and I went out. From the top of the hill I could see all over the farm. I could see there was something wrong, something out of place; then I realized. The cows had come through the gap in the hedge into the paddock, which they had never done before, although the gap was always open. In the night the tree had fallen. The curse was removed from the paddock."

I had finished ages before anyone else. I sat doodling in the margin of the composition, visualizing the tree falling in the storm.

The headmaster came into the room with a bit of paper and showed it to Sir. He said something in a worried voice and hurried out of the room again. Sir looked round and said, "Who's finished? Nobody? Oh, you have, Bird. Please will you take this to Miss Lovely in Class Three?"

I took the headmaster's bit of paper and went out. When I went into Class Three Miss Lovely was saying,

"It's a bad thing to have an accent. We've got quite a selection of accents here. To begin with, will—Oh, Rutherford! We'll have you. Read the words on the board."

I scowled at her. It wasn't as if she didn't know about our change of name. The whole school had buzzed with it. The headmaster had sent for me and talked to me about it, purely out of curiosity. He was a jolly man, and seemed fascinated by everything we did. After that interview every teacher in the school knew all about me. Even the silly young temporary Class Four teachers knew me and called me "Bird."

"Read the sentence on the board aloud so that the class can hear you, Rutherford," said Miss Lovely.

"How now, brown cow, said Jane in the train in Spain," I said loudly. I knew that I hadn't got an accent. Mummy had been careful about it. She and Daddy had commented on it.

"Now that," said Miss Lovely, "is what we call a public-school accent. It's as bad, if not worse, as any we can have. Your father did go to a public school, didn't he?"

"Yes, Miss Lovely," I growled. She had a silly affected voice. I could just imagine her saying, "Hay-oh nay-oh bray-own cay-oh."

"Yes, and you don't make a secret of it either, do you?" she said. "Now, Farley, will you repeat the words on the board? You've got what I'd call an ordinary Midland accent. It should be quite easy to overcome."

"Please, Miss Lovely," I said, "I was told to give you this."

"How exactly typical of you, Rutherford, to wait all this time before doing so," she said ferociously, turning on me. She took the bit of paper without looking at it. "It might have been something really important, and here you stood, for minutes on end, without delivering it, doing nothing. I can't imagine who was fool enough to trust you with it." She glared at me. "That's just what I'd have expected of you, Rutherford. What with your—huh—public-school parents and your—huh—gallivanting off to have a holiday just when you feel like it, before the end of term, you just haven't any sense of responsibility." She stared angrily into my face. I stared back. I badly wanted to say, "I don't see what that's got to do with it, and I wasn't doing nothing, and anyway if it's so important for goodness' sake get on and read it!" I also wanted to say, "It wasn't me that went gallivanting off, it was Daddy, so don't scold me." But I knew what she'd say: "Oh yes, I know, I know. Nothing's ever your fault, is it, Rutherford?" So I just glowered at her.

"Oh, and she doesn't attempt to apologize either, does she? Well, I don't want you sulking here. Get on back to your own class."

"Yes, Miss Lovely," I managed to say, and went out. She still hadn't read the headmaster's message. Through the door I could hear her saying: "Now, come on, Farley, we haven't got all day." She didn't sound cross as she had with me, though.

"I've corrected your compositions," Sir said, "some of them were very good. Hand them out, please, Stevens."

There was nothing on mine but a tick in red biro at the end. Johnson, who was sitting beside me that term, glanced at it enviously.

"Didn't you get any mistakes?" he asked incredulously.

"No, I don't think so."

"Coo! And just look at mine!" It was a mess of red slashes and crosses. "Twelve mistakes," said Johnson. "That's good, for me. Didn't you get any?"

"No, not in this, but to make up I didn't get any of those problems right last night," I told him.

"Didn't you? But they were easy!" He leant across and tapped Peters on the shoulder. "Bird's got no mistakes in hers. I got twelve, what about you?"

Peters stared at me. "What, none? Coo! You're the one that writes poems, though, aren't you?" he said, as though solving a mystery.

"Yes, that's me," I agreed.

"Ah, well," he said, turning away.

"We'll have the best read out. Bird, will you start with yours?" Sir said.

Pleased, I read mine out. Everyone gazed at me intently as I read, listening, absolutely silent. At least, almost everyone.

"What did the old man do down the drain?
'E went pss, pss, and fell down dead."

Roberts went quietly on from his corner all the time I was reading. But the others all listened, their eyes fixed on me. When I finished they stirred and murmured.

"Coo! That wasn't half good!"

"Wish I could write like that."

Matthews read his out, a dry little essay on the uses of trees. The class began to whisper and fidget a long time before he finished. Sir pointed out that the subject had been "A Tree", not "Trees." Nobody whispered how good it was.

I leant across and said to Matthews, "That was awfully well written." That's true, at least, I thought.

"Oh, go on," he said, "I don't write poetry."

"That's got nothing to do with it. It was jolly good."

"Bird," said Sir, "I think you could take yours up and show it to the headmaster."

We all gasped. That meant a star. A star! Sir hadn't sent anyone up for one before, all the time I had been at the school. Everybody was patting me and congratulating me. I noticed Sir was smiling.

"Take it up now," he said.

I got up with my composition. The door seemed far away in

a thick fog. I lurched out and stumbled up past the staff-room to the headmaster's study, peering at the stairs through the fog. The headmaster said, "Come in," as soon as I knocked. I staggered in.

"Please, sir, Mr.—um—Sir told me to bring my composition up to you," I said.

"Oh, he did, did he?" the headmaster said genially. "Well, let's see it." He read it slowly, twice.

"Yes," he said, "yes. I think I'll give you a star for this. It's vivid, all right. Yes, you can have a star." He took a red pencil out of his desk and drew an elaborate star at the end of the composition. He was grinning. I discovered that I was too, and wondered for how long.

"I think I'll keep this, if you don't mind. Did you know that a star's worth five house-marks and fifteen for yourself?"

"No, sir, I didn't. Thank you very much, sir." I couldn't stop grinning. Well, why should I? I wondered. He hasn't.

"It's very good, Antonia. I suppose it's what comes of having a mind for poetry," he said. I started. Mummy's told him about my poetry. Oh, niddle, I thought.

"I expect you're right, sir. It was much easier to write than a poem, though," I said.

"Was it? I'm surprised. You'd know, though. All right, off you go, and chalk up your marks on the chart."

I went, trying to remember which was my house. I plumped for Blue because I liked blue. As I began to stick the five stars on to Blue, Sir said, "You're in Yellow team, aren't you, Bird?"

"Oh," I said. I picked at the star I had stuck on Blue. It wouldn't come off. "Oh, dear."

"Never mind," said Sir, smiling at me. "Go and sit down."

I went. Everybody was grinning at me.

"Never mind, Antonia, you're in another world, aren't you?" somebody said kindly. Lynda, I guessed.

"Good old Bird, she's given us a house-mark."

"You can see she's miles away, writing a poem, I expect. Are you, Bird?"

"Mmm? Well, not exactly," I said. I was vaguely aware of dozens of friendly faces smiling at me. Not a single hostile one among them. Oh, yes, there was Tatley. Well, who cares about her, I thought. Just look at all the others. I bumbled round trying to find my desk.

"Oh, dear, Antonia, we'll have to look after you, won't we?" someone said, helping me to my seat.

"Thank you," I said into the fog.

"She's like a little lost dog, isn't she? Our mascot. That's what she is, our class mascot."

"No, not that book. You don't want to do arithmetic, do you? This one. That's right. And your dictionary. Oh, dear, I can't find it. Well, perhaps you can manage without. Now shut the desk. That's it, you're improving," somebody was saying. They were right, I was far away. I was thinking of what I had sung to Daddy in Ibiza : "Mr. Most Popular Man ! Mr. Most Popular Man !" It was going round and round inside my head now. "Miss Most Popular Girl." It's true, I thought, I'm popular. They like me. Once upon a time they wouldn't talk to me. And now, here I am, friends with everyone, and all because I stuck a star in the wrong place. Or was it that? Who cares, anyway? I'm popular, and I've got a star.

"That was crafty, Antonia," said King in play, as she juggled balls between her legs, over her shoulder, against the row of green doors.

"Crafty? What was?" I had never felt less crafty in my life.

"Putting that star in Blue. Eric Stevens is House captain of Blue."

"Oh, is he? I didn't know." I suddenly understood what she meant. "Oh ! Oh, I see what you mean. I didn't do it because of that, though."

"No, of course. All the same, it was crafty. Buying his heart, that's what it was," she giggled.

"Mmm," I said. A star ! I was thinking. Perhaps I might really get into St. Rhadigond's after all. Oh, if I could only take that eleven-plus now. Now, now, now. A star !

15

We took the eleven-plus just over a fortnight later. I felt het-up enough myself, at breakfast, but it was nothing to Mummy. She kept saying that I must calm down, look at me all tensed-up, there was really nothing to worry about, nothing at all. I smiled at her over my egg, thinking that all her remarks applied to her more than me. She was fairly palpitating. I was too, of course, but not as badly as her.

"I know what you need," she said suddenly. "Does you a world of good before an exam." She gave me a little Grand Marnier in the bottom of a tumbler, and had some herself, too. "That'll put heart into you. Oh, and I know what else you must have, too." She went out.

The liqueur was dreadfully nasty. I got it down with the help of my hot chocolate, and managed to smile wanly at Mummy when she came back.

"Look!" she said. "You can have them all, to bring you good luck." She put carefully down on the table all seven of her pink elephants, including the huge stuffed felt one I had made. I gulped, and smiled feebly again.

"Thank you very much, Mummy," I said. "I'll put them all on my desk during the exam. I'll be certain to pass, looking at them."

"Don't forget to stand them on their noses," she reminded me.

None of the boys seemed a bit excited when I got to school, and roared round, the same as ever. Of the girls, only Barker (who went round telling everyone about her collywobbles in most vivid language) and Tatley had, or admitted to having, the jitters. I was surprised by Tatley. She flopped all over her desk and wouldn't let anyone come near her. She kept crying and taking aspirins. I thought she was ill at first.

Barker said she had been sick twice that morning and thought she had a temperature.

"Well, go to Miss Lovely and take it then, and she'll give you an aspirin," I said, genuinely worried.

"Oh, no, I'm not going to take it, Antonia," said Barker tearfully. "If I've got a temperature I don't want to know. It would make it worse."

I gave up and went to see Lynda. She was quietly reading *The Heroes*. We grinned at each other.

After prayers we were all made to change our desks, and then the mascots began to appear. I hadn't noticed that it was snowing, but it must have been, because many of the boys had great snowballs on their desks, as mascots. They didn't melt for quite a long time, but when they did some of the boys quickly put them inside the desks they were at. As we had all changed, they weren't their own, of course. After a while a slow trickle of water began to come out from underneath the desks. Luckily I found that the noise of dripping and running water helped me to think, which was just as well, because it went on all through the exam. Sir didn't do anything about it. The other boys with snowballs just let them melt all over their desks, until they were writing in a great pool of water. Sir kept passing round cloths, but nobody used them. Roberts emptied his inkwell into his pool as well. I don't know what he wrote with after that. Very likely he didn't.

Sandra Pope brought an enormous wedding horseshoe, with great bouquets of artificial flowers and scrolls and Cupids and things. It took up her entire desk, and she wrote on her lap all through the exam. The other girls brought unpretentious little mascots, like my seven pink elephants. I had thought people would laugh at those, but they turned out to be a most modest mascot. I stood them on their noses in a row across my desk. They took up less than half.

Several people, boys and girls, had for mascots little lumps of coal, from the scuttle by the classroom fire, daintily wrapped in tissue paper. Usually they had several. They kept coming unwrapped, and rolling all over the desk making black marks on everything. You'd have thought they were precious relics, they were treated with such reverence.

The first exam was the arithmetic. We went on wishing each other good luck loudly for ages after the starting bell. Sir was furious, although he could only whisper about it after we had begun.

We had to fill up a form first which was an intelligence test in itself. We kept parading up to Sir, one after the other, to ask him what it meant and what we ought to write. I think he did nearly everyone's for them. I did my own.

The first section was simple arithmetic questions. I opened the paper and looked at it. This is it, I thought. This is what I've been working for, building up to, ever since I learnt how to count. This is what we've all had our eyes fixed on, Mummy and Sir and all those temporary governesses. We've all thought and worried about this, the eleven-plus arithmetic, for such years and years; and always it's been in the future, like a legend in reverse. And now, here it is, here it actually is. Four into ninety-six goes thirty-four. It seems impossible, how can it be happening, I was thinking as I wrote the first answer. It's like dying, something which you know is bound to happen and which never does.

Ninety-six divided by four was the first question, and there was my answer screaming up from the page, thirty-four. Pull yourself together, I thought. It's not time to write your composition yet, so you can just stop writing one in your head and get on. I corrected my first answer and dashed on. The first section was easy. Mummy and Sir had told me, again and again, that the questions in it carried as many marks as the harder ones and that I just had to get every one right, and I might pass. It didn't take me long, once I had started. I made sure that I hadn't made any more stupid mistakes and went on to the "mechanical" section—money, weights and measures, more complicated fractions, decimals and percentages. I knew I had to do well on these too. I did my best, but they weren't as easy as I had hoped. I really messed up the last area question.

The section on problems was just a joke. I began all of them and finished one, with a ridiculous answer in hundredths of a pint. I barely scraped through to the end of the paper, even though I only began most of the problems. I had spent far too long on both the other sections. Still, I thought, I've done all I can on the important things.

I went down to play feeling dazed and exhausted, quite forgetting to be wary as I crossed the playground. I only just escaped being caught by one of the girl-hunting gangs of boys. It hadn't occurred to me that they might be going on with things like that on such a day. Perhaps they're from Class Two, I thought, who aren't taking the exam. But no, they were all boys from my class. We were having our play late, anyway.

In the lavatories I joined a group of girls, expecting them to be discussing the exam. I felt I wanted to talk about it.

"Did your mum knit that jumper?" Wilson was saying.

"Well, she did a bit and I did a bit. I did the sleeves."

"It's a nice pattern."

"Yes, our auntie sent it to us. She usually knits her patterns herself, but she's getting stiff in the hands now. I've got a little scarf to match, blue, with ribbing down the edges. It looks ever so nice."

"You'd need a big brooch with it."

"Yes, I've got a big red butterfly. Got it from Woolworth's specially. I think yellow would have looked better, really."

I turned away.

The two intelligence exams were almost fun. They were mainly concerned with juggling letters, anagrams and so on. Many of the mascots had been put away, and there were only a few new snowballs. Everyone seemed to have got over their nerves. I felt so relieved to have got the terrible arithmetic over that I hardly felt either the intelligence or the English to be exams at all. The intelligence was really only a game, and so were many of the English questions. ("What other word means 'heavy'?" "What does 'unison' mean, in line six of the passage above?") It was always fun to write a composition. As usual I was completely absorbed in it, and was only dimly aware of the rest of the school making a tremendous racket outside the room, and not painfully, as I had been during the arithmetic. Matthews, Mason and I finished early, even though I checked through my paper again and again, and Sir let us go out into the playground. We ran and chased each other, yelling, and played snowballs. I didn't feel dazed and exhausted any more. I felt quite equal to talking about King's knitting for hours on end. The eleven-plus, that great bogey, was over, finished, for ever.

I threw a snowball at Mason and hit him full in the face. He yelled, skidded and fell over. I opened my mouth to laugh, and got it full of snowball, from Matthews. I threw one back at him. He stepped back to dodge it and tripped over Mason, and they both went flying. I heard the bell for the end of afternoon school, and ran upstairs laughing, leaving the two boys sprawling in the slush. There wasn't much snow left, after two playtimes and a lunch hour.

"Hullo, Triunfadora!" I heard a shout as I passed the Post Office, on my way home. It was Mummy, with a parcel. "Would you like to come and have hot buttered toast somewhere, while you tell me all about it? And here's a present just anyway, because you're still alive." It was a pound of coffee chocolates. "I was thinking of our Totty doing her exam, and what would she like to cheer her up, and then I saw these in the window of a shop and I wanted them for you."

"Yum yum," I said with my mouth full.

We couldn't find hot buttered toast anywhere, but I had a delicious cake instead, and kept assuring Mummy that really I was still alive, and that except for the problems I'd managed perfectly. She didn't really believe me, until I produced her pink elephants and stood them on their noses.

"Well, they look happy enough, anyway," she said.

"And so am I," I said.

I described every question to her, and my answer. She so glowed with admiration, and looked so keen and eager at everything that she almost convinced me that I really had done a brilliant paper.

"I don't believe I really did as well as you make out," I said, "I made a muddle of one or two of the intelligence questions and I just couldn't express 'held tightly' in one word when 'on to' comes after. I mean to say, you can't put 'She clutched on to the rail' or 'She gripped on to the rail,' can you? But I did enjoy it, even the first section of the arithmetic."

"You don't enjoy an exam if you've done badly," said Mummy. "Have another chocolate."

I felt perfectly well that day, better than I had for ages, in fact.

"Nerves," said Mummy gloomily. "You see, you'll have a collapse soon."

She was right. The next day I felt awful, and Mummy kept me at home, and when I felt better and Mummy was going to send me back, Daddy stepped in and said I was to have a week's holiday after the exam. So we went to our little country cottage for a week, and I went back to school on the first of February.

I felt quite skittish after my holiday, and so, "just to show 'em, and make Eric Stevens froth at the mouth." I came back to school wearing scarlet socks.

Everyone greeted me cheerfully. "Hullo, Antonia! Feeling better now?"

But Felicity Dearchild took one look at me and my socks and shouted, "Aren't they ghastly!"

She didn't say anything else to me, all day. Nobody else took any notice of the socks.

On that day the boys seemed to have gone mad. Now that the exam was over Sir gave in to Miss Lovely and took us to the downstairs hall to do P. E. Thompson had brought a transistor radio (he usually used it for listening to the cricket scores) and he turned it on to a jazz programme, very loud. Everyone shouted and began to dance, jiving, the girls with the girls and the boys with the boys. The girls were very half-hearted and soon gave up, and sat down in a circle and did hand-jive, but the boys were tremendous. I stood and watched, fascinated. Thompson's transistor wasn't really very exciting, but the boys behaved as if it were really wild rock 'n' roll. Sir stood by grinning, and didn't try to stop them. They were red and sweating, their shirts hung out loose over their shorts and they leaned right over, backwards, staring at the ceiling, thrumming on an imaginary guitar. Presently the girls came and stood round the room clapping in time to the hardly audible music.

Roberts was the best. He was in a frenzy with excitement as he leaned, stared, bent his knees, and then went off whirling and capering as he jived with his partner. Sometimes he gave a terrifying scream. Sir looked quite excited himself as he stood clapping with the girls.

There were workmen in the playground, and we had to stay indoors for play. The boys were still as wild as ever, and tore all over the school with wet knotted scarves, flicking and beating the girls and smaller boys. There was nowhere to hide except in the girls' lavatory in the back playground, and we weren't allowed to go there. I cowered behind a desk in the classroom. Stevens, charging in, found me, and was about to hit me when he saw who I was. I was trying to edge round the desk, away from him.

"It's all right, Antonia," he said soothingly, "we won't hurt you." He laid emphasis on the "you." I gaped incredulously at him.

"Oh, good," I said. "Thanks." He really did look just like a cow. He turned away and dashed after Little. What had he called me? Antonia? A boy, calling me by my Christian name? Of course, it was that star I had given accidentally to his house. But still, that surely didn't warrant such familiarity. And how could a boy possibly know my Christian name anyway? I went away to search for Lynda. She was hiding in the library. I stared at her in disgust, sitting under the Nature shelf, and then decided that it was a perfect hiding-place and joined her there.

16

"IT'LL BE VALENTINE'S DAY again tomorrow. Won't you be sending a boy a valentine *this* year?" Mummy said wistfully.

"Gosh! I hadn't thought of it. Well, it would be a laugh, wouldn't it. Shall I, just for a joke?" I wondered.

"Oh, do," Mummy begged.

"Well, all right, I will! I'll go out and see if I can find a jolly card after tea. Who shall I give it to?"

"If you like, I'll pay for the card for you," she said. "Fancy not knowing what boy to send it to." She bonked me on the head with an envelope. "You're not human."

"Oh, dear," I said apologetically. Poor Mummy, I thought, I'm a big disappointment to her. I'll have to get romantically engaged at fifteen to make up. "I know! The girls at school are cooking up an affair between me and a boy called Stevens. I'll send him a valentine. It'll keep them happy for days."

"What about keeping you happy?" Mummy said slyly.

Oh, dear, there I go again, I thought. "Why yes, of course, I should simply love it—I mean I should simply love him—oh, dear, you know what I mean," I said, wriggling in my chair.

I bought a perfect valentine card, full of desks and ink blots shaped like hearts, and a picture of a girl leap-frogging over a desk to get to her boy. I put it in Stevens' desk in the morning, amidst great ceremony. All the girls knew who it was from even before Stevens found it.

Wilson had put a valentine in too, but she hid it away in an envelope and I don't think it was ever found. I took mine out of the envelope and put it on top of his books. The poor boy found it the minute he opened his desk, amid howls of laughter. He knew at once who it was from. He couldn't not, when the whole of the rest of the class did. He blushed red all over his face and stared at it unbelievingly. I retreated to the back of the room, knowing what was bound to happen.

"Kiss him!" someone shouted, as soon as we could stop laughing.

"Kiss him! Kiss him!" shrieked the class. Half of it pinned poor Stevens, crimson to the ears, down on to his desk, and the other half rushed towards me. I pretended to struggle for a minute with Skinner, and then let myself be dragged over to Stevens.

"Kiss him!" everyone was shouting. They pushed me down towards him. Our faces were barely six inches apart. But just as the exciting moment came, with him grunting and me squealing and everyone else cheering and yelling, in marched Sir, just at the wrong time as usual.

"Come along! Get away off those front desks. What on earth's going on? You're making enough noise to be heard in Timbuctoo. Get back to your desks."

So I never got my kiss. It wouldn't be any good to bring it up again later. The time had gone past.

I glanced at Stevens. He was paling down, and didn't look cross or annoyed. His clothes were all pulled about, and he was trying to put them straight.

"We're going to change the desks round a bit," Sir said. He made us alter all the desks round so that all the girls were sitting next to boys.

"Good old Sir," Matthews said, "Trust you. On Valentine's Day, too." We all cheered Sir loudly, not really because of what he had done, I think, but because we liked him. Not that that had made us want to make a go of his Christmas concert, the year before.

While Sir was writing an exercise on the board, Skinner, on the other side of the room, stood up and sent a paper dart flying across the room. It landed at my feet. He nodded at me and sat down. Wondering, I unfolded the dart. There was something written on it. I puzzled over it, and eventually decided that it said, "I love what this is the sowing girl." It was anybody's guess, though, really. The only words that were even moderately legible were "I love." There was no mistaking them, however. In astonishment I realized that Skinner had sent me a valentine. I gaped at it, remembering how this very same day a year ago he had given me a black eye. I smiled rather uncertainly at him. He saw me all right, but he didn't smile back or anything.

I only just managed to squeeze into the lavatories at play

and had to stand almost in the doorway, so that I had a perfect view of what went on outside. I saw Skinner accusing Stevens of something. A group of boys was standing round them. I saw Stevens going red again, and then Skinner breaking away from the circle waving something brightly coloured—my valentine card, I realized with a pang. Stevens dashed after him. In the middle of the playground either Skinner turned to meet Stevens or Stevens caught up with Skinner, and they began to wrestle. The boys were still standing round in a circle. Some others seemed to have joined.

I watched at first without interest, except that it seemed to be about my card, thinking it was just another of the playful tussles that were always going on. But when after a minute or two Skinner threw Stevens on to the ground, instead of offering him a pear drop he threw himself on to Stevens and they went on fighting. I couldn't see very well for the ring of spectators, and so I crept warily out and joined them. The fight was by then the only thing going on in the playground and so I was quite safe.

The boys were hurtling to and fro, throwing each other about, punching and grappling. Sometimes one fell and sometimes the other did, but the fight went on. It wasn't just play either. Both the boys were scarlet in the face and their eyes glittered, and their faces wore the expression of intense hatred that painters sometimes give to the Damned. Everyone was shouting. I noticed that the other girls had followed my example and come out to watch.

They reeled apart for an instant, panting and glaring at each other, their clothes torn and pulled about. Stevens wasn't much bigger than Skinner, after all. Then Skinner gave a growl like an animal and leapt at Stevens, clutching at his throat. They both fell heavily at our feet, grunting and gasping and rolling over and over. Stevens suddenly managed to get on to his knees, with his hands at Skinner's throat. We were all screaming and screaming, especially the girls. Some boy prefects kept pushing through us and trying to split up the fight, but the girls, thirsty for blood, pushed them away, and though the boys kept trying, they didn't get anywhere.

Skinner suddenly rolled over and away from Stevens and jumped to his feet, and Stevens was still on his knees. I yelled and jumped up and down, like everyone else. Skinner threw himself at Stevens. They looked as if they really might murder each other. Evidently the boy prefects thought so, for they tried to push through again, but the girls wouldn't let them. A proper fight at last! We weren't going to have our fun spoilt.

Stevens, still on his knees, pushed and struggled, and suddenly Skinner gave way and fell back, and Stevens scrambled up. He jumped for Skinner in a frenzy and pushed him to the ground. As he got up again he seized him round the neck from behind. For a second the thought flitted across my mind : He'll break Skinner's neck. But then that was eclipsed by : Hurrah, my one's winning!

"Now behave yourselves. Get up and stop scrambling like children," said Andrews, a prefect, sternly. He got through the girls, and tried to pull Skinner and Stevens apart. The girls ran at him and pulled him off. By the time we had dealt with him Skinner had broken away from Stevens' neck-hold and they were rolling on the ground again, locked together. We went on shrieking and cheering, nearly as excited as the boys themselves, as now one and then the other got on top. They were breathing in great gasps. Their shirts were torn open, and their faces were deeper crimson than you'd have believed possible.

"Stevens! Go on, Stevens!" I yelled. Nobody, I noticed, was shouting for Skinner.

Stevens did seem to be winning. He was right on top of Skinner, and had him almost pinned down. His face was contorted with fury until it looked almost mad. Skinner's looked worse, for it was desperate as well.

"Stevens! Stevens!" we screamed. The boy prefects were still struggling uselessly.

"All right, that's enough of that. Come on, get up the stairs," said a man's voice authoritatively. We glanced round in dismay. It was Sir, old busybody. The crowd melted away. He went up to the boys and pulled them part. Amazingly, they allowed it. We all trooped disappointedly upstairs. Sir made us spend the last few minutes of play under his eye, in the classroom.

We all considered that Stevens had won, though, and the boys kept telling him so.

"That was all because of you, you know, Antonia," said Barker. "They were fighting about you."

"Oh, rubbish," I laughed. "How could they have been?"

In the middle of one of our P.E. lessons in the downstairs hall,

Miss Lovely came in with a note and whispered urgently to Sir. He read the note, frowned, and went hurriedly out.

"Well, now," said Miss Lovely. She caught sight of the little Indian girl and pointed at her. "Why aren't you undressed?"

"She's not allowed, Miss Lovely," we all yelled. Everyone was on her side if it was against Miss Lovely. "The headmaster says."

"Well, it seems very silly to me," she said. "I hope you've got a doctor's certificate. Now, I didn't send your Mr. Gibbs on a wild goose chase for nothing. I want to talk to you about him."

"Mr. Gibbs? Sir, do you mean?" called Matthews.

"Yes, yes, of course," said Miss Lovely impatiently. "Well, no one else knows yet, but—" she looked cautiously round and spoke lower, "he's going to be married."

"Hurrah! Good old Sir! Hurrah!" We all shouted and cheered. Miss Lovely watched us, smiling. Yes, she was actually smiling.

"Ssh, now! We're doing P.E., remember," she said. "Well, I thought that we—the whole school—might raise a subscription and buy him a wedding present, as a surprise." She looked happy, really nice, as she spoke.

"Yes, yes!" we roared enthusiastically.

"We've got a fortnight, then. He's getting married on the Saturday, and I've made him promise to be at school on Friday, and we can give it to him then."

We cheered and stamped.

"Now, if you could all manage to bring at least half-a-crown by next Wednesday, please," Miss Lovely said.

When I came home Mummy was doing the washing. She had the washing-machine, the spin-dryer and a jazz record all going full blast. I mouthed at her, and she mouthed back, and realizing we were getting nowhere I wrote her a message, and she put a wet sheet on it, so that it smudged. I had to wait till dinner to talk to her.

"Can I have some money for Sir's wedding-present? It's for next Wednesday, and I don't get any pocket money till after then."

"Why, of course, better take five shillings," she said.

Miss Lovely glared at me when I brought it.

"I ask for two and six, and so you bring five shillings. All right, we know you're rich."

"We're not," I muttered, but she didn't hear.

She bought a large, framed reproduction of some ballet dancers, by Degas, with our subscriptions, and we duly presented it to Sir on Friday afternoon. He was, or pretended to be, very surprised, and made a speech about how he adored Degas and would hang it in his sitting-room. We clapped and cheered, and some of the girls threw confetti about, and we sang "For He's a Jolly Good Fellow" with great gusto. Sir grinned and blushed. I think he was really pleased, whether he liked Degas or not.

He was away for a fortnight after that. Strange rumours went round the school about where he had gone for his honeymoon. He certainly looked a lot less harassed when he came back.

"I'm expecting your eleven-plus results next Wednesday so you'd better all come prepared," said Sir, one afternoon in the middle of April.

We all sighed and groaned and pretended to be terrified.

"I'll bring a coffin," said Matthews. We agreed that that would be what we'd all need.

To my surprise several girls, including Tatley and Barker, did come prepared. They brought aspirins and kept taking them until Sir came in.

"Well, I've got them," he said. We moaned and whimpered. "This year they've got a new fancy way of dividing you. Recommended for Academic Education and Not Recommended for Academic Education." He sounded impatient, almost disapproving. "Recommended is what they called Passed in my day and Not Recommended is virtually Failed."

He began to read out the list. I was after Valerie Barker, on the alphabetical list. When Sir read out, "Barker, not recommended," she screamed, and I didn't hear mine. I scowled at her. She was crying, and I felt sorry for her and stopped scowling. Sir paused and looked at me, and then repeated,

"Bird—recommended."

I smiled gratefully at him, still more concerned with not having heard than with the result. Then it sank in. I had passed. Instantly I thought: St. Rhadigond's! I grinned happily at Lynda. She smiled back, a little wanly. Sir was still at Matthews, recommended. She was all right, though. As I had expected, Page was recommended.

Tatley didn't pass. I was only mildly surprised, and that was only because everyone else was. I realized after a minute that I should have been more surprised if she had passed. She pouted and sulked and looked defiant and bossed everyone about more than ever. It struck me that in spite of all her aspirins, and her show of being frightened, before the results, she was very surprised indeed that she had failed.

King and Wilson and Pope had also passed and all the boys I should have expected, the ones who were so clever at arithmetic, like Johnson and Alcock and Andrews. Stevens didn't. His expression didn't alter at all as Sir read out, "Stevens, not recommended." He just went on looking like a cow and wrote it down in his rough book, "Not recmended for ackademic edducatian," in case he forgot.

There was a slight hush after Sir had finished, and he said, "That was quite good. Ten people passed, as compared to eight last year." He went on to say something about technicals and secondary moderns to "those people who weren't recommended," but that was quite drowned by the yell of triumph of the ten successful ones. We jumped on to our desks and hallooed, and threw them over and tried to hit the ceiling with our inkwells We laughed and shouted and hugged each other and danced round the room, singing and cheering. We threw all our books into the air, and tore up our exercise books and threw the pieces at each other until the whole room was covered with bits of paper and running with ink. Sir had quite a time controlling us, but being Sir, he did (Miss Lovely never could have, not even with a machine gun), and gave us a good scolding and a beastly arithmetic exercise to do. But he was half-smiling all the time, and I knew he was secretly delighted with us for passing. It was a record for ten to pass out of a class of thirty-six.

The rest of the class sat as gloomy as gloomy all through the morning, but the ten "grammars" were bubbling over with excitement and could hardly sit still. The instant the bell went for play we gave a great shout and rushed down the stairs arm-in-arm. We charged round the playground, girls and boys together, for once not caring a button for the other boys on the war-path. We sang "Auld Lang Syne" over and over again as we rushed to and fro. Everyone was laughing, and Pope and King were crying hysterically as well. We danced and capered and sang.

All the tension of those months—years—had suddenly snapped. We had been building up to it, and building up to it, and then we had waited months for our results, and now they had come and everything was all right. We were so relieved that we could have screamed. In fact we did scream.

As we were singing "Auld Lang Syne" for the third time I felt so overflowing with excitement that I began to twirl round and round with my eyes shut. I bumped into a wall, but I didn't care, and opened my eyes, preparing to dance away. I found I was in a corner at the far end of the playground, and beside me was Tatley, crying. I felt a pang of pity for her, and tried to smile consolingly.

"What a shame about your result . . ." I began, and then saw it wasn't going to work. She didn't answer, and just scowled at me. I smiled. She pouted. I gave up and went back to the nine other "passes," still celebrating madly. I joined in, but I didn't seem to feel quite so exhilarated now. I couldn't help thinking about the others, kicking stones at the other end of the playground, and especially about poor Tatley, who had obviously pinned all her hopes on passing. Just like me. Supposing I had failed? It was too awful to think of. And she had.

When I came out of school at the end of the afternoon I ran into Mrs. Tatley, Linda's mother. I had only met her once, ages ago, but we both recognized each other. She asked politely if I had passed, and I said yes, I had, and then remembered that Linda hadn't.

"But you know, this year it isn't a question of passing or failing, it's all different," I said hastily. "We're recommended for academic education or not recommended for academic education or recommended for technical training or not recommended for technical training, and anyway, the headmaster says lots of the modern technicals are almost better than grammar schools—" I ran out of breath.

"Ah, I see," said Mrs. Tatley, but I thought she was in a fine muddle. I hoped she was. I was vaguely aware of Mummy's voice calling me, but I didn't think about her. I was watching Mrs. Tatley waiting for Linda. Linda was late. I didn't blame her.

PART TWO

17

I WENT FOR MY interview at St. Rhadigond's in May, a few weeks later. I only had my dingy old pinafore dresses and my gaudy holiday clothes. I thought those would do, but Mummy panicked and bought me a grey pleated skirt specially to look earnest and worthy. I tried to seem bright and intelligent, but as before I was so overawed by the magnificence of the school (even here in the headmistress' study, which was really just like any other room) that I found it difficult. As I was telling how I had been to the concert, I had an inspiration, and said outright that I had been so impressed by the school then that I had longed ever since to come there. The headmistress, Miss Haversham, smiled brightly at me as I said this. Oh, I see now what the head girl meant when she said that everyone loved Miss Haversham, I thought. She's so friendly, and kind, and motherly, even better than I had imagined. I grinned back at her. She was small and thin, with carroty hair and slanting black-rimmed glasses, and looked jolly, I thought. She was young, too, no older than Mummy, I guessed.

She asked me about the school. I went into rhapsodies over what I had seen of it, the façade, the front hall, the great hall. She told me lots more about how it had been founded and why it had been given the name "St. Rhadigond's," and all about its customs and traditions. We had a bit more about the heroism of the school during the fire, too. I listened entranced. The only things she asked about myself were did I make a habit of working hard at school and enjoying working hard, and what were my hobbies? What did I collect? That stumped me for a moment. I longed to say "Ideas." Or "Flying horses." Perhaps even "Pink elephants." But I pulled myself together and said "Foreign dolls." It was more or less true. Whenever anyone in the family went abroad they always brought me back a doll. I had six or seven.

She didn't ask any more about my interests. We talked a bit more about the school, and then she gave me another motherly smile and said I could go now. She had Mummy in for a minute to talk to her. I expected her to look all dewy-eyed when she came out, but in fact she was frowning.

"Oh, Mummy! Isn't she nice! Isn't she clever and under-standing and wonderful! Oh, how I hope that she really will one day be my headmistress," I said, when we were outside the school. "And she's so young!"

"I don't think she's so wonderful," Mummy said. "Still, I suppose she'll do. I hope you'll get in too. It does seem a nice school, and it's got a good reputation. They ought to be glad to have you. They don't get a Totty like this one every day of the week."

"Oh, no, Mummy," I said earnestly, "if I do get in it'll be a terrific honour. What are you smiling for? I've been tremend-ously daring even wanting to come here. If I'm accepted it'll be such an honour—such an honour. . . ."

"Of course it will," said Mummy, still smiling.

We had a letter a month later saying that the headmistress was glad to inform us that I had been accepted as a pupil at the School. The term started on the ninth of September. The uni-form list and school rules were enclosed.

All of us, Mummy, Daddy and I, went wild with excitement. I spent the whole day reading and re-reading the rules and uniform list. It was all purple and black. Purple tunic, black blazer, black raincoat, purple jersey. There was a list of the staff too, all with rows of impressive initials after their names. All of them had degrees. Quite a few had been to Oxford or Cambridge.

"Oh, Mummy! Oh, just think!" I kept saying.

The school looked more imposing than ever when I arrived there on the morning of September 9th. I found myself taking a deep breath before I went in at the gates, as if I were about to do a high dive. The entrance hall was swarming with huge girls, all looking quite composed and at their ease, chatting with each other. I felt very small and lost. I had felt so important, marching out of my front door, in my beautiful purple tunic and black blazer, with the crest, the hive of St. Rhadigond, shining as if it were on fire. Here all the girls were wearing summer dresses anyway. They towered above me. I couldn't see anyone else of my own age.

"New girls, over here please," someone was shouting. From all over the hall, between the legs of the big girls, we scurried towards her, normal-sized girls, aged eleven or twelve. I might have been going to school with them just last term. The Valeries and Lindas and Sandras. I felt at home to see them all, and relaxed a bit, especially since they were all wearing tunics too.

The prefect shepherded us out of the hall, through a door into the playground (it was at least three times the size of the one at my old school and had a huge ornamental fountain at the end) and right across it into a separate wing. She divided us into two and led us into two enormous rooms full of neat desks in rows. I was in the front of my crowd, and as I stepped into the doorway of our room I suddenly hesitated. That huge room—all those desks—and all quite empty. I was used to coming in in the morning to a roomful of rampaging children. Don't be silly, I told myself, I'm not breaking in to the middle of the school this time. It's empty because we're a whole new class, and I knew it would be just like this. I wasn't really expecting it to be full of girls. I walked firmly in. Once again I felt as if I were diving off a high board.

We huddled in the doorway. Obviously we were all feeling intruders. Nobody spoke. We were all strangers. I looked round for Lynda, and to my delight saw her in the doorway, with her back to me. She hadn't seen me. I ran over to her and we talked about our interviews. They had, apparently, been identical. She seemed to be quite at her ease. We chatted for a bit, admired the building, the big rather dim room, the handsome desks. When I looked round, the other girls were talking too. The ice was broken. They were beginning to settle at desks, too.

"Come along and let's find a desk for you," Lynda said. She was fairly shining with happiness.

"Yes, you organize me," I said laughing. We chose two next to each other in the middle of the room. I felt wonderfully happy myself. We're going to get on so well here, I thought, it's the perfect school for both of us. What a beautiful room! What beautiful desks! How nice to have Lynda here! At the end of the playground was the fountain, full of gargoyles and things. I compared it all to the small stretch of muddy asphalt I was

143

used to. No, I wasn't used to that. I was used to five green doors in a row and a lot of dirty brickwork. I told Lynda so. She laughed and agreed.

A teacher came in, looking very wise and understanding, though not really motherly. She took all our names down in a register. To my surprise there were only three Sandras, two Valeries and only the one Lynda. The others were all called things like Margaret and Jennifer and Rosemary. Then she gave us detailed instructions for the daily routine. How considerate! How kind! I thought. What a wonderful school!

She introduced herself as Miss Mildon. "I ought to warn you, too, that you'll be having me for maths," she said with a sarcastic twinkle in her eye. "I'm also your form mistress." She was tall and hideous, with dandruff in her hair, and always had a little dry half-smile. Ugly and lovable, I decided.

She handed us out piles of coloured exercise books. They had "St. Rhadigond's School" printed on them, and inside the cover was written "May this school remain a holy and godly institution for maidens with willing hands and meek souls.—Agnes Winthrop." How grand, I thought admiringly.

"The orange book is French," said Miss Mildon, "Write 'French' on the cover there and your name in the top left-hand corner." She waved her arm. "In case you don't know, that's your left hand."

"Write? How can we? She hasn't given out the pens," I whispered to Lynda.

Lynda smiled and shook her head, and handed me a fountain pen out of her own pencil case. I glanced round and saw that all the other girls were using their own pens. Well, how could I know, I thought. Sir always used to give us everything we needed.

"And your form. You're IIIB. Perhaps I should say that you aren't any lower than IIIA. For the moment, at any rate, the two streams are meant to be equal." She said everything as though it were the most ridiculous thing she'd ever heard. That's to put us at our ease, I thought. How nice of her. I didn't quite like the emphasis she put on the words, "For the moment at any rate" and "are *meant* to be equal." But perhaps that was just my imagination. She told us all which House we were in. Lynda and I were both in Baxter, and our Housemistress was called Miss Mackintosh.

At nine o'clock a bell went—a beautiful electric bell, not the deafening hand-bell I was used to—and Miss Mildon led us out to prayers. We crept across the playground behind her. I thought I had never seen such a collection of frightened girls. Only Lynda seemed confident. She walked along, gazing ahead of her, glowing with enthusiasm, and looking serene and angelic, exactly as usual. I caught her eye, and she grinned at me and whispered, "Oh, dear, you do look worried. Cheer up."

"I'm quite cheerful, thank you," I whispered back. "This is my red-letter day."

"I shouldn't talk if I were you, Antonia," said Miss Mildon caustically without turning round. How on earth can she have heard, I thought, she's miles ahead and we're only whispering. I shut up, though.

We filed into the great hall where I had seen the concert and sat down in rows. The hall looked even better in the sunlight, packed full of girls in purple. There were three rows of new girls in the front. We all sat mousy quiet and stared round us, wide-eyed. I sat up straight (though that wasn't easy on the floor) and looked in front, feeling consciously proud to be here in the great hall, in my purple uniform, a scholar at St. Rhadigond's. Here I am, sitting at prayers, where so many others have sat before me, for so many generations, each one proud to be here, and I'm the proudest of the lot, I thought. I kept it up all the time we were waiting, and we waited a long time. The teachers sat on chairs in a row at the front.

Miss Haversham came in, looking very dignified in her black gown, and stood at a desk on the stage. We sang a long, dreary hymn I didn't know (I discovered that I alone out of all the new girls hadn't got a hymn book, and had to share with Lynda) and then scrambled on to our knees while Miss Haversham read some collects and things. I wondered how I could ever have thought she looked jolly. She looked very sober and serious. Then we all sat down on the floor again and she read the lesson. It wasn't from the Bible. It was an address by a pre-war bishop who had been such a very great friend to the school. It was all about unreserved devotion and glad service. We should be glad to be able to toil in the cause of a godly institution. It was very long. I glanced furtively round and saw that even Lynda had begun to slump instead of sitting up straight.

Then we all had to repeat St. Ignatius Loyola's prayer about giving and not counting the cost and toiling and not seeking for rest. I felt very tired by the time we got to the blessing, and even that was about going forth to our work with ever patient devotion. And then Miss Haversham gave a brisk smile and said, "Would the new girls stay behind for a few minutes?"

So then we had a long speech about the school and the part we were expected to play in it, and its traditions, which it was up to us to maintain. Every now and then she stopped looking serious, put on her bright smile and made a little joke. We tittered uncertainly. By a quarter to ten I had stopped even trying to think about the honour of actually being present here in the hall of St. Rhadigond's, and only longed to get back to our form-room and sit on a chair with a back.

She went over the history of the school, and told us a lot of things about the old uniform, for instance, and the school song. The dreary hymn we had had was apparently the school hymn for special occasions. The bishop whose address she had read was a great benefactor to the school. He was always coming to talk to the girls, who valued his counsel more than anything else. To him and to the headmistress they brought all their personal problems, even those not concerned with school. This had always been the tradition of St. Rhadigond's and she hoped we, too, would follow it. To encourage us, she gave us examples of the troubles that had been brought to her. The problems were intimate, all right. I fidgeted uncomfortably.

Then she told us how it was the duty of every girl to make herself a good citizen by following a really worthwhile career, such as social work. She went on about all the welfare workers she knew, and how their cheerful and willing service was an example to all of us. She hoped we would all follow in their footsteps. It should be the aim of each one of us to find for herself a similar vocation, and it was the work of the school to fit us for this, to equip us with the right character and outlook, to teach us patience, perseverance, accuracy and hard work. I stopped listening after a while. The last thing in the world I wanted was to be a welfare worker.

At five to eleven she made one last bright joke and dismissed us. We had been sitting on the cold tiled floor in that hall for nearly two hours. We marched out without a backward glance.

In the form-room, Miss Mildon gave us more instructions about labelling our exercise books. Green was English, mauve

146

was geography. The fat grey book was for rough notes. Lynda and I grinned at each other. I drew the first picture of a sequence of caricatures of Miss Haversham in the front. Lynda was drawing Miss Mildon, bonier than ever, in her frilly blouse and navy blue skirt.

"I'm going to give out the text books," said Miss Mildon, "and then we'll go on a conducted tour of the school. I'll give you your time-table now."

"Time-table!" some of us gasped. We had never had anything so grand at primary school.

"Yes, time-table," said Miss Mildon. "If you know what that is. Eight lessons a day, nine-thirty to ten-fifteen, ten-fifteen to eleven, eleven to eleven forty-five, eleven forty-five to twelve, break."

I was left waving Lynda's pen helplessly. The numbers meant nothing to me. If she had said "half past" and "quarter past" and "quarter to" I might have understood.

She covered the whole day. It sounded an awful lot of lessons when she talked in numbers like that.

"What about afternoon break?" one girl called out.

"We don't have such a thing here. You'll have to learn to survive without," said Miss Mildon, raising her eyes to the ceiling in patient resignation. "And though I can't be responsible for what went on at your last school, it's the custom here to put up your hand when you want to say something and to wait until the mistress chooses to hear your remark before making it."

The girl went scarlet and bent very low over her desk.

We had French every day on the time-table. French, of course! That should be fun, I thought. We had maths every day too, and twice on Thursday. I noticed it was "mathematics" and not "arithmetic" and was suitably impressed. We had two lessons of science on Tuesdays. That intrigued me. We had never dreamt of such things at primary school.

Miss Mildon led us all over the school. It seemed huge, though it can't really have been. There were vast and endless cloakrooms, all vaulted of course, and a special art room, and the most magnificent geography room, lined with globes and maps and diagrams and things. There was a tempting gymnasium, full of gleaming wall-bars and an astonishing variety of things to vault over. There were rows and rows of laboratories, big ones, little ones and middle-sized ones. You'd think we were the Cancer Research labs, I thought as I admired them. There was only one library, but a beautiful one, with a tiled floor and really stylish chairs, and Gothic niches in the wall, with lots of elaborate brickwork, for the bookcases. There was a separate room for the geology club, and a music room with a stage. In our wing, there was a dual-carriageway passage. We all goggled and gasped. It was more wonderful and luxurious than we had ever dreamt a school could be. Miss Mildon told us about it in a bored and contemptuous tone. I couldn't understand why the very sight of all these marvels didn't send her into raptures.

She led us to our cloakroom. It was called the "South Wing Cloakroom." It seemed to me the size of an aisle in a cathedral. We had a double peg each and a little bit of paper stuck beside it for us to write our names on. I hung all my stuff up reverently, the overall, the purple hat, the shoebag. It was all beautifully clean and tidy and everything was marked with my name in marking-ink, done by me in a fit of enthusiasm. It had taken me days. I signed my name, "Antonia Bird," on the little piece of paper beside my hook, with a flourish as if I were signing a picture. That proves that I really am actually here, in this dream school, I thought gleefully. My name written up in the cloakroom. There's no getting away from it now.

When we were all up in the form-room again that lovely silvery electric bell went again. We looked expectantly at Miss Mildon.

"Break now," she said. "At twelve come up here again for marking inspection."

A quarter of an hour! Five minutes more of play—break— than usual, I thought, wincing automatically. Then I remembered that it wasn't like that here, that there weren't any boys, and I wouldn't have to stay cooped up in the lavatories.

"Come on, Lynda!" I shouted. We went down the stairs and along the enormous passage. There was a door into the playground, and we ran through it into the open.

"Let's explore," she said. "What happens round there?"

It was a small court behind one wing. We stood admiring the elaborate architecture and the lovely brickwork and the pointed windows.

Miss Mildon came out and said to us, "Do you mind not

148

staring into the staff-room? I'd have thought you'd have more manners than that."

"Oh, dear," said Lynda. "I'm very sorry, Miss Mildon."

"I wish we'd known it was the staff-room," I said when Miss Mildon had gone. "I'd have looked much more carefully."

"Yes, I wonder what they can have been doing in there that we weren't to see," Lynda said, laughing.

We went across the playground to look at the fountain. There were just as many big girls as before, but I didn't feel shy any more now.

"Were there only us two who went for interviews here? I'd have thought everyone who passed would want to come," I said presently.

"You mean, from our school? Well, you have to have a pretty high pass-mark to qualify for an interview, even, and perhaps the other girls didn't quite get there. Anyway, it doesn't always occur to people to put themselves down for the best schools." She grinned at me. I grinned back, not because she had said anything funny, but because I felt so happy.

"Let's have a hopping race across to that yellow line," I suggested.

This is the most wonderful play I've ever had, I thought.

After break Miss Mackintosh, our Housemistress, came in and introduced herself, and explained the House system. She was pale and flabby and looked like a frog, and wore round rimless glasses that kept catching the light. She told us about things like the Inter-House Matches and the House Prefects, and then gave us a lecture on the school rules and the uniform. She said we must never wear sloppy shoes, and must always wear our hats in the street. If we didn't we were letting down the school. I wondered indignantly who could be traitorous enough to do such a thing.

I went on feeling on top of the world all day. We had our clothes inspected for marking. That caught some girls out, but Lynda's and mine were so beautifully done that Miss Mildon only grunted and sent us back to our seats. She took down all our addresses, and gave us labels to stick in our text books. Then we had lunch. It was a most gracious affair. Nobody knocked any water over, or speared other people's meat, or did any of the uncivilized things that the primary school children had done. I thought the food was delicious too, but perhaps that was only because I was used to being forced to eat the bits of fat and gristle that other people put on my plate. The other girls groaned and complained and picked at their food and said they felt sick. The mistresses wouldn't let them off any of it either. I felt sorry for them, though I did think they were making a lot of fuss over nothing, and I ate several girls' stew for them. They were pathetically grateful, and plates of stew from all over the dining-room kept being passed up to me. I couldn't eat it all, though. I hadn't felt in the slightest bit hungry even for my own stew.

18

"Oh, Mummy, it was so wonderful, you haven't any idea," I shouted as I came in, tumbling on to the sofa beside her. "It's absolutely enormous, and there's a special room for every subject, and we've got such beautiful desks, and Lynda's sitting next to me, and there are three laboratories, and it's—it's—simply perfect!"

"I'm glad it was such a success. Tell me all about it. What did you do?"

"Ooh," I rattled on eagerly. "We had prayers, and a tour of the school, and do you know there's a fountain? And a gymnasium, and all sorts of things. And our form teacher—mistress —is called Miss Mildon, she's so nice and jolly and makes little jokes all the time to make us feel at home. And there are masses of new girls all just like me, a whole other class besides the one I'm in, which is called IIIB and it's in the South Wing and we've got a wonderful view all over the playground. And tomorrow, just think! We'll be starting lessons. And Mummy, I'm going to be twelve on Saturday!"

The first lesson we had was Miss Haversham's lesson. She was late. We sat mousy quiet. One big girl put her head through the door and saw us waiting.

"Cor! Look at all those good little things just sitting there!" she exclaimed in contempt.

"Oh, they're new," said another girl outside the door. "You wait until they've been here a week or two."

We just looked at the girl in a scared way and went on sitting quiet, with our beautiful new yellow exercise books lying neatly on our desks. Lynda and I made picture sequences in our rough note books.

Miss Haversham finally came in, looking very brisk and bright and even smaller and more efficient-looking than she had seemed at the interview. She gave us her keen smile and began on yet another lecture. It was about a hospital subscribed to by the school, how so many girls had found a really worth-while vocation there and how she hoped and expected all of us would make ourselves useful in similar careers. I listened attentively. She didn't go on very long. After about twenty minutes she said,

"I want you to copy down in your rough books the list of things I'm going to write on the board, and learn them ready for a test next Tuesday."

She wrote, " 'Religious Duties of an Englishwoman,' pp. 232-234 (Chapter 9, Obedience). The school hymn. The school song . . ."

"Learn it really well by heart for Tuesday," she said.

The girl sitting in front of me turned round and mouthed : "We don't have homework for this lesson, do we? It's not on the time-table."

"No, this is extra because it'll be good for us to learn it," I mouthed back.

Miss Haversham was giving out copies of *Religious Duties of an Englishwoman*. They looked awfully old and tattered. Then I saw the name of the author : Agnes Winthrop, the founder of the school.

What an excellent headmistress, I was thinking. What a good thing to do, in their first lesson, to teach the girls all these things. This is what I'd call really worth-while work. The very learning will be a pleasure.

When she went out at the end of the lesson all the girls began to murmur in dismay.

"It'll take me hours and hours to learn all that!"

"She's no right to set us homework. It isn't on the time-table. That's about two hours' worth, what she's given us."

"Ooh, I can't stand her. She's an old so-and-so. I can't learn things by heart, how does she expect me to learn all that? Old beast."

"Well, I just shan't learn it. Why should I? It's not on the time-table."

"I think it's all excellent stuff and we jolly well ought to be pleased to learn it," I said loudly.

There was an instant's hush. Then one girl said,

"Oh, well, it's all right for you. Some people like learning by heart. But I don't and I can't and I don't see why I should."

"I wouldn't mind a line or so for proper homework. But when it comes to learning the whole of that miserable Victorian book by heart . . ."

"She's a horrible woman."

"She's nothing of the sort. She's very nice and it's the best homework she could possibly set us, to make sure we know all those good things," I said.

"Bet she doesn't know them herself."

"What do you think, Lynda?" I asked her. She had been sitting silent listening to us and looking amused.

"Well, I don't see what it matters what anyone thinks," she answered. "If we don't do it we're going to get punished and if we do do it we're not, and that's all there is to it."

I looked at her in admiration. "What it is to have common sense," I said. "Of course, you're right. I bet everyone does it."

In the other lessons we had that day, English, French, maths, science, and so on, we didn't do much work. The mistresses tried to learn all our names and gave us an outline of what we should be learning. They were all so friendly and nice. I knew I was really going to love all the lessons, and resolved to work really hard and do brilliantly well in all of them. I had felt a bit anxious about maths but Miss Mildon only dictated to us some notes on the most elementary sorts of arithmetic, and then drew some lovely pictures on the board of various geometric shapes, cones and pyramids and so on. I copied them much better than lots of girls, because they had trouble with the perspective and I didn't, much. I felt vastly relieved, realizing that I was going to do all right even in maths.

When we came into class after lunch, Miss Mildon said, "I'm going to take down your ages in years and months. Will you call them out, please, when I say your name." She began straight away with me, "Antonia Bird."

"I'm eleven and twelve months," I announced proudly.

Miss Mildon put down her pen and gazed resignedly at the ceiling, rolling her eyes.

"How many months do you think there are in a year, pray?" she said.

"Why, twelve," I said, not understanding.

"So you do know. Why not say 'twelve years' in the first place? You haven't come here just to waste my time and yours."

153

"Oh, I'm sorry, Miss Mildon," I said, "but you see, I'm not twelve yet."

"No, of course not. Only eleven and twelve months."

"My birthday's on Saturday," I explained desperately.

"I asked you, did I not, to tell me your age in years and months, not days," she said bitingly.

"I don't see where days comes into it. I'm not twelve and so I must be eleven," I growled under my breath.

"If you have a remark to make, please make it so that I can hear," said Miss Mildon. "Antonia Bird, aged twelve exactly. Jennifer Brierley?"

"You must have finished that homework by now. You've been working all the evening," Mummy said.

"I haven't got half way even," I said. "I've still got that great long thing about obedience to learn."

"You're being awfully slow."

"Oh, I'm not. You are unfair. But I had to learn these grammar notes," I said. "I'm lucky, though, in science. Miss Blandish didn't set any homework."

"Gosh, however many subjects do you have a night?" Mummy exclaimed.

"Oh, only two. The learning by heart was extra for our first lesson."

"Well, so long as it is only for tonight," she said. "And now whether you've finished or not you must go to bed."

We had our first games lesson on Wednesday. I hadn't realized how quick you were supposed to be undressing. That had been quite a leisurely affair at primary school, perhaps because of the sheer impossibility of making Roberts and O'Brien and Dearchild hurry if they didn't mean to. But at St. Rhadigond's, although I fairly ripped off my clothes and didn't even bother to tie up my plimsoll laces but rushed out all anyhow, I was miles behind the other girls and found the whole class waiting crossly for me.

"That's the first thing you must learn," said the mistress, a tiny beefy-looking woman with a pleasant face, "to hurry. If you aren't undressed and ready within three minutes it's not worth having the lesson at all."

I hung my head and mumbled apologetically. I had taken a

clear ten minutes, going full out. The other girls must have taken seven or eight minutes themselves, I reflected.

"That goes for swimming too. We have swimming this year in the summer term, instead of our Friday games lesson. Forty-five minutes we have. The journey takes ten minutes each way. Three minutes for changing you can have and no more. That includes stripping right down and drying afterwards. I don't want you looking a shambles either. So you see if you don't learn to change about three times as fast as you did today you're going to find yourselves in trouble."

I listened, shivering in my mauve aertex games blouse. In my mad rush to change I hadn't had time to put on a jersey. I wasn't liking the sound of the swimming lessons as much as I had hoped.

Miss Pratt, the mistress, lined us up and told us to run as fast as we could across the playground when she blew the whistle. She blew it before I was ready and I started behind everyone else. I tore after them, but they only got further and further away. I finished last by yards. Even Lynda beat me. Then we threw a ball about, in twos. I always missed, or dropped it. I tried like anything though. She gave us demonstrations of how to throw the ball. She looked as if she were doing ballet, going gracefully into an arabesque and making a flowing motion with her hand that sent the ball hurtling across the playground. I tried, and only dropped the ball as I overbalanced. Even when I managed the position, I couldn't seem to send the ball further than a few inches.

At the end of the lesson she called me up to her and said, "Your P.T. shirt is a mess. Tell your mother that if it isn't ironed properly—better than it is now anyway—before the next lesson, I shall have to report you to Miss Haversham."

I tried to speak, but seemed to have lost my voice. I remembered how Daddy had suddenly got keen, the night before my first day, and had spent the whole evening smoothing my blouse over a steaming kettle. We hadn't got an iron. Mummy rough-dried everything. It always looked perfectly good. I thought, no, if I give Daddy this message he'll cry. I just can't.

"In fact, I very much doubt that it's been ironed at all. That's disgraceful."

"Please, we haven't got an iron, Miss P-P-Pratt," I croaked. For one ghastly moment I had forgotten her name.

She looked at me blankly. Then she repeated, "Tell your mother to see that it's properly ironed by next lesson," and went in. She bounced as she walked so that for a moment I thought she was running.

She had used up at least half of my precious three minutes. All the other girls were almost changed by the time I got in. I had to beg Lynda to wait for me. I knew I would never find the geography room by myself. She had brought my geography books down to the cloakroom at the end of the lesson before, too. She guessed, quite rightly, that I wouldn't remember.

We abandoned the beautiful geometric shapes in maths, to my sorrow. I was really getting interested in parallel lines and vertically opposite angles, especially when you marked the angles in with coloured crayons. Instead, we moved on to things called H.C.F.s and L.C.M.s We learnt—or rather, the others learnt —a complicated system of sums which was supposed to give you the magic numbers. Miss Mildon demonstrated it on the blackboard. It looked like a lot of division sums all underneath each other, though where you started off from, and what you divided into what, I couldn't discover. Nor did I ever find out what H.C.F.s and L.C.M.s were.

I felt that if only I could understand the beginning, the lead-in to the division bit, I would be able to do it. I asked Miss Mildon to explain over and over again. She did, twice, looking very fed-up and contemptuous, which I felt was only justified, in words of one syllable. That was just what I wanted, though I suspected that she meant it as an insult. But I still didn't understand.

There was a long queue at my bus stop when I arrived there at a quarter past four, feeling tired and longing above all things to get home. Buses of every kind except my number sailed by, or drew temptingly up alongside. When one did come it was full. It seemed hours before another came. It was a quarter of an hour's walk home from our nearest bus stop. My satchel weighed me down and gave me a stiff neck. Softie! I thought, as I dragged myself along. The trees dripped water on me. It must have been raining, I registered vaguely. Pull yourself together, Scholar of St. Rhadigond's. Get a move on, stop being sorry for yourself, begin thinking about your homework. Slow-coach, everyone agrees this is a quarter of an hour's walk and you've been twenty minutes already.

But it was no good. For the first time in my life it didn't work, and it was twenty-five to six when I got in. Shameful, I taunted myself. But myself didn't respond and just sat heavily down in Daddy's armchair, which was forbidden, and refused to get up again.

"You look tired," said Mummy. "How did it go today?"

"Oh, beautifully," I said. "I'm settling down now. Of course I keep making a tremendous ass of myself, but that's nothing. Think how stupidly I behaved when I first arrived at my last school. No, everything is wonderful. I'm liking it better and better." Then I told her what Miss Pratt had said about my blouse. Daddy was downstairs painting and didn't hear. Mummy groaned and hid her face in her hands. Suddenly she jumped up and said,

"Good gracious, your letter! I'd forgotten all about it."

The letter turned out to be a magazine called *Images* accepting a poem I had written in the previous Christmas holidays, called *The Dragon in the Sky*.

"The sun was a red-hot dragon, gaping flame
That billowed and circled and roared in agony
And writhed around cold, wet Earth. Steam rose,
Smothering the light; and as Earth flinched
From the angry breath of the serpent, Time awoke.
Time is a cold-blooded monster; he came and stared.
He froze the hissing steam that wrapped Earth round,
Quenched the panting heat; till the Dragon in the Sky
Was belching blood-red ice."

It was so familiar, and yet it looked so strange in print. I lingered over every word.

"Well, Genius!" said Mummy, hugging me and reading the poem over my shoulder. "Another success! Are you pleased? I know. Take it and show it to your English mistress. She ought to be interested."

"That's an idea. All right, I will. She's such a nice woman. Mrs. Day she's called. She comes bundling in to our lesson in the morning with such a big happy grin and she's always so jolly. She's always got a great armful of books or something. It doesn't matter where she is or what she's doing, she always

157

seems to be carrying an enormous pile of something, with just her big smile showing over the top."

"She sounds nice," Mummy said. "I know! Why not take all your poems to show her? And poor little Triunfadora, I was forgetting about you. Would you like to come out to a film or something to celebrate?"

"Oh, I would, Mummy," I said, "but I've got such piles of homework. French, for a test I think, and maths, and I haven't the faintest idea how to do that and it's going to take me hours. And there's always Miss Haversham's learning, I've still got masses of that. And all the teachers want their text-books covered in brown paper. That's extra, too. And I'm so tired."

"Good gracious, you poor child," said Mummy. "No film then. You'd better get started. You must have tea first, though."

I left the maths till last because I was really dreading it. I still hadn't a notion how you began, although Lynda had taken pity on me and explained carefully. I thought I understood the dividing part, though, and that if only I could get on to that I might manage. I hoped I could skip the beginning and end bits, but it turned out that as the sums stood there wasn't anything to divide into anything. Anyway I wasn't sure that you used the same system for both L.C.M.s and H.C.F.s. I worked for my full half-hour, dividing wherever I could fiddle the numbers to make division sums, but I didn't get half the homework done. Altogether it was rather a failure. I thought about working on to the end, but I had taken all the time I was meant to and anyway it was bedtime and anyway I felt so tired.

19

Our last lesson before break the next day was English and at the end I took my folder of poems up to Mrs. Day. She always stayed a few minutes after each lesson collecting up her armful of stuff. When I came up she put it all down again, said, "Hullo, hullo, have you got something for me?" and spent all break standing at the desk reading my poems, very slowly and attentively.

She made all sorts of interesting comments, and beamed all over her face as she finished each one. When I told her about the one I had just had published she congratulated me warmly.

The bell went for the end of break, and she said, "Oh my goodness, is it as late as that? I'll have to rush now, but I tell you what, I'd like to show this one to Miss Mackintosh." She picked out one called *View from an Aeroplane*. I had only written it that summer, on the journey home from our holiday abroad. " 'The cars run up their roads like flies on poles.' I like that. Look, have you got a copy at home? Because I'd like to take this and show it to Miss Mackintosh now—you are Baxter, aren't you?"

I assured her fervently that I should love her to take whatever she liked. She took it, and began to load up with her armful of books. I tried to help her, thinking all the time : Oh, isn't she nice! So kind and jolly and helpful and I do believe she really cared about my poems.

The next lesson was maths. As Miss Mildon came stamping in, with her contemptuous little half-smile and her eyebrows raised in boredom, I couldn't help thinking for a moment that Mrs. Day was a great deal nicer. But I quickly reminded myself that Miss Mildon was nice in quite a different way and how dull it would be if everyone was the same.

Lynda leant across and flicked down a picture sequence for me. It showed Miss Mildon's eyebrows shooting up and her lip curling. What really caught my attention was the curled lip. It was exactly like Miss Mildon, and yet for a second it reminded me of the cruel sneer of Roberts. But that just passed through my mind and was gone. Lynda was smiling at me. I smiled back and nodded enthusiastically.

"Would you please come out here, Antonia," said Miss Mildon.

I went shakily up to her, my heart beating fast.

"Why did you donate this book to me?" she said, leaning forward into my face. Her breath smelt awful. I cringed away.

"Why—well—it's my last night's homework, Miss Mildon," I answered.

She opened the book at the place where I had made such a mess of the exercise on H.C.F.s and L.C.M.s.

"That?" she said.

"Y-yes, Miss Mildon."

"Do you mean to say that took you half an hour?" she said staring into my face. That, at least, I had nothing to be ashamed about.

"Yes, it did."

"You really expect me to believe that that mess is the result of thirty minutes' hard concentration."

"Well, yes, it is. I do," I said, wilting, but trying to be firm. She had big round eyes with huge whites, like a fish.

"Well, I'm sorry, but I don't." She slashed through the exercise with a red biro and gave the book back to me. "You will stay in tonight until a quarter to five in the detention room and do it again. I'm afraid you'll find you can't get away with skimping your homework in this school."

"I didn't skimp it, Miss Mildon. I just don't understand it," I said unwisely. She just raised her eyebrows and smiled.

"You'd better find out before your detention, then. Hadn't you, Antonia?"

I went back to my desk and sat hating her. I scribbled on my ruler, "Old Mildew has smelly breath. Miss Mildew is an ugly horrible unkind unfair BEAST." Then I felt better.

In the afternoon we had our first lesson at a school for nature dancing, which was only a few streets away. When we got there we put on our dainty little dancing tunics and went upstairs to a big hall. The instructress, who had an American accent, made us run round barefoot.

"Step higher! Step higher! No, don't jump, use your toes. In time to the music, now, run round as if you were going upstairs. That's better. Now use your hands and arms too. Higher! Use your whole body to go upstairs. No, don't jump! Very short quick steps. You're using your hands as if you were swimming. Make quick dabbing movements with them on a high level. No, no, you don't know what I mean, do you? Stop and I'll show you."

We stopped, panting, and watched her demonstrate light dabbing movements on a high level, and then light flicking movements on a high level. Then she showed us the same on medium and low levels.

"Now try again. Going upstairs, using dabbing movements. Use your whole body. Go on! Light dabbing movements with every muscle in your body. And that includes your torso muscles. In time to the music—one, two, three, dab, dab, dab, go on, that's better, you in the red tunic, dab, dab, dab."

I spent at least half of my detention time trailing round the school with my hat and raincoat and satchel, looking for the detention room. It turned out to be Remove in the north wing and it wasn't marked "Detention," so that I never would have found it if Mrs. Day hadn't come by and seen me looking lost, and taken pity on me and led me there. Anyway, I only just managed to copy out my homework all over again, without correcting it at all. I had meant to offer up some variations on it. I had seen at least two places where I might be able to divide something different. But when I sat down in the detention room and looked at my book I suddenly felt tired and hopeless. I realized that a variation on the homework wouldn't go down any better than the original homework had. So I just copied it out. Well, it's Mildew's own fault, I thought. She wouldn't explain even though I told her I didn't understand.

It was well and truly into the rush hour when I got to the bus stop at five. When I came wearily into sight of it and saw the queue I suddenly, unreasonably, hated the school for landing me in the rush hour through an unfair detention. It only lasted a second. I went docilely to the back of the queue and waited. I didn't get home till half-past six. Mummy scolded me at first for being so late, and said that Daddy had been about to go out and look for me. I told her about the detention, and then she poured abuse on the school for giving her so much worry. For the first time I didn't try to defend it.

On Saturday, the fourteenth, my birthday, we suddenly remembered my games blouse, which still hadn't been ironed. I had gym on Monday, and needed it for that. Daddy said that there was only one thing we could do, and he took us out in Paydirt, the bubble car, and we bought an iron. We got it second-hand from a funny little shop in a back street. While we were about it we bought a lot of things for my birthday, too, and neither Daddy nor Mummy seemed to mind very much about having to buy an iron. We carried it home in triumph and put it on top of my presents. In gym on Monday we only did exercises, cartwheels and things, at which I was excruciatingly bad. Miss Pratt didn't even glance at my really truly ironed blouse, which was just as well, as the iron had been rusty underneath and left marks all over it.

When I arrived at school on Tuesday there was a great streamer pinned across the notice board. It said "HAPPY HUNDREDTH BIRTHDAY ST. RHADIGOND'S!" I stood looking at it, puzzled. The older girls were pouring along the corridor behind me. Every one of them was grinning and looking as if they were bubbling over with suppressed excitement. I said to one who didn't look too old and superior, "What is all this, about the birthday?"

"Oh, don't you know?" she said. "The school was founded a hundred years ago today and we'll be celebrating—no lessons —perhaps some sort of show—Hi, Jane!" She flew away to join her friend.

I went on to my own classroom. All the girls there were infected with the general feeling of hilarity and were sitting in groups singing, or else writing things like, "Happy Birthday to the Best School in the World" on the blackboard. I supposed they had got it, like me, from the older girls. Lynda was there, outlining in red chalk a birthday greeting that had already been outlined in blue, green, white and mauve.

"Happy birthday!" she greeted me. I said, "Happy birthday" back. All the girls were saying it instead of "Good morning."

Lynda and I began to draw a huge birthday cake with a hundred candles, in different coloured chalk, with a great frill. One by one all the other girls joined us, and soon the whole class was drawing candles and decorating the frill. We were all laughing and friendly. The ice was really and truly broken with that cake. I suddenly found I knew everyone's name.

"Well, really," said Miss Mildon as she came in. "I didn't think you were as childish as that. I thought it was only in the primary schools that people had no scruples about wasting chalk. Rub it out."

There was a sudden silence. We gazed at her, dismayed. But she was ten minutes late, and before we had time to begin rubbing it out the prayer bell went and she had to leave it. Prayers were specially long that day, almost as long as at the beginning of term. No one in my class, at least, listened. We were all desperately trying to learn the school hymn, hiding our books behind the girls in the row in front. Miss Haversham's lesson was supposed to be the first that morning.

In the passage I suddenly remembered what the girl had said.

"No lessons! There won't be any lessons!" I shouted. "We won't have Miss Haversham's test till next week."

All the girls took up the cry, and we ran into the classroom. We went on decorating the birthday cake on the blackboard. Presently a thin old teacher—mistress—came in and said, "What are you doing? You're supposed to be in the gym, having a talk on probation-work. Everyone's waiting for you."

The talk was meant to be very inspiring, but we were all so excited that it made no impression on us. We ran singing up the stairs afterwards, to put our rough books away. Luckily there weren't any mistresses about.

As Lynda and I came down together afterwards I said, "Let's pretend we're going upstairs instead of down."

She immediately turned round and started going backwards, down the stairs. "Yes," she said. "We must be about on the third floor by now."

I turned round too and tried to work it out. "I suppose we would be," I said. "No, wait, we didn't start at the top of the stairs. We're at the landing above our form-room."

"I suppose if we go upstairs we'd be going downstairs," said Lynda, looking as if she were about to burst out laughing.

Christine Hudson came by and gave us a startled look. "Whatever are you going backwards for?"

"It's to make us think we're really going upstairs," Lynda explained. Snap, I thought. We've clicked. All I said was, "Let's

163

pretend we're going upstairs"—and she understood perfectly. I don't believe Mummy or Daddy, even, could have done that. And she knew about Felias before I told her, too. We're soul-mates. I don't have to cast off my world to fit into hers, as I did with Tatley and Barker. We fit as we are. I suppose that's why I couldn't be friends with them. I had to play-act all the time, alter myself to suit them. They wouldn't come even a tiny bit of the way towards me. They wouldn't do anything to fit in with me. But with Lynda I don't have to go out of my way at all to be friends with her. We suit each other naturally.

When we reached the bottom of the stairs Lynda said, "We must have reached the top floor by now. The science labs, I suppose."

"And through here—that would be—gosh—the biology lab," I said, as we went backwards through the door into the playground.

"But we aren't allowed in there without a member of staff," Lynda giggled.

I was thinking hard. "If we've been going backwards all this time we must be nearly into last week."

"Quick, turn round!" said Lynda. "Otherwise I'll be going to tea with my aunt all over again, the whole of Saturday after-noon. Oh, how horrible."

"Well, you can turn round," I laughed. "Saturday was my birthday. I wouldn't mind having that again."

After break we had a film strip of the Oberammergau Passion Play. When we came out into the playground from that for the lunch hour, Lynda and I were swept off our feet by a chain of shouting girls rushing by. For one ghastly second I thought they were playing Chain-He. But the last girl in the chain waved to us and shouted,

"Happy birthday! Come and join on!"

"What is it?" I asked, as Lynda and I took hands and joined the chain.

"A dragon. Ghost train. Follow-my-leader," the girl explained. It was our turn to shout to the other girls to join. They did too, hundreds of them. We all went whooping and singing, follow-my-leader-ing all over the grounds. I hardly knew any of the others, though that didn't matter. The whole school was in the dragon, except for a few big girls who were still trying to play netball with the "ghost train" winding in and out between

164

them. Soon we were long enough to go several times round the playground. The whole school was a tangle of laughing girls. We ran and sang and shouted. The chain was so long that different bits of it were singing different things. My bit was singing "Nine Green Bottles." I joined in at the top of my voice, regardless of the fact that, owing to a bend in the chain just ahead, there was a piece of dragon running alongside us singing "Auld Lang Syne." The girls in that were trying to outsing us, but we shouted back.

"Seven—green—BOTTLES—hanging on the WALL!"

This is the real St. Rhadigond's spirit, I thought as we capered about. I could see Mrs. Day and some other mistresses standing in the doorways laughing with us, and the others looking sourly out of the staff-room windows. Who cares about them, I thought. My bit of the dragon was squeezing between an iron pillar and the wall. There was only a tiny space, and the girls were pushing and squashing to get through, while the others were doubled up with laughter. I slipped through without any trouble, and that made us laugh more than ever.

We had Miss Haversham's test on her extra homework the next Tuesday. I had spent all the previous evening cramming it in preference to my proper homework, which as it happened was maths and history. I just about managed in the test, but I was scared of the maths. It had been even worse than the work that had got me detention before. It was a similar exercise, called "Harder L.C.M.s." I hadn't understood it any better, although Mummy, too, had explained. I was sure she did it differently from Miss Mildon, but she wouldn't hear of that. She said I must be mixing it up with H.C.F.s. Anyway, she made it no clearer. I laboured away for twenty minutes, and then remembered Miss Haversham. I looked over her work, found I hardly remembered any of it, and got in a panic. I spent the rest of the evening trying to learn it, thinking that I could make up the extra ten minutes on the maths afterwards. But Mummy sent me to bed, and wouldn't let me stay up to finish. She didn't seem to understand.

When the test papers had been collected Miss Haversham said, "I want you to learn the catechism by heart and I'll test you next Tuesday. Open your prayer books and look at it now."

We looked. Some of the girls groaned and gasped as they

turned over page after page. We weren't quite so "new" any more now, and were a bit more daring. Even I thought it was rather a lot, though of course it was excellent stuff, really worth while, a pleasure to learn. There was even more of an outburst against Miss Haversham after she had left than there had been before. I didn't stand up for her, this time. I just sat apart and looked shocked while the other girls abused her.

Miss Mildon had already marked our maths homework when we had her lesson. She came stumping towards me and put my book on my desk herself, her round white eyes twinkling nastily. She gave me her little dry smile and said, "Come and get some paper from me at dinner-time." I opened my book. There was one word, "Detention," written in red underneath my homework. I shut the book violently and drew a picture sequence on the edges of the pages to let off my feelings. It's perfectly fair this time, I told myself. I didn't spend the full time on that homework. What on earth can the poor woman do with me but keep me in? It's not as if I wasn't expecting it, either.

20

"I STILL CAN'T GET over being able to go out in the open playground safely," I said to Lynda as we balanced, walking along the brick edge of the path.

"You couldn't go anywhere safely at the other school," said Lynda, edging along behind me.

"It's like being in heaven," I said dreamily. "Oops! Mind this loose brick."

A thin, pale girl, not looking much older than us, came up and said, "You'd better not walk on there, Miss Haversham doesn't like it and she's teaching in the room looking out over the playground."

"Oh, my goodness, I didn't know," I said, hopping off. "Thank you."

"I got into trouble myself for doing that last year, when I was new," the girl explained.

"And nobody warned you. How disgusting," said Lynda.

"I know! You catch the same bus as me, don't you?" I said. "I thought you looked familiar."

"I catch the 2a," the girl said.

The end-of-break bell went and she screwed up her face in worry. "Geography. Oh, no! We'll be getting our essays back."

"Poor you. We've only got French, that's right, isn't it Lynda? And that's great fun."

"Fun? French? You mean to say you like it? Wish I did. Well, goodbye, then."

"Goodbye, perhaps I'll see you on the bus," I said.

I did, in fact, for she came toiling up to the bus stop at the same time as me and we got on the same bus. I slung my satchel over my shoulder and held on tightly as we stood in the gangway, but she was carrying so much that she hadn't any hands free to hold on with, and kept over-balancing. I looked at her stuff. A satchel and a case. The satchel was quite big, and crammed so full of books that one of the seams was splitting, and the case looked as if it were about to burst its locks too. Two netballs in string bags. A vast cake-tin.

"What on earth is all that you've got?" I asked her.

"Oh, just my homework, and things. We were making buns in domestic science, that's the cake-tin. I carry stuff like my art overall and my games things in the suitcase," she explained. "Why?"

"Well, it just seemed an awful lot."

"It's not as bad as on hockey days, when I have my hockey stick as well, or in the summer with my swimming things and tennis racquet," she said laughing. She looked dreadfully tired and pale, and she kept frowning and screwing up her face in anxiety.

"Is that really all your homework?" I said, nodding at the satchel. "Why didn't you bring the whole desk?" I pulled out one book and looked at it. It said "Pauline West. Latin."

"Some of it's homework, but a lot of it's work I'm making up. I was absent for most of last summer term with pneumonia, you see, and that's all the notes and what not I'm copying up. I've done most of it though."

"Oh, what a shame. You mean to say, you come tottering back out of hospital and they let you take on masses of extra work?"

She smiled uncertainly. "Well, of course I do have to make up the work I've missed. I'd never keep up with the class if I'd missed some of the work."

"No, I suppose not."

"I got B for everything except geography on my last report and this term I'm working for B for everything, so I just have to work hard," she said, looking more worried than ever. "I think I'm doing better in geography, but now I'm dropping behind in science."

"Do you work all the evening?" I asked.

"Yes, as a rule I don't finish my homework until about eight, even if I start the moment I get in, and then there's making up work. In fact I have to do most of that over the weekend, and then it interferes with Guides and the canteen on Saturday, and with doing the church on Sunday."

"Gosh, you do do a lot," I said. "You must have a lot of homework, if it takes you all that time."

"Oh, it gets more all the way up the school. You wait till

you're in the lower fourth, it'll be just the same. My sister in the fifth form has three hours' homework a night."

I felt sick. I said, "What's the canteen, I mean what do you do there?" to change the subject.

"Oh, the school sends some girls every year to go and make tea for the staff in the orphanage canteen on Saturdays. It's a sort of club. There are all sorts of clubs, you're expected to join some. There's the French Club and the Music Club, I'm in that because I take extra violin lessons. Oh, dozens of clubs. I'm only in three. There's the St. Rhadigond's Girl Guide company. That's the one I'm in. Aren't you in any after-school societies?" she asked.

"Not yet. Do you bring your violin home on the bus too?" If she won't stop talking about school, I shall scream, I thought.

She didn't laugh. "Oh no, it's a school violin. You aren't supposed to take it home."

"Is your name Pauline West?" I asked, screaming quietly to myself.

"Yes, that's right. It's awfully funny, because there's another girl in my class called Judith North, and there's a prefect called Sandra Eastley." She tittered nervously, her face screwing up.

I smiled politely. "My name's Antonia Bird. I'm in Baxter."

"Oh, are you? As a matter of fact, so am I. Well, goodbye, I get off here," Pauline said. She picked up her case and hoisted her satchel on to her shoulder. Her finger-nails were bitten so far down that she hadn't really got any. " 'Bye, Antonia."

"Goodbye, see you tomorrow," I said. I watched her stumbling down the bus, apologizing nervously to the people she tripped over, and suddenly I felt dreadfully depressed. It struck me that perhaps it wasn't so much a case of "she won't stop talking about school," as "she can't stop talking about school."

As I was struggling to change after games a prefect burst into the cloakroom and shouted, "Antonia Bird! Miss Mackintosh would like to see Antonia Bird."

My heart suddenly began to beat very fast. It's the maths, I thought. I had just got five out of ten in a test and barely escaped detention. All the marks I got were for identifying cylinders and cuboids and things. I threw on my blouse without doing it up and wriggled into my tunic.

The prefect led me up to Miss Mackintosh's study and left

me outside. I knocked and tiptoed in. Miss Mackintosh was sitting at her desk facing me, smiling briskly.

"Sit down, Antonia," she said. She looked at something she was holding. "Mrs. Day brought me a poem you'd written. I showed it to the deputy headmistress."

"Oh, good," I said. "Did she like it?"

She ignored me and went on. "You have a very valuable talent, Antonia. I hope you realize that."

"Oh, thank you," I said, flushing with pleasure.

"But such a gift is also a very heavy responsibility. You must treat it as such. It's a burden that isn't just for play and enjoyment. The greater the talent, the greater the responsibility. You must strive to live up to your own talent. And that means working hard." She gave me another bright smile. I smiled back, a little uncertainly.

"And one of the ways in which you must fulfil it is not to give way to your weaknesses." She switched off the smile and looked grim. "What's all this about the maths?"

I suddenly felt very glad indeed that I was sitting down. I leant against the chair back and said, "I'm afraid I'm not very good at it. I mean it's awfully difficult, I can't understand it at all when Miss Mildon explains to the rest of the class." That's bad, I thought. I said something wrong there.

"You can't understand it?" said Miss Mackintosh sharply. She looked paler and colder than ever in the pale olive suit she was wearing.

"Only—only after it's been explained to me several times. I'm slow at understanding, though I do try."

"Well, so long as you do try," she said. "I only want you to do your best. But this extraordinary ability of yours puts you under an obligation to do all you can in everything. And I'm sure you can do a great deal better in maths than you are doing at the moment. This poem proves that you're far from stupid, you're an extremely clever child. But it's no use just being clever at one thing and letting the others go. Unless you do your very best in everything you are letting down your talent. You see that, don't you?"

"Oh yes, I do. I really will try," I said fervently.

"I'm sure you will." She suddenly beamed at me again. "Well, we'll see how you improve in maths now. You'll do a lot better in future, won't you?" She got up from her desk and came round to my side. I jumped up hastily.

"I hope I will," I said. She went over to the door and opened it for me. I said something about trying really hard and stumbled out. She had kept my poem, I remembered gleefully. What a compliment! What a kind, wise Housemistress, gently rebuking and inspiring and controlling her girls like one great family. If only we could move on soon from H.C.F.s and L.C.M.s how perfect everything would be, I thought, and ran up the stairs to my classroom.

Miss Mackintosh wrote to Daddy too. When I got home that evening he seemed all ruffled up over something. I asked what was wrong.

"I just don't like being got at by shouting women," he complained.

"Your Housemistress wrote to us," Mummy explained, "about a poem of yours she'd seen, saying what a pity it is that such a gifted child should ruin her talent by refusing to work at a subject she doesn't like, maths, and would we make you, or words to that effect. She thinks you're an Oxford possible for her."

"Oh, no!" I cried. "Haven't you explained that wild horses wouldn't make me?"

"She sounds tremendously determined," said Mummy. "I don't think she'll be half as obliging as your late headmaster. He understood at once when I explained that we wanted you to have minimal schooling as you simply haven't the temperament for it. But now this woman's got the idea into her head that you're a natural for university, I don't think she'll give it up easily. I'm afraid she'll just go on bullying us."

"I'm not going to university and that's final," I said. "It won't help me at all, especially if I want to take up art as a career." I'd been thinking about that a lot, and was almost sure.

"Well, I think she can wait for my answer," Daddy said. "I'm trying to finish that picture of the pub scene."

In history we were learning the history of the school. We were learning about the founder, a well-to-do Victorian woman, and drawing imaginary portraits of her. I drew her with a long face and a tight bun and long mauve clothes, all very straight and thin and with the corners of her mouth turning down.

We covered the whole century in great detail. Lesson after lesson, we went on studying the vicissitudes of the school, writing our own histories of it. When we went on to Ancient Egypt at the end of three weeks, it was really quite a relief.

One morning I came into the classroom, and saw a crowd of girls round the notice-board at the back of the room. I went over to investigate. There was pinned up a large coloured photograph of the gold mask of Tutankhamen.

"Hullo, Antonia! Isn't he gorgeous?" called Rosemary. She leant across and kissed the photograph. "I bet if you looked at him through a microscope, he'd be all covered in kiss-marks."

"Isn't he *handsome?*" Jennifer sighed, leaning her cheek against the picture. I thought it looked gruesome and horrid.

At the same time in maths we moved on to a chapter in the text book headed, "Harder Fractions."

It wasn't remotely related to the fractions I was used to. I had been a bit scared by the word "Harder" at first, but I soon decided it wasn't harder, really, just different. At least, that was what Miss Mildon said. It was all to do with a magic word called "Bodmas." There was a line, and lots and lots of fractions and things in brackets on top and underneath, and you just worked it out quite simply by Bodmas. If you were clever you could fiddle it to come down to just one ordinary fraction, like a sort of patience. Miss Mildon spent both maths lessons on Thursday doing sample questions on the board. They really did look remarkably easy when she did them. She set us ten questions from the text book for homework.

$$10\tfrac{1}{2} \quad \dfrac{\left(\dfrac{2\frac{1}{2}}{7}+\dfrac{3\frac{1}{2}}{9}\right)-\dfrac{4\frac{1}{7}-2\frac{1}{4}}{6\frac{1}{2}+2\frac{1}{7}}\times\left(4+\dfrac{1}{1\frac{1}{16}+\frac{3}{8}}\right)}{\dfrac{6\frac{2}{3}}{7\frac{3}{8}}-\left(2\frac{1}{8}+1\frac{1}{4}\right)}$$

That was the first. I started it that evening quite blithely, confident that I understood perfectly and was sure to get it right. You did the two halves separately. I started with the top one, and worked it out methodically, first the brackets and then everything else, and then all the answers, bringing it down further and further. I seemed to be juggling enormous numbers of incredible fractions. Never mind, I told myself, slogging on. It'll come right in a minute, when all this working is finished. I had covered the whole page with sums. It was a mess of cancelled fractions. My mind swam for a minute, and I lost the thread. I kicked myself under the table, turned over and started again.

I tried to work through, putting everything down very neatly and correctly, and got my answer to the top half of the sum. It was a cloud of impossible things like seventy-four and nineteen twenty-fourths. That wasn't all, either. I couldn't think how that could be, for I knew the answer had to come out one number. But there it was. And that one number wasn't meant to have a fraction in it, either. Or was it? Wearily I tried to cancel. It wouldn't. I stared hopelessly at it. Then again my concentration snapped and the sum became a meaningless jumbled pattern. I buried my head in my arms and shut my eyes. They were tingling and my face was hot.

I pulled myself together and started on the bottom half. It worked out all right until about half way along, and then I got lost. I went over it, but again at the same place I got confused. I put my head on my hands and stared at the page. A hot tear ran down my cheek. I noticed guiltily that I'd already been an hour and I hadn't even done the first question. The whole ten were only meant to take half an hour. I gave it up and went on to the second question.

It was no better. I filled up page after page with sums which, far from bringing the question down to one number, only seemed to increase the morass of figures and fractions and meaningless signs. I had five brackets, all inside each other, curly brackets and square brackets and curved brackets and cornery brackets. I worked out the inside one, but I hadn't a notion what to do with the rest. Work them out too, I supposed, but what were their relations with the inside one? Should I multiply them all together? I was crying in real earnest now. I gazed at the page and suddenly my mind began to race and buzz, but with words, not figures.

"There are catherine-wheels behind my eyes
And the air mills round me in tiny sparks;
Dimly through the neon lights I see
The mass of dancing figures on my page.
They twist, they turn, they drag my tired mind with them.
Dancing through a maze which never ends,
Racking my aching brain as they whirl through . . .
Dance then! but I can dance no more, I must return
Back to that dog-tired world outside my dreams."

I came out of my daydream and realized that it was nine o'clock and I was still only half way through the second question.

I picked up my pen and tried to go on, but I couldn't remember or concentrate. I laid my head down on my arms and began to cry and cry.

Mummy came over and said, "What, you're not still working at that maths? You've been there for hours. You must go to bed now. Why, you're not crying? Whatever's the matter?"

"I can't do it, Mummy," I sobbed. "I thought I could, I thought I understood, but I don't, and I can't do it. I just can't do it."

"Oh, my poor child," she said. "Is this it? What a ghastly sum. Do you really have to do it?"

"Y-yes—and not only that one, there are eight others and I haven't done any, and now Miss Mildon will keep me in—and—oh!"

"But you started at six, didn't you? Haven't you done anything?" She flicked over my pages of wrong working. "Oh, my poor child! Look at all this! What do you mean, you've done nothing?"

"It counts as nothing. I didn't get any answers, not any. It's all wrong."

"Well, hand it in and explain you didn't understand."

"She won't believe me. She didn't before. It wouldn't take her a minute to do all that and she won't believe it did me."

"What's this?" said Mummy, pulling towards her the piece of paper with my poem on it. "You haven't written another poem? Oh, you'll kill yourself." She read it and said again, "Oh, my poor child!"

"I've just written it," I said. "Instead of getting on with my homework I just went into a dream for twenty minutes and wrote a poem."

"Well, show it to your maths mistress, that'll make her understand. And tell her you worked for three hours. She might even sympathize," suggested Mummy. I just shook my head. The very idea made me start crying again.

"Oh, it's a shame to pile you up with so much homework," she said. "You look like a little sick bird, all pale and woebegone. You mustn't work any more now. Run and have your bath. You can have one of my special champagne bubble baths to cheer you up. Oh and I know what! I bought some strawberry mousse for dinner. You'd like that, wouldn't you?"

"Oh, thank you, Mummy, I'd love that," I said, hugging her.

21

IN FACT MISS Mildon didn't give me detention, perhaps because of all those pages of working. Instead she gave my homework back marked "Returned" and told me to do it all again at home, which was one better. "And mind you finish the exercise this time, Antonia," she said. Then she set our ordinary Monday night homework. A further exercise of Harder Fractions, only a bit more difficult.

After the lesson she called me up to her and gave me some extra sums to do for practice, if I really couldn't do them, although as they were so purely mechanical she found that hard to believe. So then I had three lots of maths homework to do that night, and I couldn't do any of it. There was geography as well, of course.

"Poor old Antonia, you do have a time," laughed Lynda when I complained after the lesson. "And they weren't very hard, either. There were an awful lot, it's true, but I did finish them all."

"Oh, you are lucky," I sighed. I bet she sat up late, though, I thought. She looks tired.

"Never mind," she said. "Maths isn't everything. You write poetry."

"Why, of course, so I do, you've just reminded me," I said, and showed her the copy of the poem I had written on Thursday. While she was reading it and commenting on it I copied out in my rough note book,

"O wa ta na Siam!
O wa ta na Siam!
O wa ta nas!"

"It's effective, anyway," said Lynda. "You've certainly got your message over. I understand now what you mean about your maths."

"Oh, good. Now perhaps you see why I'm not looking forward to that triple homework." I handed her my rough book. "That is the Siamese National Anthem. Do sing it for me."

"I will if you do too," she said grinning.

"Oh, all right," I said. We sat on our desks and sang it loudly as a duet. The other girls laughed and threw exercise books at us. There was quite a riot when Mrs. Day came in for the English lesson. We were getting bolder and rowdier every day.

I did my English composition and read through the chapter in the grammar book as quickly as I could, and was finished by six o'clock. Then I took out my maths books glumly and prepared to live through Thursday night again.

"What's the matter, Antoninda-Belinda? You look sad," said Daddy.

"Cheer up," Mummy said. "First day of the week's over."

"Oh, no, it isn't," I said. "If only it were!"

"Why, haven't you almost finished your homework? You've been nearly an hour already."

"I thought you were only meant to work an hour," Daddy said.

"I am, but I've got extra work tonight, you see. Maths. Two lots of extra and the ordinary. It's punishment for my Thursday night's homework that I did so badly," I explained.

"Oh, how mean! And you worked so hard," Mummy exclaimed.

"Wait a minute," said Daddy. "How long will each of these three mathses take you?"

"Well, I suppose they're meant to take half an hour, but they'll take me much longer."

"How much longer?"

"Her last maths homework took three hours, but she didn't finish," said Mummy.

"All right, three hours each. And you're only supposed to take half an hour altogether?" Daddy went on.

"Yes, according to the time-table, that is."

"All right. Take a letter to your maths mistress."

I goggled at him, and then fetched a piece of paper and stammered, "Yes?"

"Write: 'Dear Miss Mildon, Antonia was unable to do all three maths homeworks set, as each one takes her three hours,

176

full stop. They would therefore take her nine hours to do, and as her maximum time for one night's homework is one hour, including another subject, this is mathematically impossible. Yours sincerely,' and type that out and I'll sign it."

I burst out laughing. "Oh Daddy, I'll so enjoy giving her that."

"It's that word 'mathematically' that makes it so perfect," said Mummy laughing. "Oh Man, you're wonderful."

I typed out the letter and then did my legal half hour of maths. I tackled the first question in the new exercise and got an answer to the top part, seventeen and forty-three sixtieths, that looked sort of moderately right.

I gave Miss Mildon the note before prayers, when she came in to call the register. She read it and put it on one side, without looking up at me. She didn't refer to it later, in the lesson, either. However, she didn't punish me any more, or say anything more about my homework, so it did the trick all right.

Everyone was in a panic, feverishly reading and re-reading the catechism. I had forgotten all about Miss Haversham's test, but luckily I had learnt it well at the weekend and still remembered it, with a bit of conning over during prayers. Miss Haversham didn't make us write it out at once, though. She discussed the previous week's test and gave detention to half the class. Then we had another talk about how she had visited a girl in hospital who had said that the almoner had been such a source of inspiration and cheerfulness to her that she was now determined to become a social worker herself. Little prig, I thought, and scribbled in my rough book, "I'M FED UP WITH WELFARE WORKERS."

While we were trying to write out the catechism Miss Haversham came past my desk and stopped beside me. She picked up my rough note book and looked at it. I had painted a big golden ornamental key on the cover. I supposed it intrigued her, and went on writing.

"Oh, what an ass I am!" said Miss Haversham suddenly. I jumped half out of my chair and looked up at her in alarm. All the other girls began to simper and giggle. Miss Haversham was frowning and looking grim.

"What's all this?" she asked me, pointing to where I'd written the Siamese National Anthem in my rough book for Lynda to sing.

"It's the Siamese National Anthem," I quavered. She looked grimmer than ever and flicked on through the book. I suddenly remembered what I had filled it with. There were picture sequences on the edges of all the pages. Some of them were flying horses, but the others were all of mistresses. I wondered if she would recognize any. Miss Mildon was unmistakable. I must have drawn hundreds of pictures of her, all of course in almost the same ridiculous position. Then there was what I had just written about the social worker. Well, I'm glad she's seen all that, I thought defiantly. Perhaps now they'll stop thinking I'm an Oxford possible.

"This is an appalling mess and a disgusting waste of paper," Miss Haversham said. Her tone sent shivers down my back. "I think I'll take it." She marched up to the front and put my rough book in her bag. Oh help, I thought, now it'll go round the whole staff and all the mistresses will see it. I sighed and went on writing.

It was really quite cold for only October. I stood and shivered as Miss Pratt picked people for the netball teams for that lesson. I hoped she would make me Centre. I had been that in all the games so far and was just beginning to get the idea of what to do.

Miss Pratt looked at me and said, "Oh, yes, Antonia. You can be Shooter."

I gaped at her. What on earth did Shooter do? As we ran into the playground to take up our positions I belted after Lynda and asked frantically, "Quick! Where do I go? What do I do? Which way do I throw?" That was important. Several times when I was Centre, having actually caught the ball I had thrown it towards the wrong goal, or to someone in the other team.

"You stand there and that's your goal," Lynda whispered, giving me a hasty push. Miss Pratt was standing holding the whistle, waiting for me, with her hands on her hips, tapping her foot. I dashed to and fro miserably, until one girl finally took me by the shoulders and pushed me into my place. Then Miss Pratt blew the whistle, and everyone began to rush about. I stood and watched. It had been easy, when I was Centre, just to hop up and down and look busy, but I didn't know what a Shooter did. I leant against the goal-post.

In fact, not once did I even touch the ball, let alone shoot. At one moment, however, my assistant shooter got the ball. She complained she couldn't shoot from where she was. Eager to help her, I stepped politely out of her way. She looked furiously at me, shot, missed, and whispered, "You silly dope! You should have stood in front of me and then I'd have passed to you, you'd have passed to me, and I'd have shot."

"Oh, dear, I'm sorry!" I whispered back, feeling mortified. I'd thought I was being so sensible. I just haven't got the mind for netball, I decided sadly, and began to feel awfully sorry for Miss Pratt.

It was even colder by lunchtime. We'd had quite warm weather up till then and had always spent our lunch hour in the playground. But today Lynda and I decided to go to the library. "It's miles away in the other wing though," I said. "Do you know the way?"

"As a matter of fact, it's awfully handy, there's a door leading into the back of the library about half way down the south wing passage," she said. We went across the landing and down the passage. There was the door into the library, sure enough, with two steps leading up to it. We went in.

"No, I'm sorry, you can't come in that way," said an enormous prefect, getting up and barring our way. "You aren't allowed to come through there. You've got to go round and come in through the other door."

"But why—why—" I said, bewildered. We were standing actually in the library. All round us were tables and bookcases.

"This is the south wing passage, and this library's in the east wing," said the girl. "You've got to go to the end and come round the wing and come back along the east wing passage.

"What a stupid, ridiculous nuisance," said Lynda as we trudged back and along and round and along and round again. "And our form-room's about a yard away from that door, and half a mile away from the other."

"I know. There's no point. Just school being bossy," I agreed.

When I got home I went down to the kitchen where Daddy and Mummy were having tea, and did a slow flicking movement on the low level. "Total triumph with Mildew," I said. "Not another word about that maths."

"Didn't she say anything?" asked Daddy, making a soft expanding movement with his arms.

"No, what could she say?" I said gleefully. I did a lyrical flowing movement on the high level. "You should have seen her face when she read the letter. Oh Man, what it is to have you for a father!"

"Yes, I bet he took her by surprise," Mummy said, joining in with a dabbing movement on the medium level. "I don't suppose she's ever had to face anyone's father before. Big bully."

"Yes, so she is! So she is, a big bully," I said and went backwards across the kitchen with a slow straining movement. "Well, I mean to say, it was a shocking homework, but really, what good could it do just to triple it up?"

"Ugh, schoolmistresses!" said Daddy scornfully, expanding away with a rhythmic movement and using his facial muscles too, in a way that would have sent our American instructress into raptures.

"I know, haven't I always said as much?" Mummy said, dabbing gracefully on both the high and the medium levels. "What is this silly dance we're doing?"

"It's nature dancing," I explained, doing a vertical extended reaching movement and flicking with my feet. "We have a lesson every other Monday at a place that teaches it and I must say my opinion of nature is dropping steadily. That's a dabbing movement you're doing, Mummy. This is an expanded angular movement and this is a contracted angular movement, and this is a continuous flowing movement ... Oh Daddy, you're wonderful!" He was doing a beautiful movement all over the table, scowling with his facial muscles. Mummy and I clapped and made sudden applauding movements.

"And do you know, it was awful, in the middle of the test Miss Haversham confiscated my rough book and took it away to read," I said presently. "And it was all full of pictures of the mistresses, and flying horses and things, and that thing about O wa ta na Siam, and something rude I wrote about her pet hobby-horse, and I bet she'll expel me."

"You mean to say she scolded you for that?" Mummy said. "Well, if she won't let you be escapist in your own rough books she's just asking for you all to start writing on the walls."

"Hey, steady on, steady on, Man," laughed Daddy, patting her.

"Well, I feel for her," I said. "After all, it was a school book. She was quite right, of course she was. I just hadn't realized that rough books aren't for letting off steam in here. They were at the other school. I think I'll stick to writing on my ruler."

"No, no, for heaven's sake don't restrict yourself," Daddy said. "Give her something to be escapist in, Man. I want her to be able to write all the rude things she likes in peace."

"Yes, certainly, it's important. I know! There's that old exercise book I had when we were married to write recipes in. I only used one page, I think. You shall have that to escape in as much as you like and keep sane."

"Oh, thank you, Mummy," I said gratefully. My ruler was already so scribbled on that it was inked over quite solidly and was no use for anything any more, and anyway you couldn't make picture sequences with it. My mouth fairly watered at the thought of all those lovely blank page edges just asking to be licked over.

So, apparently, did Lynda's. When I showed her my beautiful new book, with "Name: Antonia Bird. Subject: Escapism" written in squiggly writing on the cover, she straight away christened it with a wonderful picture sequence of me on seven of the best top corners. But it was so funny that I didn't mind. The other girls all came crowding round to scribble too. None of them had dared to write anything in their rough note books since mine had been confiscated, and they were all terribly suppressed. Soon they were all bringing their own blocks and pads to act as rough books, and scribbling and drawing in them in a way that would have shocked Miss Haversham if she had known. The things they drew would have shocked her even more; they were far worse than my mild little picture sequences.

One day after lunch Miss Mackintosh handed out little duplicated notices for our parents, requesting them to come to a Parents' Night to meet the staff and discuss their daughters' progress. Mummy dutifully went, although it was on a Saturday and meant not going to the country that weekend. She came back fuming.

"That bossy, conceited creature! We spent most of the evening listening to her, and mind you the invitation said nothing about a speech. It was about correcting the characters of the girls and giving them a strong foundation to build a useful life on—you can imagine. And just listen to this—this is what she

said : 'Of course we get girls from all sorts of homes, and it i
our task to counteract any bad influences.' You bet it is. Bu
just imagine saying such a thing to the parents' face! And th
whole speech was like that." Mummy looked really angry.

"Oh, how awful," I said, shocked. I could indeed imagin
perfectly.

"No, that wasn't good, was it?" Daddy said. "And anyway
that's letting the cat out of the bag. Now that she's warned a
the parents that she means to alter all the girls to suit the Hous
pattern, they'll be on their guard against her."

"Will they?" I said. "You might, but you're special and extra
ordinary. I mean, you might if you had a girl there who you
could see obviously wasn't going to fit the House pattern. Bu
I think most parents are much more docile. Miss Mackintosh i
probably used to parents who just knuckle under and come i
with her against girls who don't fit." I was thinking of Paulin
West, the poor tired girl with her mountains of homework an
thousands of school activities, who would undoubtedly end up a
an almoner if she stuck it out at all.

22

DADDY EXCELLED HIMSELF that Christmas. He booked us all for a winter sports holiday in Austria by a cheap tour for a fortnight, so that after our usual jolly Christmas in the country we could leave without any anti-climax for "sun and snow and sleigh-bells and real live Christmas trees all weighed down with snow" as he put it.

When he began to get Christmassy that year, which as it happened was during the two days' holiday I had for half term, out came a perfectly gorgeous display of ski-ing brochures and catalogues, all full of dazzling mountains and pretty girls falling about and ski-tracks. They covered the whole of the main table in the drawing-room, and Daddy would stand for hours chuckling to himself, just looking at them, or reading one, though of course he knew them all by heart anyway. They flustered Mummy a bit at first, because she used that table a lot, but she soon got used to them. Daddy had them up from late October to the end of December, so she just had to. When we moved down to the cottage at the end of term Daddy took all the brochures with him and set them up in another permanent display on the kitchen table, together with the Christmas cake, shaped like a little chalet, and the beautiful crackers we never pulled, and a coaching scene. Mummy didn't mind, though. She was as keen as him, and in fact she set up the coaching scene.

We chose a little resort called Damuels which looked fubsy, a proper villagey village with wooden houses buried in snow and a church with an onion spire and lots of sunny nursery slopes and cosy Kellers to have après-ski in. We knew all that about it long before we went. I even painted an enormous picture of it, complete with pretty girls falling about, and we covered the only other useful table in the house with that. Every evening when I came in from school, for all the second half of term,

Daddy would greet me with a cry of "Hullo, Ski-ing Girl!" and hug me, while we both shouted "Damuels! Oh Damuels!"

The first time that happened Mummy called up from the kitchen in a shocked voice, "What did I hear you say, Antonia?" But when we assured her that I hadn't been damning anyone, she understood and was just as enthusiastic as us. We all hugged all of us together while we pointed out the Keller we would go to, and thought that that might be an ice-rink, and Daddy found a new picture in another brochure which showed a horse-sleigh coming round the corner of a perfectly adorable little chalet in the snow that made us start all over again, "Oh, Damuels!"

Not content with the table displays, Daddy covered the sofa with our new ski-ing clothes, our beanies, vorlages, ankle-length tomato coloured pants, Mummy's furry earmuffs, their anoraks and my parka. It really was a bright red parka, and not just an anorak like everyone else's, and I felt very superior. So we couldn't sit down either. And when our ski-boots arrived, just before Christmas, they took up the floor and we couldn't walk across the room. We were tremendously happy. All the ski-ing was extra, of course, and we still kept on with our carols, decorations, tree, just as usual. The room was as much a jungle of tinsel as ever, and what with that and the ski-ing stuff and the Salvation Army who came and sang carols twice, with lanterns and trombones and carol-sheets, Daddy got so Christmassy that he was every bit as happy as he had been in Ibiza; and that's saying a lot. He and I went round all day singing and dancing, a wonderful mixture of carols and nature dancing. Mummy did a version of her own, a little heel-kicking tail-wagging dance in the kitchen while she basted the meat and planted her new weed in the goldfish tanks.

Mummy always spent more time in the kitchen feeding the goldfish or changing their water or something than she spent cooking. Often when you went in she would jump guiltily away from her tanks and start filling kettles and things, which you thought she'd been doing all the time. Nobody minded, though. Her goldfish really were lovely.

School seemed positively grim for the rest of term while all this was going on at home, but then so would any lessons have, in contrast to such festivity. All the same, I really wasn't enjoying being a Scholar of St. Rhadigond's as much as I had expected. I would get wearily up in the morning and traipse through the grey streets and queue or dash and just miss the bus, and stand all the way with my satchel giving me backache, and march proudly into that beautiful hall and up and up and up and up the stairs to my classroom. And we would file in for those interminable prayers, and kneel on the hard floor while Miss Haversham droned on and on about toiling and not seeking for rest, until I would find myself wishing and longing to faint and be carried out. Girls regularly were. I used to watch them enviously.

Then I would drag through the day that always seemed like a week, especially the maths lessons that were always six or seven times as long as the others. And when the longed-for end of school bell went I would just pack up my satchel again and go home. I usually managed to do the walk to the bus stop in fifteen minutes in the morning, but it took me half an hour in the evening and seemed several miles. The days got darker and greyer and drearier. All the evening I did my homework. It was funny that it always did take the whole evening, because it was meant to take only an hour, and I worked out that the evening was three hours, from five till eight. But all the same I was lucky if I got twenty minutes to myself. And I was always so tired.

I realized, of course, that I didn't mind all that in itself. I was still as keen to work hard and get ahead as I ever had been. It was just that any lessons just then, so near Christmas, with Mummy and Daddy and all the shops already celebrating, seemed somehow unfair. Of course I was really enjoying the actual lessons. Science was fascinating, French was fun, the poetry lessons sheer joy. Even Miss Mildon seemed to be resigned to me, and restricted herself to making fun of me in class. I didn't get any more detentions. And the school of course was beauty itself. All the same, when we finished our last lesson on the last day of term I felt as if I had been let out of prison. All the class was breaking up all the rulers available into tiny bits in the door hinges, in excitement and espièglerie, and I joined in, yelling and shrieking. When finally a mistress came and told us off, the floor was thickly covered with tiny splinters of wood.

Miss Mildon handed out another batch of compulsory invitations to a special Parents' Night and Christmas Ceremony, in commemoration of the great fire of 1923 at St. Rhadigond's. The girls were to go to a St. Rhadigond's School Christmas Service in All Saints' Church, while the parents talked to the staff and were addressed by Miss Haversham. It was to be an event of re-dedication to the Spirit of the Founder. The date was to be December 30th, and we were to leave on the 27th for Austria.

Daddy wrote a polite letter to Miss Mackintosh next day explaining why we couldn't go.

"We couldn't very well have a better excuse," Mummy said. "Anyway, I don't suppose we're missing much. And I think it's a bit much to expect you to go to school in the holidays."

The day after Boxing Day we caught the train to London, wearing our ski clothes and dangling ski boots like baubles on a Christmas tree. When we got there we piled into a taxi and drove to Victoria, shouting, "We're off! Damuels, here we come!" to everyone we passed, all the way.

We reached Damuels in the post bus from Feldkirch the next day. We gobbled down our sausage and dumplings in the hotel and ran out again, to the horror of the maids and waitresses, who insisted that we ought to rest now after our journey and explore the village tomorrow. But the sight of all the other people in the hotel tramping out in their gay anoraks and skin-tight vorlages to afternoon ski-school was too much for us. We couldn't wait. We explored every nook and corner of the village, found the hotel that had dancing, surveyed the slopes (we couldn't help doing that, the village was surrounded by them), decided the snow was definitely new snow but would become powder snow with one night of frost. We were right about the powder snow, as a matter of fact, which wasn't bad considering we'd never seen any snow worth calling snow before. Everything, as we kept saying, was absolutely perfect, exactly as we had imagined it, the most darling little village in the world except Tedford where our country cottage was. We sang loudly as we wandered round, Christmas carols and "A Partridge in a Pear Tree" right through. There were several other groups of jolly people doing the same.

After dinner Daddy wanted to go out and dance, but Mummy persuaded him not to, so as not to be tired for ski-school tomorrow. He was fairly bubbling over with happiness. He sat chuckling and talking about snow and chalets called Friedegg and coaching scenes and lowly cattle sheds and sun and sleigh

186

bells and stem-christies, with his big smile that looked like the grin on the sun on the catalogue cover.

About half way through the holiday Daddy's suntan was really spectacular, and he had gone up several classes in ski-school and had a masterly traversing position. Mummy and I were tagging along behind. We always sat for a while outside the hotel in the sun before lunch, and it was then that Mummy was supposed to hand out all our letters sent on from England, but in fact there hadn't been any all the holiday until today. Now. there was one for Daddy, and it was from Miss Mackintosh. She said that she was unable to give permission for me to miss the Christmas Fire Commemoration Service, as it was an invaluable experience that I would regret missing all my life.

"Bad luck, the service was four days ago," Mummy laughed.

"Take this," said Daddy, handing me the letter, "wrap it up in a snowball, and throw the snowball at the knobble on the top of that ski rack."

I laughed and obeyed. The snowball hit the knobble and splashed snow all over us, and the letter fell out and blew across the road.

"Really, Man!" said Mummy, laughing. "Pick it up, Child, I'd better have it."

"Let's send Miss Mackintosh a postcard saying 'Lots of snow here, we're all learning to ski fast,' " I suggested, coming back with the soggy bit of paper and depositing it in Mummy's lap.

"And add that it's wonderful character-training and that the kick turn is an invaluable experience," Daddy said.

"Not half as invaluable as knowing how to get up when you've fallen down," said Mummy. "What a stupid woman she is, really."

By the end of our fortnight Daddy was a real champion skier, and had actually gone up on a drag-lift and done a run. Mummy and I were deeply impressed. We were still soldiering on on the nursery slopes, ploughing and stemming. Daddy would have loved to stay on right to the end of the season, and at one moment we really thought he would. That was the night when we went out in a horse-sleigh in the dark to a place high up in the mountains where we drank hot spiced wine. We sat snuggled up together under a rug, and sang carols as we jingled along, and when we got back to the hotel at about midnight Daddy suddenly said, "Don't let's go home!" But he was a dutiful father really, and back we went on the day we had said, the day before my term started.

All that night I was so excited at the thought of going back to my dream school that I could hardly sleep. In Damuels I had been sorry when we didn't stay on, but now I was too het-up to think about Damuels. I tossed and turned and watched the orange street light coming round the edge of the curtain and making a pink glow on the wall above my dressing-table. It was a very familiar sight. I was used to spending hours on end lying awake looking at it. It was the light from the moat of fire round Spinazzolala, and because it was magic fire it was magic light and I always got twice as excited watching it.

The other girls at school were all just as excited, and we sat on our desks discussing this and trying to decide why. Only Lynda sat quietly apart on her chair. I went over to see her and found she was reading our geography text book, the chapter about the rotation of crops in East Anglia. In deep disgust I snatched the book away and threw it across the room and told her to read something sensible. She burst out laughing and said, "Naughty girl! Now go and pick it up."

I went over to the book, picked it up off the floor and threw it out of the room on to the landing. "Now I demand an explanation," I said, coming back to Lynda and sitting down beside her. "You can't even not have done your geography homework because we didn't have any."

She just grinned at me and shook her head, and then suddenly leant over on to my desk and threw up the lid, to grab my copy of the text book. But my desk was in such havoc that she couldn't find it, and we both laughed and started talking about our holidays.

Margaret Evans came over holding Lynda's geography book by the corner and dropped it on her desk.

"Tiresome girl," she said. "It was lying on the landing. I picked it up half a second before Miss Mildon came round the corner. She'd have blown you sky-high if she'd seen it. Really, Lynda, and you're the good girl of the form, too."

"Left your book lying on the stairs, did you? Tut, tut!" I said, wagging my finger at her. She giggled.

Miss Mildon greeted us very drily and barely said "Good morning" before she started collecting our reports. They were very grand, with "St. Rhadigond's School" and that quotation

188

from Agnes Winthrop printe d on them about willing hands and
meek souls. You got an A, B, C, D, or E for each subject. A was
the best and E was the equivalent of nought. I had an A for
English, Lit. and Lang., French, history and scripture. I had
D for maths. Miss Mildon and Miss Mackintosh put more or
less the same thing, "Must try harder in her weak subjects."
They didn't put anything about my good ones.

Lynda had A for every single subject, and "Good" for games
and needlework. Poor Miss Pratt had made a series of dots on
my report, as if she had started to write something and hadn't
known what to say, and had finally written "Fair." Sewing was
just "weak" and indeed what else was there to say?

When we came in after prayers, which of course were extra
long for the beginning of term, Miss Mildon was giving out
pieces of foolscap paper duplicated on both sides. I went to my
desk and looked at the paper on it. It was a long list of books. I
ran my eye down it. *The Story of the Wheel. Know About Sheep.
Singing by Sight. Clothes of the Old Testament. The Story of
Leather. How Baskets Began. History is Fun! (Book Three,
Roman Britain).* They were all very familiar. I glanced at
Lynda. She was reading the list with a look of absolute horror
on her face. When she had finished, she looked up at me and
whispered,

"So someone did look at our library catalogue after all!"

"Cheer up," I whispered back. "They can't have been offended
by the picture sequences, or they wouldn't have sent copies of it
all round this school."

"I wonder what it's for," said Lynda apprehensively.

Miss Mildon said, "This is the third form reading list. I'm
sorry it's a term late, but that's because we were altering all our
library stocks." Telling me you were, I thought. There had been
a great bookcase in the library for Fiction. Every day during
the past term a few more shelves of this had been emptied and
replaced with encyclopaedias and things. By the end of term,
there was only one shelf of Fiction left.

"Every girl has to read fifteen books from this list before the
end of the year. You get a new list in the Lower Fourth," said
Miss Mildon.

"What! Fifteen books in two terms?" we all gasped indignantly.

"Well, if I were you I should just get on and read them and

189

stop screaming like children in an infants' school," said Miss
Mildon, rolling her round fish's eyes and gazing at the ceiling in
exasperation.

"Please, Miss Mildon," said Rosemary Sanderson, "I'll never
be able to read all those books—um—I mean I don't have any
time for reading. I read about—oh, three or four books a year—
um—my father gives me books and—um—well, you see I just
haven't time—um—"

"If you would kindly repeat that omitting the word 'um' I
might understand you," Miss Mildon said.

"Oh, well—um—oh dear, I'm sorry, Miss Mildon. I mean I
haven't got time to—um—oh, my goodness, I'm very sorry,
Miss Mildon—um—I'll never be able to read fifteen books. I
read ever so slowly—um—"

"I am unable to understand you," Miss Mildon said, "but if
you are complaining that you cannot read I suggest you take a
course at an elementary school."

"Oh no, I didn't mean that," Rosemary said. "I just meant
to say—um—I only have time to read a few books a year and—
um—I'll never finish fifteen. I mean I have so much to do, I
never have—um—time to read."

"If you mean that you haven't any time in the evening (though
as you insist on umming you don't make yourself at all clear) I
suggest you get up a little earlier," said Miss Mildon sardonically.
"Perhaps you may even have to cancel some of your tennis
parties this summer. I'll come to your funeral."

I scribbled ferociously in my escapism book.

Then we started again on our treadmill of lessons. Of course,
I kept reminding myself, the only ones I didn't enjoy were
maths and games and needlework. All the other lessons were fun,
like French, fascinating, like science, or really enjoyable, like
English. Even in maths we were only doing tremendously complicated areas. We were finding the areas of all the letters in the
alphabet, or of jagged pieces of paper, and at least, thanks to
Sir, I understood the theory, even though I couldn't always
manage to apply it. In fact, every lesson in itself was really great
fun. I told myself so all the time. The mistresses, I noticed,
always went to great pains to keep us all happy and entertained,
constantly cracking jokes, letting us play with magnets in science,
letting us draw imaginary portraits of all the great men we came
across in history. They really were all so kind and nice, and so

clever too. We were learning a tremendous amount quite pain-lessly, thanks to the jokes, the magnets and the portraits. I was already laying down the law to Mummy and Daddy about all sorts of things.

I went over the day every evening on my way home, thinking like this, and could never quite pin down to anything my feeling of boredom, depression and tiredness. Perhaps it was because the real work of the day, homework, was still to come.

Of course, being rid of Roberts and O'Brien and the rest of them was sheer joy. Every day, as Lynda and I wandered round the playground free and unmolested, I thought about that and compared it to the other playground, which still gave me night-mares. No football, no Chain-He, no fighting, no Class Fourers, no boys. It was wonderful, no boys! Just a few hundred of the most intelligent girls in the district walking decorously round the grounds of a beautiful school, or else playing netball in the most ladylike way possible. Every break it would strike me afresh, and Lynda and I would walk proudly round, our blazer badges shining and glittering.

23

"Let's see," I said, trying to look over Lynda's shoulder at the picture sequence I thought she was drawing in her escapism book.

She held up the book for a second for me to see. The page was filled with neat writing.

"Oh, I thought you were drawing in your rubbish book. Sorry," I said.

"This is my rubbish book," she said.

"Oh, oh I see. You're—are you writing a story or something?"

Lynda put down her pen and began flicking through a little blue book she had on her desk. "What's that? A story? Well, perhaps. No, not really."

I craned over and looked at her book. I caught a glimpse of the words "dimanche je vais chez ma tante." And so neatly written. Why, she had actually ruled a margin. In her escapism book, too.

"Is it—it's not in French?" I asked incredulously.

"Yes. Why not?" she answered. "There, that'll do. How do you say 'in bed'?"

"Au lit," I murmured mechanically.

"Don't look so horrified, Antonia. I haven't committed a crime. I just wanted to practise a bit on an extra composition."

"Of course, why not? I'm not horrified. I was just admiring you for being so earnest and hardworking."

"Well, I enjoy it. Honestly I do. Anyway, Mrs. Day said lots of the older girls do extra homework voluntarily."

"Old before your years, I knew it. Bad habit, don't cultivate it," I muttered, but luckily she didn't hear.

"Look at this, Daddy. My reading matter for this year," I said, giving him the school reading list.

Daddy read it, looking more and more as if he were going to

be sick as he went on. When he had finished he said faintly, "Did you say you want to read all this?"

"No, Daddy, I said I'm going to. It's the school reading list."

He looked at it with an expression of total horror, as if it were a woman about to come and shout at him, and then suddenly said, "Give me some paper."

I hastily found him a blank page in my rubbish book. He put a line through the school book list, and began to write another.

"See here," he said. "I, your father, forbid you to read this stuff. Instead, you will read these. Right?"

"Wonderful!" I said. "Oh, Man, thank you so much." I looked at his list. It began: *Wuthering Heights; Jane Eyre; The Odyssey; Murder in the Cathedral.*

I had another detention a few weeks later. We had had a test in maths, and when the papers were returned I had two out of ten, and on the bottom of the page was the word "Detention" in red biro. I was getting to hate the sight of red biro on blue ink.

When I trailed out afterwards to queue at the bus stop at a quarter to five, there, to my surprise, was Pauline West, only one ahead of me in the queue.

"Hullo, how do you come to be so late?" I said.

"I've been having a music lesson," she said. She looked thin and grey and pathetically tired.

"Oh yes, of course, your violin. Are you going to be a violinist or anything?"

"Oh no, nothing like that. I'm just learning it to play a bit because Miss Mackintosh said it's a good thing to be able to play a musical instrument. Sounds good, you know."

"Are you interested in music?"

"I told you, I can't play very well. It's far more difficult than you'd think. Besides, there's such a lot to learn. I'm not much good. And I haven't got time to practise properly, and anyway, you know, I really don't like it much. In fact I simply hate it."

"What a shame, and you work so hard too," I said. "I really meant, though, are you interested in listening to music, not just your violin?"

"Oh, you mean that sort of music! Yes, I used to be, I've got a huge collection of seventy-eight records that I had before I came here, but I don't play them now. I just haven't got time. Anyway, Miss Trent, she teaches me the violin—she said listening is a sheer waste of time. It's true, of course. If I messed about with records I shouldn't be able to practise so much. That's what she meant. D'you know, when I was very small I always said that when I grew up I'd listen to all the music that's ever been written. I really meant to, when I was just little." She burst out laughing, and I suddenly realized that that had been a joke.

"You had detention, I suppose," Pauline said. "You look tired. Who was it for?"

"Oh, the usual. Miss Mildon. Two out of ten for a maths test. I just don't seem to be able to manage at all. I'm doing much worse here than I did at my primary school. It's simply frightful. Of course we had an awfully good teacher there, but then Miss Mildon's very clever too. But you know, she doesn't really explain so well. I mean, she won't say it more simply if I ask her, she just repeats what she said before. I don't think she really believes I need it to be said simply, she thinks I'm just fooling."

"It's a pity you can't do any better," said Pauline. "It must pull down your good subjects."

"Yes, and the teachers seem only to be interested in your bad subject. Even Miss Haversham."

"Well, she would be interested in your maths, wouldn't she? Didn't you know? She's maths herself. It's a school tradition, the headmistresses always are."

"Of course, they would be," I groaned. "Just my luck."

A bus came up. I couldn't see its number, but I didn't need to. Whatever it was, it wouldn't be mine. It wasn't, either.

Lynda got ill soon before the summer half-term. She looked wretched, and when I pressed her admitted that she had a raging headache. A day or two later, on the last Thursday, she was absent. The summer exams were due to start on the following Tuesday, when we came back to school. All the girls brought great suitcases to school on Thursday, and took every book in their desks home. They were obviously going to spend their entire holiday revising frantically. I did the same, but stupidly I had told Mummy some time ago that it was my "half-term holiday" (as it was officially, of course) and she would keep on treating it like a holiday. She didn't seem to understand about the revision.

On Saturday she said,

"Well, Child, as you worked so hard all yesterday you must have finished that homework, and I've arranged with Papa to take us out for a drive somewhere and a long walk. So pack up those books quickly because Daddy's only got to finish dressing and we'll leave." We had gone down to the country for my long weekend, of course.

"Oh Mummy, how lovely. When will we be back?"

"Oh, late. I don't know. You know Daddy, he might go anywhere. Past bedtime, anyway."

"Well, the thing is, Mummy," I explained desperately, "I've got so much revision left—I'd really counted on having all today to work in. The exams start on Tuesday, you see, and I'd meant to do all my science, and it's only two o'clock and I've still got masses to do."

"Well, that's too bad of you. You should have started weeks ago if you've got so much. This is a holiday and I'm not having you working."

"Oh, I did, Mummy, I did," I gabbled, "I've been working on this revision for weeks, only there was tons of homework as well and anyway I've simply got to go over it all again, just before the exam, I did before the eleven-plus and that's how I managed to remember everything, everyone else is going to, oh please Mummy please!"

"Oh very well, we'll leave you behind to stew," said Mummy crossly. "If we're not back for supper there's frozen chicken. But we'll only leave you on condition that you do this homework in the garden and stop for tea and don't get tired."

"Oh yes, I'll do all that, thank you, Mummy," I said, greatly relieved, although in fact I was tired already. When she had gone I wrote in big black letters in my escapism book "IT'S NOT FAIR IT'S NOT FAIR IT'S NOT FAIR the school scolds me for not working and Mummy scolds me for working and IT'S ALL A BIG NIDDLE."

I hadn't really hoped to get away with working on Sunday, but even on Monday, when we'd got back from the cottage, Mummy said, "Why don't you go out and play on Felias? It's such a lovely day and there's a nice breeze for your flying horses." I went out there and worked all day, and it was quite true about the lovely breeze. It was almost impossible to read, the pages kept blowing over. It really would have been perfect for the flying horses. Mummy kept calling up to ask if I was happy, and

I always answered yes, but it wasn't true. I was strongly tempted to stop revising and blow bubbles, but I didn't and by seven o'clock I was very tired. But I had covered everything we'd done in the year three times, and it was all fresh in my mind, so it was worth while.

We had exams the whole week. Lynda was there, but in the middle of the history exam on Thursday she went out and was sick. She came back and finished, but she had her lowest mark for that exam, only 79 per cent. She was in the eighties in every other subject and came top of the form.

I was really exhausted by the end of the week, and got ill during the weekend and was away with a temperature, septic throat and swollen glands for the whole of the week after the exams. When I came back the results were out. I was only third in form order because I was bottom by miles in maths and needlework. I had spent all my time in maths doing one geometrical problem, constructing triangles, and hadn't had time even to try the others, though I probably couldn't have done them if I had. I did get 30 per cent for that one question, but it wasn't anywhere near the pass-mark and I was scared. My other subjects all had at least 70 per cent and I was top in English, literature and language, and French and history. But it was the maths that worried me. It was the one that mattered, I had learnt that by now.

I was ill again on Wednesday of the following week, and Mummy kept me at home again on Thursday and Friday.

"Well, it's just what you'd expect," she said. "She wore herself to a shadow for the exams and she hasn't recovered yet. It's perfectly natural."

Lynda still hadn't come back to school when I went back on Monday, and we heard she was in hospital with tonsilitis. I was really worried about her. I remembered how I had been out of hospital within a week when I had my own tonsils out, and she had already been a fortnight. She wasn't back on the next Monday either, and that made three weeks. I got more and more worried.

We really just marked time all the rest of the term, though we still had to work as hard as ever, so it was boring as well as exhausting. I felt ill again next Wednesday, and prayed that when I got home Mummy wouldn't say I looked tired and how thin I was and look at those circles under her eyes and better take her temperature and a day in bed's what you need. I bounded in that evening, trying to look healthy, and she didn't, but the next week I caught a cold and was ill yet again during the second half of the week.

We had prize-giving on the last day of term. Lynda still hadn't come back, but she got a form prize and a special Merit Prize. There, so that's all right, I thought unhappily, wondering what had happened to her.

Miss Mackintosh summoned all the Baxter prize-winners up to her study in the morning, before the prize-giving. The others all went in in a bunch, but she had me in separately. I had got the special English Prize for the first year, and a Form Prize too.

I went in last. Miss Mackintosh gave me her bright smile and told me to sit down. The palms of my hands were wet.

"You've got the English Prize," she said. "That's very good. Keep it up."

"Oh, thank you. I will. I love English," I said, trying very hard to sound mad keen.

"That's obvious. And what's equally obvious is that you don't love maths."

It hit me in the pit of my stomach. I burst out sweating all over, and suddenly thought I was going to be sick.

"As you've made it perfectly clear that you've neither tried nor cared, Miss Mildon and I were very reluctant to give you a Form Prize. However, we've done so, in the hope that you'll mend your ways."

I wanted to shout out, "It's not true, I do care and I try like anything." But I only made a silly croak.

"You've no excuses. You have the ability, the brains. The very fact that you've won this English prize is proof of that. You did well in every subject except maths. That proves that it's sheer laziness which prevents you doing well in that too. You could easily have come second, perhaps even first, in your form. Well, I will not tolerate such laziness. In future I expect to see your maths brought up to the standard of the subjects you like. History, for example, you've done well all the year in that."

"But please, Miss Mackintosh, I really do find it so difficult—worse than difficult," I began, and then stopped, realizing the impossibility of getting across to Miss Mackintosh what maths actually was to me. She would never understand that it wasn't just "hard." Nobody ever understood. It was always the same.

"Oh, but surely, with a little work, a clever girl like you—you can write poems, can't you?" Work took you so far and no further. It had been so far when it was simple arithmetic. Now it was maths, it was further.

"No doubt you do find it difficult. That's why I call it laziness when you don't try. There are plenty of girls in the school who find many subjects difficult. They haven't your ability. But they don't just sit back, as you do. They work. They get perhaps only half marks, but it's obvious they really work to do it. If they took up your attitude they also would do as badly as you. Therefore it's obvious you haven't worked. You owed it to your gift for English to succeed at maths. I hope you are ashamed."

She waited for me to say I was, but I couldn't. It was too much to ask. Anyway, I *had* tried.

"All right, you can go now," she said. I said "Goodbye, Miss Mackintosh," and went.

There were six girls who won form prizes, out of sixty in my year, and only one English Prize, and so when I went up for it I was clapped the loudest of all. Miss Haversham gave me her broad smile as she handed me the book and shook my hand warmly. She said "Well done!" and beamed at me. You would never have guessed that I had been told to be ashamed. I did the silly little bob I had been told to do, smiled proudly back, and marched down from the platform with my book. All the girls grinned at me and clapped as I went by. That was all right. I grinned back.

I looked at my prizes. One was a biography of Elizabeth Fry, "the prisoners' friend, the greatest social worker the world has seen. . . ." I glanced at the blurb and decided it was definitely in the category of Daddy's banned books. Still, it would look good in my bookcase.

"Well done, Antonia," said Margaret Riley afterwards. "That was the best prize of all, what you got."

"Well, I'm glad somebody thinks so," I said. "You've no idea what a rowing Miss Mackintosh gave me."

"She rowed you? What for?"

"My maths, of course. Can't you guess?"

"Gosh, and you did so well in everything else. Goodness, if she blows you up for just one subject—oh help! D'you know, I didn't get above fifty per cent in anything?"

"Well, perhaps she won't notice you. I hope she doesn't. She half killed me," I said.

"What's that?" said Christine, coming up. "You, of all people."

"Yes," Margaret said anxiously, "and she only did badly in one subject, so think what's coming to us."

"No, thank you, I daren't," said Christine. "Perhaps I won't come back next term."

"It was today she blew me up," I pointed out.

"I expect she'll send for us," said Margaret, looking scared. She spread the news, and half the class spent the rest of the day waiting in suspense to be sent for. But in fact nobody was.

24

I GOT A POSTCARD from Lynda during the summer holidays. It had been sent out to us in Tangier from England and said:

"Congratulations on all your prizes (I know you must have got some). Everything is perfectly all right with me, I feel marvellous and have almost finished *The Bassoon—Clown of the Orchestra*—the eleventh book on our library list! I'm leaving hospital tomorrow. For goodness' sake take care not to walk backwards, won't you, and send me back again, wherever in the world you may be."

I didn't say anything to Daddy, and hid the postcard away. His opinion of Lynda had been so high ever since she came to tea that it seemed a shame to spoil it all. I knew what he would think if he heard she was reading his banned book list earnestly in hospital when she ought to have been reading something jolly and getting better. I felt pretty disgusted with her myself. No doubt she had made herself much worse, working away on top of an operation.

She was there, on the first day of the new term. We were all huddled miserably in that grand front hall, trying hard to feel superior now that we had been there a whole year and were Lower Fourths. It was difficult when we hadn't got a classroom and didn't know where to go. At least we knew better this time than to wear our tunics. We were all wearing our summer dresses, like the other big girls, and that made us able to look down slightly on the tunicked new girls.

"Are you going to be a naughty Lower Fourth?" Louise Carter asked me. The Lower Fourths had a reputation for being naughty.

"Oh, I don't know," I answered. "I'll see if I have the energy."

"I am," said Louise with great relish.

"I know who won't be," I said, looking at Lynda beside me. She didn't answer, just went on smiling brightly. She insisted that she was perfectly well now, but I didn't believe her. I compared her with the Lynda who had sorted books with me a year ago, or was it more? She was thinner and paler, but then so were all the girls. She looked even more enthusiastic and good, in fact there wasn't anything to her but enthusiasm and goodness. She looked as if she were about to fly away with a halo. I know! I thought suddenly. She looks old. About seventy. I bet she ought still to be in hospital. Mummy calls me a shadow, but it's nothing to her.

We were finally told we were Lower Four A this time, and were led up to a classroom at the very top of the north wing. To our dismay Miss Mildon was again our form mistress. When she came in she just looked slowly round, smiling her little smile and nodding, and said, "Well, well, So we meet again. Now let's see who's died." Then she called the register.

The marking-ink had washed out of my clothes, and I hadn't noticed, and she gave me detention.

"Typical you," said Lynda. I looked at her, hoping she was laughing. But she wasn't.

This year we added Latin to our curriculum, but otherwise our time-table was pretty well unchanged. That was the awful thing. It was too much unchanged. We still had our double lesson of maths right at the end of the week, on Friday this time.

"Isn't that joy?" I said to Lynda. "So if I get ill any more times half-way through the week I'll still be missing the double dose of the one lesson I don't dare miss."

She ignored me, and just went on looking thoughtfully at the ceiling.

"Lynda?" I said, perplexed. "Don't you think it's just what would happen?" She still didn't answer. Then suddenly I understood. She couldn't hear me. I hadn't been whispering, either, only speaking quietly as we always used to in the lessons. Could this be the result of her illness, with her slaving away in hospital on top of it?

A gaunt mistress I didn't know came in and said, "Now, every year some girls from the Lower Fourth form volunteer to help in the libraries, sorting the books and so on, and dealing with the tickets and catalogue. Who would like to be the helpers this year?"

I burst out in silent laughter, and nudged Lynda. But she wasn't laughing. She was glowing with enthusiasm, and had shot her hand up. She turned in response to my nudge and grinned, but it was only her usual keen smile, and there she was, straining up her arm to be chosen as a library helper. Of course she hasn't heard, I thought, and scribbled a note : "You dope, you've volunteered to SORT BOOKS IN THE LIBRARY." She glanced at it and pushed it impatiently aside.

"Yes, all right. Lynda Page," said the mistress, writing her down.

"Now then, what are you accusing me of?" said Lynda, turning brightly to me.

"Never mind," I said dully.

"All right then I'll accuse you. Why didn't you volunteer?"

"Why didn't I volunteer?" I gasped.

"Yes, keep me company. Anyway, I think you ought to have. She obviously expected you to. Everyone else did."

"Yes, you always do what the school expects, don't you," I growled. "Well, I don't." But she didn't hear.

After the House meeting Miss Mackintosh said, "Now I want you all to stay behind for a few minutes. I have something to say to you, and it applies to every one of you. I know that a great many of you waste a lot of valuable time on boy-friends."

We fidgeted miserably on the floor. "It's going to be one of them," groaned Angela in my ear.

"And the rest of you waste your time worrying because you haven't got boy-friends. This is a very wrong attitude." She suddenly looked extra grim. Her spectacles had caught the light, and you couldn't see her eyes. "There is one girl here who has disgraced herself. She has broken down the foundation of her life that the school has spent five years in giving her. The rest of her life will be a wreck, as a result of her action. She had just achieved some really good results in her G.C.E. She could have gone to university, she could have had a really worth-while life. All this is lost."

She paused and stared hard at the back of the hall where the fifth form sat, and then said, "The girl is Janet Finley in Upper V B. She is pregnant, and she will not be continuing her studies at this school after today. I have talked to her and shown her how she has ruined her prospects. She was an intelligent girl and her G.C.E. results were really excellent. I hope that she sees now how everything is wasted."

The entire school was gazing at the back of the hall, following Miss Mackintosh's look. I stole a glance myself. It was obvious which one Janet Finley was. She was crouched down with her head in her hands, shaking with sobs.

Miss Mackintosh said, when the school had had a good stare, "I hope you all take this girl's lesson to heart." Then we had an anti-boy lecture for half an hour. Everyone went on looking at poor Janet Finley throughout. So, as a matter of fact, did Miss Mackintosh.

As we came out afterwards all the girls were talking angrily.

"Silly old fool, what does she know about it?" Angela said to me. "If she had any idea of what goes on, she wouldn't make such a fuss about just one girl."

"You mean everybody—" I said.

"Of course. Well, she's asking for it, isn't she. I mean to say, she goes on and on about boys. You heard. So of course we all have boy-friends. And what's wrong with that, anyway?"

"It takes up time you could be using to do more homework," I said, imitating Miss Mackintosh.

Angela giggled. "I'd like to say: Homework takes up time I could be spending with boys."

"Oh, it does, doesn't it!" Jennifer said fervently, joining us. "This place is an absolute nunnery."

"And how can that Mackintosh woman know anything about boys anyway?" Angela said. "She's never had a boy-friend."

"I know; the way she goes on you'd think boys were some sort of disease."

"I expect that's the idea of the homework, to stop us ever meeting a boy. I must say I don't know how you manage it at all," I said, thinking of the fifteen minutes I got to myself in the evening if I was lucky.

"I'll tell you how, but it means detention next day," giggled Jennifer.

"Oh, she makes me absolutely sick, and the whole of this stinking rotten nunnery too," said Angela, so violently that I was startled.

We stopped in the passage outside the cloakroom, underneath the stairs, and Angela began to run a comb ferociously through her hair. "I feel for that girl, Janet Finley, I tell you. And I bet every girl in the school feels the same."

Louise Carter joined us and said anxiously, "Do I look as if I had a cold?"

"Mmm. No, not really. Why?"

"I've forgotten my purple top-knickers and I'm going to get into such trouble for games when Miss Pratt sees I've only got these." She held up her skirt and showed us her frilly, shocking-pink briefs. "She'll probably confiscate them."

"She'll be shocked stiff. Perhaps you had better have a cold. You could forge a note," I suggested.

"Go out in them and let her jolly well be shocked," Angela said.

I glanced up and saw Miss Mackintosh leaning over the banisters above us. I nudged Angela violently. She looked up and saw her, and we ran up to the classroom. There she exploded again.

"The old so-and-so. Snooping about. Well, I jolly well hope she heard everything."

"She can't have. We were only under her a bit of the time," I pointed out regretfully. "Let's go back, and say it all again."

Margaret came over to me and said, "You know, she still hasn't sent for me about my exams, Antonia. I'm almost beginning to hope she won't.

"Well, I don't know," I said. "Oh, yes I do, though! I expect she just hasn't got you listed as an Oxford possible, and so she leaves you alone. I know she wants to get me into university, and perhaps that's why she keeps on at me."

"Well, I don't understand it. I never thought I'd get away with only passing in three subjects," Margaret said. "And you were top in four!"

25

I LASTED THROUGH THE first three weeks of term without being absent. But it was perfectly true what Pauline West had said. Homework was getting more and more all the time. We had four subjects now at weekends, and each one was always a special bumper pack, and between them all they ate up even Saturday. The weekday evenings were a lost cause, of course. Even my fifteen minutes had dwindled to five. It was odd how the mistresses could deal out what was obviously at least an hour's work for a half-hour prep without turning a hair. No apologies, no "and if you can't finish in the time . . ." The evening's work that Mummy had started by making such a fuss about had become a matter of course now. All the girls got through it somehow, but you could see them all getting thinner and more subdued every day.

Lynda was making up all the work she had missed during her illness as well. She admitted that she often worked till eleven. "Well, my parents don't mind. The work's got to be done, there's no other time, and they let me do it. So just you pipe down, Antonia."

Once when I admitted to her that I wasn't reading this year's book list either (which was identical with the other, except that the books were longer and prosier—I glanced at some of the ones Lynda was reading) she burst out :

"Honestly, Antonia, the way you keep on, shirking work— that's what you're doing, you know. Shirking work. You say you're a poet and shelter behind that. Yes, you do, you know. And when did you last write a poem, anyway?"

"Oh, Lynda !" I said. "I know I haven't written any poems for ages. Not since I've been at this school. It's because I'm so up to my eyes in school that I haven't time to think. Whose fault is that? I don't just turn out poems like a machine, you know. I'm always so tired—and I've got to think to write poems. I used to think for hours and hours and then I wrote poems. But now it's homework, homework, always behind in something, always something on my mind—"

"I'm ashamed of you, Antonia. You've got so lazy. You don't write poems, you don't work at school. If you've stopped being a poet and come down to earth *at last* you can start working. Maths, for instance, if you did a few hours' work on that a night you could come right up. Yes, you could, it's just good hard work you need, but you're so bone lazy you don't mind letting all your talent go to seed...."

I put my elbows on my desk and rested my head on my hands while she scolded me. She shouted so, now. I supposed it was because she was deaf. Of course, she was right. Miss Mildon was right. Miss Mackintosh was right. Well, let them all be right, I thought. I feel awful. I've got a sore throat. I'm so tired, I just don't care. If only it could be the weekend soon. But it was only Tuesday, and anyway even when the weekend did come it would be no better.

When I had finished my homework that night and came to say goodnight Mummy took my temperature, as I had dreaded she would. She kept me in bed all the rest of the week. I had a bad cold and it affected my glands. I went back on Monday but was ill again on Thursday, just one day before the double maths this time. My temperature was only just over a hundred, but my glands were swollen again, and I did feel dreadful. Mummy was right really, I supposed.

On Friday afternoon a letter arrived from Miss Mackintosh asking for a doctor's certificate. Daddy wrote back that I was never absent without his knowledge and consent, and that he never kept me at home unless I showed definite symptoms and had a temperature, when he felt it would be injurious to my health for me to go to school. If Miss Mackintosh was not satisfied, however, he would send her a certificate if I should be ill again.

I went back to school on Monday, in time for Miss Haversham's special lesson (that was on Monday this year). Before she arrived Miss Mackintosh came in. She came over to me and said, "Well, I'm glad to see you back, Antonia. I had your father's letter this morning."

"I'm better now, thank you," I said.

"Well, we must hope you won't be away so much in future," Miss Mackintosh said briskly. I gulped and finally managed to say, "Well, I hope not, Miss Mackintosh, but I can't help being ill." I sat and glowered at her while she scolded us for being noisy, thinking how like a frog she looked and how much I would enjoy to put my tongue out at her.

That evening I finished my homework at eight o'clock, and was just getting out my books to start copying up the science notes they had had while I was away when Mummy came in and said, "No more work now. You must go to bed."

"What, so soon?" I said in horror. "But I've only just started these notes."

"Well, I'm sorry," said Mummy. "You'll just have to leave them. Ever since we let you work until dinner and have your bath afterwards you've been getting to bed so late, it's no wonder at all you're ill all the time. Daddy and I have decided that you're not to work later than eight."

"Oh, no!" I wailed. "But other girls work till ten—they told me so. Not just Lynda. Rosemary and Jennifer Lucas and the other Jennifer, they all do—nine isn't late—"

"Oh, isn't it!" Mummy said. "Well, off you go to bed. I'm sorry about your homework, but they can't blame you for your mad parents. It's not your fault that your mother's the only one in the school with an ounce of common sense."

But at the next science lesson, when Miss Blandish said as usual, "And you've made up the work you missed all right, then, Antonia," and I was bound to admit I hadn't, she was very cross, and didn't seem to think Mummy's unreasonableness any excuse at all.

Then in maths we began algebra. Miss Mildon said, "Now we come on to the easiest part of mathematics of all," and began to explain the fundamental principles. It made no sense at all. It was far, far worse than problems had ever been. It was sheer gibberish. As she plunged on through a crazy upside-down morass of x's and z's, with here and there little numbers like gargoyles making faces up in the air, I felt simply terrified. Nothing that Sir had ever taught me, none of those magic spells, worked here. You popped in pluses and minuses just where you felt like it and they meant nothing, or you fiddled things about without rhyme or reason just to make something equal what it didn't really equal. There were malevolent little numbers that suddenly made everything less than nothing, and then you were multiplying less than nothing by less than nothing for ages, and

will-o'-the-wisps kept appearing in the sky and making everything to the power of themselves. Then Miss Mildon would say,
"So?" (muttering the Lord's Prayer backwards no doubt) and
the others would all shout enthusiastically "Three!" or "Seven!"
or whatever black number they felt inspired to say, and that
would be the answer to that paticular sum.

At the end of the lesson Miss Mildon set us ten questions
from the text-book. "They're exactly like the ones we've just
done. A minute each, they'll take you. This is a cushy homework."

I spent an hour and a half that evening frantically reading
and re-reading the examples I had copied from the board, trying
to find out how you began, even. Finally I decided you performed a miracle, and swopped over what was really there to
what you wanted it to be. I gave up the first question and tried
the second, mixed the numbers about and got stuck again, went
on to the third, and so on. At the end of two hours I had done
all ten and hadn't begun any of them. That was at seven o'clock.
I was about to try again when I remembered this awful eight
o'clock time limit, and that I had several hours' worth of French
and geography still to do. So I gave up the maths altogether,
though I did put a little note for Miss Mildon : "Please could
you explain again some time, as I don't understand anything
at all."

Inevitably, I got detention, and though Miss Mildon did
explain I still didn't understand. The rest of the class were romp-
ing ahead, and were doing things with all sorts of weird brackets
and other assorted instruments of torture. I didn't get home till
half-past six and only had time to skimp the three essays I had
that night. For once I took the time marked on the time-table.

I was really hopelessly lost in maths, but somehow I seemed
to be dropping behind in most of the other subjects too. I got
very low marks and made stupid mistakes and kept on skimping
my homework. I simply couldn't do it properly in just a couple
of hours or so; not all three subjects, anyway.

One weekend I left my satchel full of homework at our country
cottage. I didn't notice until I was getting ready for school the
next morning, and there was nothing I could do. All the four
teachers whose homework I had left behind thought I had done
it on purpose, and I got detention from all of them (except Mrs.
Day, who was too nice) bang bang bang, three nights in succes-

sion. I got desperately behind in all my homework, being late home three nights in one week. I could have managed except that Mummy made me go to bed so early.

On the Thursday of that week Miss Mackintosh sent for me, about my homework and about the algebra. I tried to explain that there was always more homework than I could manage in one evening, and told her about the eight o'clock time limit, but I couldn't somehow get through to her. On my way out I noticed I was wearing one long grey sock and one short white.

On Friday I was ill with yet another bad cold, sore throat and gland trouble. Our letter with the doctor's certificate crossed with one from the school demanding it. On Monday another letter came from Miss Mackintosh : she wanted me to be examined by the school doctor. That was fixed for Wednesday, when my own doctor said I would be fit to get up.

On Wednesday morning our third letter in succession from Miss Mackintosh arrived. It was more or less what she had said to me about my homework. She did not feel I was putting my full energy into it, and she could only remind us what a very important part of the school syllabus homework was, and how wrong it was for us to regard it as something that need not be taken too seriously and if convenient could be cut or neglected. She disapproved most strongly of my own lazy attitude, and asked Daddy to see that in future I spent all the time necessary on my homework, especially on my maths. It was perfectly obvious that I had made up my mind not to try at algebra, and she urged him to make me finish every exercise in this that was set for homework, as it was very important that I should excel at maths.

Daddy read out the letter at breakfast. He drafted his answer as he ate : "I regret that I cannot allow minor school rules to endanger Antonia's health, however inflexibly they may be enforced. I cannot permit her to work later than eight o'clock at her homework, whatever it may be." He enclosed my homework poem that I had written a year ago when I first became a Scholar of St. Rhadigond's and had first begun on my nightly three-hour orgies.

The school doctor said exactly the same as our own : that I showed signs of gland trouble, that I must on no account overwork, attend school when I was ill, or sit up late. She added sympathetically, "Well, don't you worry. You mustn't try to be top in everything. Just sit back and be a cabbage. Don't let it upset you."

It did upset me, though. All this fighting and struggling, fighting and struggling. I thought it was about time Miss Mackintosh paid some attention to some of the other hundred girls in Baxter. Was it possible that she really spent her entire time trying to knock the corners off me, trying to reduce me to the dreary, worn-down, good-all-rounder who was the Type Baxter Turns Out, wretched girls like Lynda and Pauline West? I decided it was not only possible, but fact.

When I came next to school and walked in through the front door there was that great stained glass window in front of me, with that founder woman and her dreary great book. I remembered what she had said about the school remaining a holy and godly institution for maidens with willing hands and meek souls. You bet, I thought sullenly. Just at that particular moment I should very much have liked to throw a stone through that grim founder, with her grim motto. I understood now why that girl in the poem had tried to murder a mistress.

Our first lesson was maths. As Miss Mildon went through a new version of her black mass, with some girls looking keen and shooting their hands up continually and the rest just sitting and looking miserable like me, I suddenly had a fit of nostalgia for Sir. He would have had us out in front of the class pretending to be x and y and z, and then you could have seen exactly what conjuring tricks they were up to. Or he'd have made you understand somehow, not just by nagging and punishing you like Miss Mildon and Miss Mackintosh. He never used to let anyone sit and look miserable without understanding, except perhaps Roberts. I nearly laughed out loud at the memory of Roberts, and realized that suddenly, astonishingly, I was having a fit of nostalgia for him too, and for Skinner and O'Brien and the fighting in the playground and silly harmless Miss Lovely and that row of green doors in the lavatory and everything to do with that jolly school.

At lunchtime I stopped half way down the stairs and looked out of the window on the landing. From that height you could see out over the high wall round the playground, and you could see the street outside. Across the road was a little street turning off, and the window looked right into it. I didn't know what it was called or anything about it. It was solid with fruit and vegetable stalls lining the kerb, with happy men serving who never stopped grinning. All the little shops were bright and gay, with awnings out and notices saying "Bargains" in the windows, and the whole street was crammed with people wearing jolly clothes, stopping to look at something they fancied in a shop window just exactly as they felt inclined, with nobody telling them to stop that and do something dreary. It was really a sweet little street. I stared hungrily at it through my barred window. Suddenly I thought, it's the Promised Land I used to send flying horses to from Felias. The Promised Land. And here was I shut up in my prison. I was used to hearing girls calling the school a prison, but I hadn't really seen what they meant till now.

26

Suddenly summer had arrived, down in the country at Tedford. Now in May the weather turned fine, the oaks came out at last, candles blossomed on the great chestnut, and the ashes turned thick, thick green. Daddy went round quoting bits of Falstaff and banging his fist down and saying, "Ha! 'twas a merry jape!" Then we would go out and he would quaff tankards of ale at all the village pubs round about, and drive through "green tunnels," narrow sunken lanes with the trees meeting overhead.

At one village, as I sat in the sun outside the pub (I was still a few months off being fourteen), Daddy came out with a huge toby-jug. "Hold this," he said, "have it and love it," and went inside again. It was the jolliest toby-jug I had ever seen. It was fairly splitting its sides with laughter. My hands wouldn't meet round it.

As I was admiring it Daddy came out again with three more, just as big and happy. "Take these," he said, "have them and love them." I stood them in a row on the bench beside me, wondering mildly how Daddy had conjured them up. I filled them with clover and dandelions, muttering "Ha! 'twas a merry jape."

When Mummy and Daddy finally came out they brought two more toby-jugs with them. We each hugged two and carried them all the way down the hill to where we had left Paydirt, the bubble car, and then I had to look after all six on the back seat.

"Daddy saw them behind the bar and loved them," Mummy explained. "He said so to the man, and he said he'd been meaning to sell them for months but hadn't got round to it. So Daddy bought them."

"Oh Man, they're wonderful," I said. "I don't suppose they ever stop eating whole capons."

"Oh Man!" said Daddy. "Do you suppose that if I ate enough whole capons too I could look like that?"

"Perhaps you could," I said.

"Oh, no, Man!" Mummy said in horror. "You don't want to be fat and ugly like them."

"But they're beautiful!" said Daddy and I together.

"All right, all right," Mummy said hastily.

"As a matter of fact," I said, "figure apart, you look just like them anyway, Daddy. The expression, I mean." I could see his face in the driving mirror. It was the proper shade of brown. His eyes were all creased up as he laughed, and he had a real Toby grin. Yes, he looked just right.

We stood them all over the kitchen table. Mummy looked harassed when she saw them there, but she didn't say anything and soon got used to them.

Meanwhile the term went on. Every Sunday, as Daddy got ready to leave Tedford and drive back to town for my week, he said, "Oh Child, why do you have to do this thing to me?" And I would say, "Perhaps we needn't go back." But Mummy always brushed that aside and went on steadily: "Now, you've got your satchel? Your hat? Your blazer? Your pen? All your homework?"

The wearisome school drudgery was exactly the same as it had ever been. It was all very well for the doctor to say, "Don't overwork. Be a cabbage." It simply wasn't practicable. Every homework was vital and urgent and took hours. Daddy was always very annoyed at my working all Saturday when he wanted to take me out, and put all the blame on me, but I couldn't help it.

In the middle of May I caught flu, and was away for a whole week. When I came back, somehow the work seemed to have doubled. There were pages and pages of notes to make up, that I had missed. They must have done several terms' work in that week. I had missed Miss Haversham's test and she made me do it in detention (not as a punishment) and she also made me learn all her last week's homework, pages of a Victorian religious poem. It was the first time I had ever had to do homework I had missed, too, essays and so on. I was a bit surprised, though I dutifully did it all. Then my flu came back, complete with gland trouble and everything I had hoped had been cured by the Easter holidays. When I came back I was piled up with more work, and after a few days I promptly went down again. I went on like that for weeks. I was absent more than I was at school. Finally Daddy got fed up and went to see Miss Mackintosh. He put on a bow tie and looked so smart and terrifying that he quite scared even Mummy and me. I thought Miss Mackintosh would just crumple up when she saw him, let alone when he began to speak "words of exquisitely poised irony," as Daddy said he was going to.

When he came back I ran downstairs to him. "Hullo, Man! Did you cow her into utter submission?"

"No, I'm bound to say I didn't. On the contrary, she said quite baldly that she had no intention of letting you slack on any grounds, and she stuck to that. In fact, see here, Antoniella-Mariella, I won't have you going to that school any more."

"What!" gasped Mummy.

"Oh!" I said.

"She's obstinate and conceited. I'm not going to have my Totty bullied by a woman like that any longer."

"Gosh! I didn't think she was as bad as that," said Mummy goggling. "But where else is Antonia to go?"

"Well, there's a very good grammar-school, I've heard, at Bennington, with a bus from door to door. Only about a half-hour's ride."

"But—" Mummy pulled herself together and said, "Oh, very well, Man."

"I've wanted to do this for ages, go and live at Tedford, I mean," said Daddy, cheering up a bit. "I only kept back because of this boring school. But now I think Antonia would do well to get right out of the place, so there's nothing to stop us going."

"Oh, lovely! Oh, wonderful!" I said.

"Have you got anything at school?" Daddy asked me.

"Only my clothes, I think."

"All right, you can go tomorrow and finish off, and then we'll go down straight away and look for fish in the river and listen to cuckoos." He looked as happy and excited as he had been when he was planning the Damuels holiday. "Can you be ready by tomorrow evening to move down permanently to the country, Man?"

Mummy blinked and rubbed her forehead and said, "Yes, I

214

suppose so, if you want." I knew she was thinking about the goldfish.

"You would like to do this thing, wouldn't you?" he asked anxiously.

"Oh, yes, I would!" I said fervently.

"I only want to please, myself as well as others," he said, looking appealingly at Mummy.

She laughed. "Why, of course, it'll be simply heavenly. I love Tedford. And I think Antonia will be happier too at a less strenuous school."

Daddy looked happy again. "Oh good. She can start at it on Monday then, if we arrive on Thursday night."

"But Man, we haven't got her uniform or seen the headmaster or—or anything," said Mummy, looking harassed.

"That doesn't matter," Daddy said. He rolled over on his tummy on the sofa and looked up at us over a cushion. I could tell he was laughing because his eyes were all creased up. "We can do all that sort of stuff on Saturday."

"Oh! I've just thought," I said, bouncing on the sofa, "if I leave tomorrow I'll miss Friday and the double maths."

I hardly slept at all that night. Although it seemed obvious now, I had never dreamt of leaving St. Rhadigond's before. I had vaguely pictured myself battling on there till I left, aged about twenty. All the other girls did this, though in fact I probably wouldn't have because I had definitely decided to go to art school afterwards. But that was a long, long way off, three years at least. To leave now—just like that—finis! I could hardly believe it, even now.

When I said goodbye to the girls at school they were surprised, too. As usual there were about eight away. And then there were nine, I thought jubilantly as I broke my news.

"You're not really going? Oh, Antonia! Who'll write our form play for us now?"

I said to Lynda, "Well, goodbye."

"But you can't go now, in the middle of the term."

"Well, I will be going to school down there," I said, trying to laugh, although I knew really that she wasn't joking.

"I think it's mean of your father. Making you spoil your whole school career like that. Why don't you just say you don't want to leave?"

"I do want to, though," I said, but she didn't hear.

I hesitated, watching her busily packing up her satchel, and then said, "Will you make me a picture sequence, Lynda, as a memento?" But she didn't hear that either. It was no use anyway. It was over a year since she had last made a picture sequence.

PART THREE

27

We went to see the headmaster of Bennington Grammar
School as soon as we were installed in Tedford. Mummy had
been right about him being a headmaster. It was a mixed school.
I told him that would be a nice change. He laughed. I thought
he was a jolly man.

He fired questions at me about my work, but I was able to
answer them all and he seemed pleased. He didn't ask me my
age, only what form I would have been in next year at St.
Rhadigond's. I said Upper Four, and he said, "Right, I'll put
you into the fourth form here then next year, and for the rest
of this term you'd better go in the Third." I didn't understand
what he meant at the time.

He put me in the B stream, the stupid stream. "I do automatically with newcomers, just temporarily," he said apologetically.

He said there was still some paperwork to be done, especially
as I was transferring counties as well as schools, but that I
might as well come to the school while all that went forward. It
was settled that I should start on Monday.

On Monday morning, just before I left, a letter arrived from
Miss Mackintosh, answering Daddy's telling her I was leaving.
She could not give me permission to absent myself for the rest of
the term, and had reported me to the headmistress who would
no doubt place the affair in the hands of the Governors.

"Oh, how terrifying," I said. "She's quite right. I missed
Friday between schools. The Governors will be very angry."
Then I left to catch my bus.

It was wonderful. The bus stop was a couple of hundred
yards away, as compared with that twenty minutes' walk I
had had before. And none of those hideous streets of villas
either. I hadn't realized how I hated them. Here there were
just a row of sweet little cottages on the other side of the road,

and those great ash trees to walk under. It felt very peculiar to be walking under them wearing my St. Rhadigond's uniform, and with my satchel bumping on my back.

The bus came just when it said it would, and there wasn't any queueing or anything. It was lovely.

Inside the school the girls of my form, the third, took me in charge and led me to the form-room. It was small and snug and sweet, and on the first floor, again a wonderful contrast to St. Rhadigond's, which had lately come to seem like a skyscraper. We sat round on the desks talking. To my intense surprise there were no boys. Perhaps this is really the girls' lavatory, I thought, laughing to myself as I remembered my first day at primary school.

"What do you think of Bennington? Doesn't it seem dull after a big town?" one girl asked me.

"Well, I didn't find the town wildly exciting," I answered. "Anyway not the bit between home and school. Besides, Bennington isn't exactly new. We've been weekending at Tedford for years."

"Have you?" another girl said. "Isn't there anything new we can tell you about then?"

"Yes, the school, I don't know anything about that."

"Well, nor do we, really. It's just sort of school."

We grinned at each other. No school-worship here, I realized delightedly.

"It seems enormous, anyway," I said.

"But it's weeny! It's a sweet little school, actually." You'd never hear anyone saying that at St. Rhadigond's.

"Wasn't your last school big?"

"Yes, I still don't know my way round it, but it doesn't seem any bigger than this."

"You wait till you've been here a week. It's always like that when you're new," another girl said kindly. I thought I had never met such nice girls. Where were the boys, though? I was waiting apprehensively to see them again.

Another girl came in, dangling a magazine and swinging her hips. "Oh, hullo," she said gaily. "Are you the new girl? They were saying you'd come, in the cloakroom. I was new last term, too. Don't you think big towns are gorgeous?"

"No, as a matter of fact, I don't," I laughed.

"Better than this place, anyway. One coffee bar and the Girl

Guides. Give me Liverpool any day." She perched on a desk and swung her legs. She didn't look very miserable.

"There's one thing I don't understand," I said. "That's why this is called the third form."

"Well," said the kindly girl, "form one, first year; form two, second year; form three, third year."

"Third year?" I gasped. "But I've just come out of the second year at my last school."

"Gosh! How old are you then?"

"Thirteen and ten months."

"Why, that's only a month younger than me," a girl said. "You must have been the oldest in the class, before."

"Well, now I'll be the youngest."

"Will you be leaving us then?" another girl said, sounding genuinely heartbroken.

"Oh, easily not," I said. "You can't ever tell with my parents."

I asked their names. They were called things like Poppy and Apple and Chicken and Turnip. The girl from Liverpool was called Peacock. There was also a section called Bobbles and Tiddles and Baggles and things like that.

Suddenly a bell went, and the boys poured in. Except for their neat blazers, and the long trousers that almost all were wearing, they looked exactly the same as ever. They tore in, yelling and fighting even in the doorway, and proceeded to knock over the desks and smash each other's rulers, just as always. They turned left at the door and kept all their activities strictly to that half of the room. They came nowhere near the girls' half, to my surprise and relief. The other girls didn't seem even to have noticed them. Peacock and Frankie drifted off and were chatting together. Frankie, I noticed, had the same half-selfconscious expression as Peacock, and the same swing of the hips.

"Flirts, both of them," Baggles proclaimed loud enough for them to hear, with a twinkle in her eye. "Don't you have anything to do with them, Antonia. Bad lots, they are. They'll cor-rupt your inn-o-cence."

"Oh, you!" Frankie giggled, pretending to throw a book at Baggles. I couldn't help wondering somehow who they flirted with. Obviously with none of these boys, who might still have been nine or ten, judging by their appearance and behaviour.

Our form master—yes, a master, quite like old times for me

—came in. He looked young and shy, not at all what I had expected.

"Oh, that's Mr. Murphy," Baggles said to me in what just passed as a low voice but which Mr. Murphy could hear perfectly. "He's a darling, but he can't do anything with us and we all tease him like anything."

"Rosemary!" Mr. Murphy said reproachfully.

"Oh, sorry, sir," said Baggles. "I was just telling Antonia—she's new and doesn't know what to do."

"Now just keep quiet, will you," he begged. Baggles said very sorry, yes of course, sir, but within a minute she was at it again nineteen to the dozen with Turnip.

Mr. Murphy called me out and took down my name and address. Then he said, "You'll be having me for physics."

"Oh, no!" I groaned. Physics was as bad as maths ever since my first term. In fact, it *was* all maths.

He looked startled. "Why, don't you like physics or something?"

This was most uncomfortable. I didn't know what to say. Luckily Baggles said for me, "Of course she will, sir. Everyone likes your physics." The other girls cheered and the boys guffawed.

The poor man blushed scarlet and sent me back to my seat. I decided to say nothing about being in the wrong class till I'd seen Daddy.

"He's Irish," Baggles told me.

"I can hear that!" I said. He looked imploringly at us, blushing and sweating. I felt sorry for him. After all, his accent was really no stronger than the others' Midland ones.

The prayer bell went. We trooped across the passage into a big classroom, tripping over satchels and edging our way between chairs and desks. It was a wonderful change from the awe-inspiring great hall at St. Rhadigond's. Here too the boys went into a completely separate part of the room. So far I hadn't seen a boy speak to a girl, or in fact appear to be aware of the existence of girls at all. Perhaps they had changed, after all. At the primary school there had been no barriers. The boys treated the girls just like other boys (except when they were bullying them, of course).

I felt conspicuous in my purple among all the navy blue. It was obvious I was new. People turned and smiled at me, offering to share their hymn-books with me, or showing me the place when they saw I'd got one. Again I thought I'd never met such nice girls.

Prayers were short and sweet too; they lasted ten minutes instead of forty. There was none of the undignified scrambling I was used to either, up, down, up, down. When in French afterwards the girls asked me if I was liking the school any better yet, I said I certainly was, I liked it far better than my last school. "This is so sort of free-and-easy," I said. "There, it was so solid with red tape ... Anyway, it was a grim place, the girls called it a nunnery."

"Well, I wouldn't like that," Peacock admitted, grinning. "I knew a girl who went to a school she called a nunnery, d'you know, the girls weren't allowed to have boy-friends? If they were seen with a boy they were blown up."

"Oh, I forgot to tell you," Frankie said, leaning backwards on to Peacock's desk. "I saw Ken Saturday, it was ever so funny, I was wearing my new shoes with heels—you know. Well, we were walking down from the coffee bar ..."

I flicked over the pages of the text book the mistress had given me and swung back on my chair to ask the girl behind me, Apple, what we were meant to be doing. She opened my book at the place for me and showed me. I thanked her, and started the exercise.

The mistress, who looked withered and ancient but seemed kind, said, "I see they've got you into bad habits already, Antonia." She was laughing.

"No, we haven't!" Baggles said indignantly. "Look at her sitting there all good."

"Wait till you've finished with her," the mistress said.

"J'ay bow coo de fam," Baggles pronounced triumphantly, writing away. "There! I've finished."

"You aren't the first, Rosemary," the mistress pointed out. "Has anyone ever tried gagging you?"

"Oh yes! Never stop!" Apple said. "But it doesn't work."

Frankie was going steadily on :

"I don't know what I can wear. The yellow skirt, but then the pink petticoat looks awful if it shows and the blue doesn't flounce any more. What're you going to wear, Peac?"

All the same, she seemed to have finished too.

I scribbled my last answer. The questions were hard, but I

just managed. I was pleased by that, remembering that I had skipped a year. But then French had been my good subject.

In break I joined on to Apple and Bobbles and tagged on behind them. They strolled into what appeared at first to be a series of great lawns, surrounded by trees. Then I noticed tennis nets, and realized they were just super-beautiful tennis courts, but to myself I still thought of them as "lawns."

We walked round them. The trees really were lovely. It was still fine; the weather had held since May. One of the tennis courts, at the far end, didn't look as if it had been mown for a long time. The grass was thick and luxuriant. "The Verdant Pasture," I thought of it to myself.

"The gardener doesn't often get up here. It's too far away," Bobbles told me.

"Have you had your exams?" I asked. They were about to start them at St. Rhadigond's.

"Yes, we have, you lucky beggar," Apple said. "We always have them at the end of June."

"Ooh!" I said, delighted. "Who was top?"

"Baggles, of course. She always is. She's awfully clever. That's why the teachers put up with her. She was top in all their subjects."

I thought sadly of Lynda. So it was possible to be top without being dull.

The other lessons we had that day didn't seem too hard. In geography we started on a new country, and I was no worse off than the others. In games I just ran about and made a fool of myself. It was rounders, which I'd never played before, and I didn't know the rules or anything. But I didn't care. It was all so beautiful, with the sun and the trees, and the glorious view, and the other girls were all so friendly. Turnip said to me at one moment when the ball was comfortably out of sight, "You don't seem to mind being new very much."

"Not here, I don't," I said. "I don't feel new."

I didn't feel too wretched even in maths. It was so far beyond me that it was simply a joke. They were doing some mad kind of geometry all tangled up with some mad kind of algebra. When it came to physics, Mr. Murphy did try to explain, but he looked more and more miserable, and tore his hair and groaned, until I had pity on him and said I understood, though in fact I didn't. He had gone over it again and again, giving me a brief course in the whole subject while he was about it, but I still didn't see how, where and why linear coefficients expanded. Although he explained very carefully in words of one syllable and although I listened hard I couldn't discern any rhyme or reason in it anywhere. In the end he told me to "use logs," whatever that meant, and left me.

I looked round, and saw everyone talking hard. Two boys were fighting. Mr. Murphy stood in front of the class and looked flustered. He said weakly, "Now just get on with a bit of honest work, will you?" But everyone just shouted back, "Oh, we are, sir," and went on as before.

Baggles was saying to Tiddles, "Well, what about that girl of twelve in the paper, who was going to have a baby, but she didn't know which of the five boys was the father?"

"Rosemary!" said Mr. Murphy, blushing all over his face.

"Sorry, sir," Baggles said cheerfully, "I was just telling Janet about this diagram, because she doesn't understand it."

"Yes, we all heard that," Mr. Murphy said.

"Oh, he's too innocent. He doesn't know what she's talking about," said one of the boys.

"Shut up, you're making him blush," Chicken yelled.

Mr. Murphy blushed more than ever and said, "Just keep quiet, the lot of you. I don't mind people who are stupid and keep quiet, but when they're stupid and noisy it's too much. You're stupid and noisy."

"Which are you, sir?" another boy called.

"Steve's going to sell his motor-bike," said Peacock to Frankie. "I don't suppose he will really, though. I don't think he could live without it. He says a smash once a week is as good as going to the pictures. Coo, look at Antonia! She looks quite shocked. Don't worry," she said to me, grinning, "he doesn't really. I wish he did."

When the bell at the end of the afternoon went, they all seemed to have done plenty of work, however. Baggles announced to no one in particular that she had finished number three. Mr. Murphy looked quite pleased when he heard. Everyone else started saying that they'd done number three, too. Peacock admitted shamefacedly that she'd only done two. A boy shouted out that he'd done all four. I was deeply impressed. When they asked me how far I'd got, I was forced to admit I'd only got as far as copying the first one.

I ran up into the town to the children's clothes shop. Mummy was there, waiting for me.

"Hullo," she said. "You look happy."

"I am," I said. "It's the nicest school I could ever have dreamed up. It's all so jolly, and the girls are so nice..."

I talked hard while the assistant came and put things on me. We just had time to buy the school summer dress before our bus went back to Tedford. Mummy obviously wasn't listening, as she tried to decide whether it was too short or too long or too tight or too big, but I hoped she might be taking it in subconsciously and went on telling her about Baggles and Peacock and all the teachers.

The next day we got the school hat. I thought I looked really striking in my blue dress, purple blazer and navy-blue hat, with the gold St. Rhadigond's hive on the blazer and "B.G.S." in white on my hatband. People winced visibly when they saw me in the street. I grinned at them. It was all such fun. I was almost sorry when Mummy bought me the proper blazer.

The wonderful thing was the homework. Even for me, a year behind, it only took the regulation hour and a half. French did take a bit longer, of course, but I was catching up quite quickly now. The stuff in English was new too, but it didn't seem particularly hard once I had got the hang of it. Maths was hopeless, but I muddled about for half-an-hour and always managed to serve up something, even if it was only the questions written backwards. Nobody seemed to care too much.

When I told Daddy I was in the year ahead he just shrugged and said, "I want my Totty to have everything she wants."

Mummy looked delighted, and said, "Oh, what a bit of luck. You mean to say you've managed to miss a whole year's school? Well, for goodness' sake don't tell anyone, or they might put you back."

So I said nothing and next term went up with the others into the fourth form, still a year ahead.

28

As we came out of the changing-rooms Baggles said, "Did you see Peacock's love-bites?"

"Yes! Hasn't she got a lot?" Chicken said. "All round her neck, whopping great ones."

"It's that boy, Steve, she goes with," Baggles told us. "Every Friday he gives them to her, and by next Friday they've faded, so he gives them to her again."

"She'll end up with a tattoo, if she's not careful," I said.

"Yes, you've got a point there, Birdie," Chicken answered. "She will. Anyway, I think it's revolting. I wouldn't go out with that boy if I were paid."

"No, he's filthy, isn't he?" Baggles said vehemently. "Just the sort Peacock would go with, though. Honestly, I think the way she carries on is disgusting."

I went down to the lawns to look for Fishscale and her friend Slinky. I had joined up with them because they seemed so jolly, and such a wonderful change from Lynda. I caught up with them wandering past the nearest tennis-court with their arms round each other. Slinky was whispering something in Fishscale's ear. She was chuckling and giggling into her handkerchief, when she saw me.

"Go away, Birdie! This isn't suitable for your ears."

"Oh, shut up, Fishscale," Slinky said. "Poor old Birdie, no one ever tells you anything, do they. Come here and listen to this one :

> 'Shakespeare was a man of wit
> And on his shirt he had some shit—' "

I pushed her away and said to Fishscale, "I just wanted to ask you about that book you were reading last week, that you said I could have after you. Have you finished with it?"

"I don't know. I've forgotten. Do you mean *Lady Chatterley's Lover*?" She tittered.

"*Lord of the Flies,*" I said wearily. "Was it out of the library? Oh, look, you must remember."

"I don't." As I turned away hopelessly she said, "Aren't we terrible? Look, Slinky, doesn't she look disgusted. Have we shocked you, Birdie?"

"Oh, no end," I called back. "I'm going away to be sick."

I walked all round the lawns to give them time to change the subject, before I went back. I examined all the trees to see if they had begun to turn yet. The chestnut had flickers of yellow all over it, but the other trees were still green. I looked across the fields at the wooded hill, but there were only a few patches of yellow there too. Probably more chestnuts, I thought.

Fishscale and Slinky had lain down on their raincoats and were cuddled up together. As I walked past I heard Fishscale say, "I wish you were somebody else."

"Mmm, so do I," Slinky sighed, snuggling up closer. "I'm imagining you are. Rock Hudson, now."

I went quickly past them. They both had their eyes shut and didn't see me. I broke into a run, and ran as fast as I could across the lawns to the Verdant Pasture. There I threw myself down in the long lush grass and rolled over and over in it. The tennis courts were in full view of the school, and for all I knew all the prefects and the entire staff were watching. I squirmed on my tummy, and tore up a mouthful of grass with my teeth. It was sopping wet. I turned over and lay looking up into the clouds. They were dark and wild. Just above me was a great bright hole in them, and I stared through it into a dazzling spiral of cloud. The rest of the sky was deep grey. I hoped it would rain hard.

The lesson bell went, and I got up and walked slowly back towards school. The girls all shouted at me as I came into the classroom, and rushed up to rub me with handkerchiefs.

"Oh, Birdie, you are hopeless. You're wet right through your blazer. What on earth have you been doing—having a bath?"

I was a bit wet, I supposed. I didn't think it mattered that much. I remembered something I had made a mental note to find out more about, and said to Peacock,

"Tell me about Steve."

She looked surprised. "What d'you want to know about him for?"

"I'm just interested. I've never met any boys—not proper

boys, I mean. Only primary school boys and this lot." I waved contemptuously at the boys' side of the room.

"Oh, them!" said Peacock, equally contemptuously. "You don't want to go by them."

"No. Tell me about Steve."

"Well, he's the biggest layabout in town. He's unemployed. He's been through about eight jobs since he started taking me out, but he won't go to work and misses whenever he gets the chance, so he just keeps being sacked."

"Oh," I said, feeling that there certainly was an awful lot I didn't know about. "Go on."

"Well, he swears like a trooper . . . drinks and smokes and all the rest of it. He did have a motor-bike but he couldn't keep up the payments and they took it back, what was left of it. He lives in blue jeans and a shiny jacket. He's got beetle-crushers, or brothel-creepers, if that means anything to you. Oh! I know. He's got a hobby. He's mad keen on barns."

"Barns?"

"Oh, give up, Birdie," Frankie giggled. "You're too innocent."

"No, no, I know what you mean," I said hastily. "I just didn't click for a minute because I've usually heard it as 'haystacks.' Go on, I'm just beginning to get a picture of this boy. He sounds a character."

"He's that, all right," Peacock said, lying back on the desk and stretching out her arms. "He's the filthiest, lousiest, laziest tough in Bennington."

"Oh, I see," I said, reeling.

"And all the girls are scared stiff of him, but they go with him just the same."

"Ah," I said, nodding wisely. "Thank you very much."

I stared out of the window on the other side of the classroom, feeling that I certainly was leading a Sheltered Life, capital S, capital L. I didn't even know what brothel-creepers were. The window was a small high one. I could just see a strip of slate-grey cloud, almost black in paces, with the top of a great yew tree swinging and swaying against it. I snatched open my rubbish book and scrawled across two pages "WOW! YIPPEE!" and scribbled across it a huge criss-cross pattern. Then I suddenly cooled off, and spent the physics lesson drawing a complicated little design in the corner. It was only doodle really, but it seemed beautiful to me and I worked away at it in between the examples I was copying from the blackboard. I got all Mr. Murphy's fascinating diagrams down, and most of the dull writing, and finished my design.

There was a fuse that night in our cottage, and we ate romantically by candlelight, and went round making weird shadows on the wall with our hands. When I went upstairs to bed with my candle I suddenly got hypnotized by it, and sat on the bed for hours watching the still flame and the luminous wax. Next day I took some old Christmas tree candles to school, so as to continue my study between lessons.

They didn't look quite so good by daylight, and there were draughts and the flame kept flickering. People came up to me every now and then and said, "Really, Birdie, you're madder than all of us put together." After a while I stopped trying to explain how beautiful it was and just answered, "Ah, well, simple pleasures for simple souls, you know." Then they always just shook their heads and smiled indulgently and left me to it.

The boys were hopeless. They never tired of shouting at me and cracking jokes and throwing things at my poor candle. They really did seem to be mentally about ten years old. One or two of the girls took them on and shouted rude things back, but the boys had staying-power, and were capable of going on long after the girls were ready to scream from boredom.

In the lunch hour I went to the library. As I was searching through the fiction bookcase I heard a silly titter. Two boys were standing in front of a picture pointing and sniggering at it. It was a picture I particularly loathed, painted in white on black to look extra gruesome, of a group of refugees dying from starvation. Their clothes were worn right down to an occasional rag here and there, and you saw every bone in their bodies sticking out. One of the boys was pencilling on the glass round the outlines of the mother refugee.

"Oh, naughty, naughty!" the other boy was giggling. "Look, you can see everything. Just shows what sort of a mind the headmaster's got."

What with them, and Peacock's Steve, I was beginning to wonder what girls were supposed to see in the other sex. Still, they did liven things up a bit, with their continual shouting and fighting and guffawing.

On the bus home I suddenly had a happy thought, and lit my candle again. A boy leant over the back of the seat, and blew it out, amid much noise and laughter. I lit it again, and he blew it out again.

"Vandal!" I shouted, trying to shelter it with my hat.

"Look at Birdie, she's trying to burn her hat," remarked Poppy. I grinned across at her.

"I can't quite make it catch," I said. "Here, you have a go."

By an unwritten law, the top of that particular bus was reserved for schoolchildren who lived on the road to Tedford and beyond. Nobody but schoolchildren ever dreamt of going up there, anyway. The noise was deafening. Ross and his lot passed the time singing in chorus at the top of their voices, and Hardy rolled all over the seats doubled up with laughter, while the rest of the boys just scrambled and yelled generally. On the other side of the bus, the girls spent the entire journey bounding around trying to decide who to sit next to, bawling jokes at each other, or doing each other's homework. Poor Apple, who had to get off early because she only lived just outside Bennington, always had to do feats of gymnastics to get to the stairs.

That bus ride was always the jolliest part of the whole day. It was such a mad, good-natured riot. I remembered the dismal journeys on the bus with Pauline West and girls like her, and thought it said much for this school that we all had so much spirit. I felt so well and happy lately, I could rattle through my homework in a sensible time. It didn't seem so difficult now. I had even, to my great surprise, written a poem one evening, which Daddy said was my best ever. Mummy didn't like it much, which I couldn't understand, because there weren't any horrors in it. It was called

The Valley of the Shadow

"It's those tall chimneys that are the trouble.
So much smoke, everything's grey, even the sun,
The whole place is thick with it, it's dark all the time.

In the blackness the light stabs and sears, the flashes
Burn, the fire falls stinging through the murk...

It's that bright, when you come in, it hurts your eyes
You're dazzled, want to hide, go back outside.
Even when there's no smoke, it's just as grey

It's like that anyway, 'tisn't just the chimneys
The air's so thick, it's twilight all day long
Lightning can kill you, it's dangerous, you know.

Haven't you heard? That riot in Trafalgar Square
Some fanatic was killed—a carpenter
The people did it—just the other day
I'd have thought you'd know, it was in all the papers
... And who are you anyway, if you don't mind my asking?

Don't be frightened, that's what the doctor said,
One little prick, there's nothing to be scared of.
Just keep still and let me do it, he said,
But it's no use, I can't take the needle.

Still the grey blackness falls, silting in the gutters,
Settling heavily past the chimneys into the streets
That stagnate obstinate under a dim sky."

Mummy just said that she didn't see why I had had to write a poem about factory fog when we had just moved out to the country. I tried to explain that it wasn't really about smoke, but she didn't seem to understand. She also wanted me to take out the bit about the doctor, because, she said, it had nothing to do with the rest of the poem. Daddy understood it a lot better. But anyway I knew somehow inside myself that it was written now and to alter it would be worse than forgery. I didn't know myself where it had come from. I hardly dared to put my own name at the bottom.

Once Daddy brought home from somewhere a magazine, with a huge picture of a girl in blue tights and a boater, hugging a book nearly as big as herself with "Down with School" written on the cover. I cut her out and stuck her inside my desk lid, to brighten it up. My desk soon collected dozens of inscriptions from forms who had lessons in our classroom, "Hear Hear," "Seconded," and so on.

Then I stuck on the top of the desk a headline from a newspaper, "SOLVE IT WITH VITALITY PLUS!" It cheered me up an awful lot in the duller lessons. I always kept a bunch of wild flowers and leaves in the inkwell. The teachers looked at me queerly when they went by, but they didn't say anything. I'd have thought a great deal less of them if they had. It looked really pretty, especially when I lit my candle.

The leaves had all turned now, and were falling too. I spent all my break and lunch hour running about trying to catch them. There were all sorts of trees, oaks and acacias and chestnuts, and leaves never stopped floating down. It was all a great improvement on those dreary trees I had caught leaves under on the pavements.

In the middle of October the weather had turned fine again; but it only lasted a week or two. One day when I ran out to catch leaves early in November it was wild and stormy, with the sky so dark that the trees on the hill looked pale and mad against it. It looked like a negative. Usually trees look tones and tones darker than the sky, but now they had caught the light somehow.

There was a tremendous gale blowing in gusts too. I ran and shouted, while the leaves flew by me so fast that when they hit me they stung. Everyone else had gone indoors, and I was all alone. Suddenly it began to hail too, specks of ice that burnt my face and hands. The torrent of leaves was rushing by me faster than I could run, all mixed in with hailstones. The air was so thick with them that I could hardly see anything. I stood facing into the wind with my arms flung out, trying to catch the leaves as they whirled past. I found I was laughing hysterically. There was ice in my mouth.

The bell went, and reluctantly I pulled myself together and went back to the school. It seemed just then a very long, steeply uphill journey, though in fact it was perfectly flat. I found the other girls huddled together in the cloakroom, all without exception doing their hair. I couldn't help giggling at Peacock. She was back-combing her hair, and it stood upright on her head, like a golliwog's.

"I know, you're laughing at me," she said. "It's a dreadful habit. Don't you try it, Birdie. It's ruined my hair."

"Oh, mine too," Frankie said, back-combing energetically. "It's split all the ends. You won't do it, Birdie, will you?"

"Oh, very well," I laughed, watching as Peacock gave a few pats to her hair, and suddenly from looking ridiculous it looked glamorous and beautiful. She was pretty, except when she looked sulky. She looked sulky all the time in the lessons.

Apple and Bobbles were doing their hair in the doorway, staring out.

"I love this weather," Bobbles was saying. "It makes me feel all desperate and gorgeous."

"Oh, it does, doesn't it!" I agreed fervently. "I wish we could have our lessons out in it."

Fishscale was doing Slinky's hair for her. I went across to say hullo.

"And her daddy began to undress, you see," Slinky was saying. "So the little girl said 'What's that?' And he said, 'That's my golliwog'. So she said, 'Can I play with it?' . . ."

I ran upstairs and flung open the classroom door. There were a couple of boys there, to my amazement sitting with Chicken in the girls' half. When I came in they scuttled away to their own corner with the transistor radio they had been playing.

" 'Listen with Mother'," Chicken said cheerfully to me. "Typical, isn't it? By the way, what on earth were you doing, running about in the rain down on the tennis courts, Birdie? I saw you chasing about in the wet grass, and I wondered if you'd gone quite batty, or what."

"I wasn't being batty at all," I said indignantly. "I was just enjoying myself. It wasn't rain, it was hail, you see. I was having a lovely time."

Chicken looked at me, mystified. I went over to the window and stared out. The light had gone off the trees and everything was just dark. I stared up at the black clouds for a rainbow, but I couldn't see one, although the sun was shining quite brightly through a gap in the clouds on the other side of the room. Then I thought I saw the ghost of one, but it might just have been that I had been staring too long.

29

Peacock stormed into the classroom and flung her satchel down without speaking to anyone.

"What's up, Peac?" asked Frankie, alarmed.

"It's Mum. Oh, it was row, row, row all night because I'd gone to that dance without telling her who with. 'Who'd you go with?' she said and I said, 'It's none of your business, Mum, so just you leave off,' so she says, 'I'm not having you going out if I don't know who with,' and I said, 'See here, I was in by eleven o'clock, so I don't see why I should tell you,' you see, and she said 'All right, tomorrow you can stay at home then'." Peacock was nearly crying. "And she went on and on—all night."

"And then this morning—honestly, I only wanted some biscuits, you see. 'Can I have some biscuits for my break, Mum?' I said, and she flies off the handle."

"What a time you have. I never have any rows with my mum," I said.

"Oh, well, you're lucky. You must have a decent mum," said Peacock. "My mum's horrible."

"My mum's lovely," I said. I noticed that the top two buttons of Peacock's V-necked summer dress were undone again. I hesitated, wondering whether to tell her, but decided against it. Frankie's dress was the same and so were Fishscale's and Slinky's. Twice yesterday I had pointed it out to them, they had giggled and said, "Oh, look, I'm indecent," and ten minutes later they'd had three buttons undone. They might as well not have bothered, for all the attention the boys paid. Only the girls noticed.

I couldn't understand why they all wore the summer uniform anyway, so late in the autumn. It was bitterly cold, and I was wearing a thick jersey under my winter blouse.

I made friends with Apple and Bobbles soon afterwards. They were enthusiastic Girl Guides and never ever mentioned boys or sex. It wasn't that I didn't like Fishscale and Slinky, I was just getting a little tired of their sole topic of conversation. Apple and Bobbles talked about the Guide jumble sale and the number of recruits to go in the Kingfisher Patrol and the best sort of knot to use on the new washing-up gadget Captain had told them to make and whether they could use it at camp next year.

After a while I joined their Guide company. It was no use being friends with them if you weren't in it. Bobbles put me in her patrol, and was awfully pleased with me at first because I was so keen and sent for my uniform direct from Headquarters so that I had it at once. Then the Tenderfoot test was all learning by heart, or almost all, and I got through that in no time.

"You're going to be a really good Guide, Birdie," she said. "We're all expecting you to set an example to the company so that all the slackers will pull themselves together." That was a bit frightening, to begin with.

I couldn't tie my tie. Apple and Bobbles spent all the meeting-time and hours and hours of break at school trying to teach me, but it was no use. When I came home to try for myself I simply couldn't remember. Finally I got Bobbles to tie it beautifully for me, and never undid it, just ran our old iron over it. I thought I had found a perfect solution, but Bobbles caught me out and made me stop. I didn't, in fact, which meant breaking the Guide Law about obedience every week.

I couldn't seem to make myself look neat. Whatever I did there was always something wrong. Bobbles admitted to me that it didn't matter what the Guides did so long as they always looked as if they'd come straight off parade. I couldn't help feeling there was something wrong there. So she made me wear my belt too tight, to look nice. All the other things I stupidly did, like forgetting to brush my beret, or getting my shoes muddy on the way, were my fault of course, but Bobbles made them out to be of such primary importance, and kept on and on at me about them even at school, that life became one long inspection parade. But it was the stalking that really finished me.

We had prize-giving at the end of the term, about a week before we broke up for Christmas. There weren't many actual prizes, only games colours and things, and they presented a lot of certificates. I thought it was dull and didn't attend much, but Mummy, who had gone out of duty, was tremendously enthusiastic.

"I feel awfully bucked about that, I really do," she kept saying. "I counted—there were five boys with seven O levels and two with nine, and masses of girls with eight. One had nine too I think. Yes, but did you notice all the A levels? There were three distinctions. That's really something. I bet Haversham couldn't beat that."

"I don't know, Mummy," I said.

"Don't sound so bored. You see, I was afraid when we moved here that we were doing you out of your education, and that a little country grammar school like this mightn't come up to standard. I'm really quite relieved. Three A level distinctions!"

"You don't want me to do that, do you?" I said, alarmed.

"Good gracious, no. It's perfectly maddening that you've got to take any G.C.E. at all. I only wish you didn't have to. But there, your art school man said you needed it, though I really don't see why, but I suppose he knows what he's talking about."

"I suppose he does," I said. "I think we've started the G.C.E. syllabus in English already."

"Have you indeed?" Mummy said. "Well, I'm delighted they take it so seriously."

As we got on to the bus Mummy tripped over the coat she was carrying over her arm and it fell on to the floor, exposing the basket she had covered with it. I had been wondering what she could possibly want a basket at prize-giving for, because she did all her shopping by telephone, and except for special occasions never left Tedford. In the basket were three vile-looking jam-jars and some bottles filled with some sort of green filth.

"Yes, I think I've been brilliant getting that. I want to be admired," said Mummy proudly. "You've no idea the trouble it was. Wading about in horrible stagnant mud in the freezing cold scooping up scum in a tablespoon, and all the slimiest scum was out of reach so that I got soaked getting it. Ugh! Ugh!"

I admired her suitably.

"All right, you can stop now," she said laughing. "I do think it was sheer genius though. I got Mr. Evans to lend me his waders, and then I found that lovely smelly backwater I pointed out to you from the bus a while ago, you remember. It was miles, right the other side of Bennington, and I had to go through someone's back garden, but I found it—" She looked eagerly at me. I praised her a bit more for her perseverance, ingenuity, resourcefulness, determination—

"Oh, thank you," she said gratefully. "It's for the goldfish, you see. I think they're getting frankly anaemic on that horrid dried Daphnia I've been giving them."

"Oh! Ah!" I said, light dawning.

"You're supposed to give them live pond food," Mummy explained. "But it's just struck me that perhaps dried fleas don't count as live pond food. So I got them this as a treat."

"You're so good to them, Mummy. I only hope they're grateful."

"Oh, I think they are. I shouldn't be surprised if two of those red ones in Daddy's room were ready to spawn soon."

We all sat in a row at the back bench for chemistry, Peacock, Frankie, Tiddles, Poppy, Baggles, Chicken and me, and none of us ever stopped talking. Fishscale and Slinky sat round the corner. It was a daunting sight for the poor chemistry master. Occasionally he threw bits of chalk at us, or came and bonked us on the head with his long ruler, but as a rule he just tried to ignore us and kept his eyes firmly fixed on the boys in front. They took a bit more interest than us, because they did some practical chemistry while the girls did domestic science.

Fishscale and Slinky played consequences together. I could hear them going on incessantly, "They met in the ladies, and he said, 'Your face needs washing', and she said blank blank blank, and the consequence was they ended up with three littluns..." The trouble with them was that they were suffering from wish-unfulfilment. Neither of them had a boy-friend. Slinky once asked me pathetically, "What have other girls got that I haven't got?" It was impossible to answer, but whatever it was, she didn't have it.

The rest of us just gossiped. The chemistry master was remarkably patient, really.

"I'll tell you who I like—Mick Thurloe, in the sixth form. Oh, I think he's gorgeous!"

"He took June Dobson out once. She said he was slimy."

"Oh, she would, she's like that. He isn't a bit slimy. Nor's Jeff, and she called him a drip. She just finds fault with everyone."

238

"Haven't you got a boy-friend, Birdie?"

"Oh, dear me, no," I said. "I just haven't any sex-appeal."

They all tittered and giggled.

"Poor old Birdie," said Baggles. "Aren't you interested in boys then?"

"I wouldn't know," I hedged. "They aren't interested in me."

"Well, put it this way: would you say boys were your speciality?"

"Oh, yes. No doubt at all. I'm an expert on boys. I can tell one at sight," I laughed.

"Well, never mind, Birdie," Baggles said kindly. "One day there'll come along a nice young man and he'll hear you reciting poetry to yourself or something and he'll carry you off."

"So come in, my Eric Stevens dear," I sang, remembering the rhyme at primary school, but of course nobody understood.

I spent my spare time painting. I did dozens of huge stylized pictures and books and books of pencil sketches. Most of them were appallingly bad, and Mummy always took my pictures away from me as soon as I had finished them and kept them safe in case I tore them up.

It really was a very cold winter, though there wasn't much snow, and the wind howled through our wretchedly thin tunics. They weren't nearly as warm as the one I was used to, the St. Rhadigond's tunic. All the same, I wasn't away once all the Spring term, and didn't get flu or gland trouble or anything more than a cold. Every day I expected to feel that familiar pain in my jaw, but I never did. It was wonderful. I noticed that it was quite unusual for anyone to be away. Mr. Murphy never bothered to call the register. If anyone was absent, you couldn't help noticing. It was news. At St. Rhadigond's a full class was a great rarity, but here it was expected.

When we came back after our summer half-term holiday at the beginning of June, there was a notice pinned to the board in the hall headed "Time-table. Summer examinations, June 21st-28th." That threw everyone into a panic. We went round gasping and fanning ourselves and saying "Only three weeks more to live," as if the summer exams were the last thing we had been expecting.

"It's like this every year," Baggles confided to me. "We get all scared and have heart failures and make a lot of fuss about nothing. I'm always the worst."

She was quite right. For three solid weeks she kept up the hysterics, taking home whole deskfuls of books and sitting up till eleven at night revising. Turnip, who was clever too, and Tiddles were nearly as bad, and Poppy was the worst of all. She was continually having fits and going out to be sick. She would come staggering out in the lessons, panting romantically and scarlet in the face, and sometimes she would be found in a dead faint in the cloakroom by Baggles, who went out to look after her, and sometimes she would just be sick all over the senior mistress's study. She did one or the other regularly, every day, especially in chemistry, when the bad egg fumes were too much for her.

I did some rather half-hearted revision for the first week, and some really concentrated hard work all the rest of the time. I summarized our year's work again and again, I made notes from the prosy useless textbook and learnt them in rhymes, I drew little maps that looked like things I could remember. You drew Popeye in profile and marked his mouth "Red Earth Region," and you had a lovely map of China. I really did work hard, though not as hard as Baggles. But she made everything twice as difficult by learning it all straight from the textbook, which was no more use than a sick headache.

We finally had the exams, and it was a wonder that Baggles and Poppy ever got anything written at all. They were out somewhere being sick the whole time. I kept myself going with my motto "SOLVE IT WITH VITALITY PLUS!" In fact I almost enjoyed some of the exams, the ones like English and French and history. Maths and science were ridiculous. We had made a dreadful jump in physics from the (comparatively) easy things we had been doing to electricity. I got as far as copying the diagram, and then got stuck. I couldn't imagine how to start any of the other questions, they were all calculations. So I drew Mummy's Black Moor goldfish in my diagram, which was meant to be a tank of electro-plate.

That took up five minutes. I was settling in to an hour and twenty minutes of boredom when Poppy rushed out of the room, stumbling and choking. For once Baggles was reluctant to go with her, as she had only begun her own exam. I put up my hand.

"I'll go, sir," I said to Mr. Murphy. "I can't do any more of this."

The class laughed, and the poor man winced. He had gone bravely on all through the year, trying to explain to me, tearing his hair and groaning. I didn't mean to be so beastly to him.

When we came to the end of the exams I was so tired that for the first time I was away from that school for two days, with a bad cold. When I came back most of the results were out.. I had had one per cent in physics, everyone told me that at once. Some of the boys actually spoke to me, congratulating me warmly. I wondered very much how I had got the one per cent. Most probably I owed it to the goldfish. In spite of me, our form had beaten the A stream by quite a bit in physics. That was really a triumph for Mr. Murphy, who was a first-class teacher.

A little later, when the ribaldry had had a chance to die down, Baggles disclosed to me that I had pipped her by one mark in history, and was top, that she had pipped me by one mark in scripture and I was second, and that she had made a mess of geography and again I had just beaten her. That was undoubtedly all Popeye's doing. I had also apparently come top in English and French. I was very surprised about the French, but there was no doubt about it, I was a clear three per cent ahead of Baggles. I was bottom with a per cent or so for luck in maths and chemistry. Fishscale had beaten me and was second to bottom. Slinky was bottom with me. I think she was bottom in everything, but I didn't like to ask.

That meant I was in the first three in everything but maths and science, and that I was top in five subjects and second in form order. I felt triumphant. I didn't need my vitality plus motto any more; I took it down and put it inside my desk. I had vitality plus anyway. I scribbled a few more "Hear Hears" inside my desk lid beside my blue-stocking, who was still stuck there with her slogan "Down with School," and ran outside.

"Did you know you're wearing odd socks, Birdie?" Baggles called out.

"Am I?" I said. Now that I looked at them closely, I could see that one of them was sort of ridgy and embroidered and the other was plain. "Oh, I don't think they're that bad. They're the same colour at least."

"Oh, well, the boys'll like you just as much," said Baggles, smiling indulgently. I grinned at her, and ran down on to the lawns. I sat down in a nice comfortable position so that I could spend the whole lunch hour watching the light all green under the trees, or in staring up into the great chestnut.

In music we suddenly went Irish and learnt a whole batch of Irish songs—"In Dublin's fair city," the "Londonderry Air," the one about the harp in Tara's halls, and so on. It was a coincidence that our music lesson came directly before the physics lesson. When we were let out we romped upstairs to the physics lab, shouting out, "Hurrah! Hurrah! for the girls of Dubelin town! Hurrah for the bonny green flag, the harp without a crown."

As we knew perfectly well, Mr. Murphy always arrived early for that lesson. He was waiting there when we came in. We all started to stamp our feet and bang on the benches, still singing loudly. Baggles did a beautiful descant. Poor Mr. Murphy shouted at us, blushing and running his hand through his hair.

"Hurrah—Hurrah—for the girls of Dubelin town!" we bawled, stamping in time.

"Oh, come on, sir, join in. This ought to interest you," Jones called out.

"Yes, sir, tell us about them!" shouted Chicken.

Mr. Murphy waved his arms about despairingly. I could guess he was saying "Just keep quiet, the lot of you," but in that din you could only see his mouth moving.

Suddenly a grim face appeared scowling in the pane in the door. It was the headmaster. We all shut up instantly and cowered behind the benches. To our intense relief he turned away and didn't come in, but the very sight of his face left us sitting quiet and subdued.

"Now," said Mr. Murphy, "as a punishment you're going to do some work."

In maths we went on to a peculiar thing called "Relative Speed." It wasn't too bad at all. There was no algebra in it anywhere. It was practically back to those golden days of simple arithmetic and problems. Here at last is something I can do, I thought in delight.

When Mr. Dearn had finished explaining I started on a question by myself. It said, "A train leaves Newcastle at 2.30 p.m. travelling at 25 m.p.h. At 3.14 another train leaves in the same direction, travelling at 50 m.p.h. When will the express overtake the first train?"

Eagerly I started. The method was obvious. I worked out how far the first train had got when the second one left, with much effort. When I had managed that I worked out how long it took the second train to get to wherever the first train had been when the other left. It was all very laborious and difficult, but I felt determined to get at least one sum right for the first time since I had left primary school. Then I found how far the first train had got in that time, and how long it took the express to cover that distance, and how far the slow train went in that time, and how long the other took to go that far, and how far the first train went in that time, and ... My brain was in a whirl. It didn't seem to be so simple after all. Why, at this rate the express'll never even catch up with the other, I thought. I seem to be going on and on without ever getting anywhere.

I pulled myself together and went on. When the lesson ended the first train was only a little bit ahead. But in the next lesson we went back to algebra, and I never did finish the sum. I knew there was only a small bit left to do, but somehow I had got discouraged. I tried to get it done in break, but I didn't quite, and anyway everyone else had finished ages ago and kept telling me the answer when they saw me still working.

When I came home Daddy was gloating over a beautiful new art book he had bought, with coloured reproductions of pictures by his favourite artist, Modigliani. We all agreed they were fascinating. I did a weird Modigliani-style picture myself, and we all began to talk excitedly about Montparnasse and pernod. Daddy said he only objected to one thing in Modigliani, and that was that he shouted out "Italy!" on his deathbed, when there he was penniless and dying of drink in Paris, and what more could any painter want? Mummy winced at that, but I sympathized.

We spent our summer holiday in Paris, naturally enough, in a little hotel in a side street on the Left Bank, and we filled the bedrooms with wet pictures and palettes to make it look more realistic. Daddy painted his pictures in a smock with a huge bohemian bow, which Mummy had found for him. I wore jeans and a loose shirt, and painted like Modigliani, only

243

I carried it even further, and my pictures were even more extraordinary.

"What I like about us," I said, as we sat in the Dome, watching Daddy's pernod go milky as he poured the water into it, "is that we're such splendidly typical trippers."

"Unashamedly so!" laughed Mummy.

"Oh, of course. But who but us would take it in such earnest, sitting in this café of all cafés, thinking everyone we see is really a destitute poet?"

"Oh, well, if it makes us happy," said Daddy. "Anyway, I like to feel I'm following in Modigliani's footsteps."

"Don't!" said Mummy.

"I'd like you to be a student. Why aren't you at the Sorbonne?" said Daddy suddenly, turning to me.

"Well," I said, "if you want me to change schools again—"

"Oh, yes, I'd forgotten, we live in England, don't we? Still, listen, Antonessa-Vanessa, some time you shall come and be a student at the Sorbonne and wear startling jeans and go to lectures about Molière's incorrect use of the subjunctive, so you'd better be practising your French."

"Oh, Man, what wonderful ideas you have," I said enthusiastically. "I'll look forward to that."

30

WE STARTED THE G.C.E. course next term, ready to take it the following June. Somehow, by degrees, I began to feel tension in the atmosphere again. It was in sharp contrast to our happy relaxation just after the exams. Within a week of coming back from the summer holidays Poppy began to have attacks again. You couldn't pin it down to anything, but we were getting nervier and nervier. Work was increasing too, naturally enough. But it wasn't just due to that that we were all so ridiculously strung-up.

There was some rumour put out by someone that the world was going to end on that Saturday, and the newspapers gave it publicity, treating it as a joke. When we came to school on Friday I was surprised to see Turnip in a worse state than usual, pale and shivering. Poppy, apparently, was so bad that she hadn't come to school at all. Everyone felt vaguely uncomfortable and didn't know what to say to Turnip. Baggles hardly spoke, either, which cast quite a gloom even over the teachers.

In break Turnip broke down altogether and began to cry. Everyone scuttled nervously out of the classroom, including the prefect who was supposed to be forcing us all to go outside. Baggles ran up to Turnip and put her arms round her.

"Oh, Turnsie, what's the matter? What is it, dearie?" I heard her say as I slunk out of the door.

When I came back in ten minutes and wandered past the window I saw Turnip still sobbing away on Baggles' shoulder. I didn't dare do more than glance, but I thought Baggles was crying too. They weren't in class when we had to go back at the end of break. I heard later they finished their cry in the cloakroom, miles away.

Turnip and Poppy still looked rather shaken and subdued even on Monday. I wondered if they were ill. But Poppy said to me in break,

"Honestly, Turnip and I were so scared all Saturday, we just sat in each other's houses all day. We just had to be together. Quaking in our shoes, we were. You know, we sat up till all hours, Turnip wouldn't go to bed alone, so we just sat there scared stiff, waiting for the world to end."

"But these rumours crop up every other year," I said. "You don't mean to say you believe them all?"

She laughed, a nervous high-pitched laugh. "Oh, I know it was silly. But honestly, we were in such a state. I felt too sick to eat anything—oh, it was awful."

"What a time you have," I said. I could hardly believe that anyone could get into such a tizzy about something so silly. But it was just the sort of thing Turnip might get worked up about, I supposed. She was always worrying about her work, too, trying to keep in the first three in form order. I could just imagine her and Poppy huddling in their fall-out shelters. Poor things, I thought, they'll never live to leave school.

"You know I only came seventeenth in the exams," Poppy said anxiously. "Do you think I've got a hope for G.C.E.? D'you know, I'm really scared about that."

"Well, I don't see that you've any need to be, you do awfully well in class. It was just that you were ill during the exams. Nobody can do well in an exam if they're ill."

"Oh, no, Birdie, you don't understand at all. I was only ill because of the exams. And I'm not going to get any better for G.C.E. I just know I'm going to fail, I just know it."

I could think of nothing better to say than "Well, don't make up your mind about it now."

"Hi, Bags," Poppy called. "I was just telling Birdie about how I'm scared of G.C.E."

"Oh, Poppy!" said Baggles, looking as if she'd been hit. "If you're scared, what about me? Everyone expects me to do well. You know, I dream about it every night. Aren't you scared, Birdie?"

"Well, no," I said. "I hadn't thought about it much, really. After all, we were at the top of the class. You were first. And it's a year off anyway. I always make a point of not getting scared till the day before the exam." I looked hopefully at them to see if they looked reassured.

We were doing Keats in English and were in the middle of

going through *Ode to a Nightingale* when the prefect came in. "Now just concentrate on those lines," said Miss Fairbanks.

" 'Charmed magic casements, opening on the foam
Of perilous seas, in faery lands forlorn'."

"The headmaster would like to see Antonia Bird, please," said the prefect.

Miss Fairbanks nodded. "Just think to yourself what image those lines bring into your mind. Perilous seas . . . faery lands forlorn . . . what do they bring to your imagination? Perilous seas . . ."

I jumped out of the magic casement and sailed in my faery barque towards the prefect, who galloped ahead on a flying horse and led me towards the enchanted portal of the Study Dolorous. I knocked, and the headmaster said, "Come in." I went in, feeling a bit shaky round the knees.

"Now, madam," he said. "I take it you know your exam marks in maths, physics and chemistry?"

"Yes, Sir Saracen—yes sir," I stammered.

He stared at me with black, black eyes that went right through me and nailed me to the wall.

"And what have you to say for yourself?"

"W-well—I really do find maths awfully hard, sir."

"Oh, you do, do you?"

I gulped. "Yes, sir."

"Now I find that very hard to understand. You're an intelligent girl, in fact you're an extremely clever girl, as your other results show. Now it's quite natural that you should have some slight difficulty in maths. I'm the same myself. But I really cannot believe that you are as bad as you have been making yourself out to be."

"Well, sir, it's algebra," I managed to gasp out. "I just can't begin to make sense of it. And physics is all algebra, too."

"You can't understand algebra? But an intelligent girl should have no difficulty with that. After all, it's basically common sense."

"But I do, Mr. Deane explains one sum to me, and I try to go over it five minutes later and I just can't remember one word, not even how he began or anything."

"But that's ridiculous. It's forty years since I did any algebra, and I can remember it perfectly. Now listen. I don't think you

can realize how important it is to you to do well in every subject, not just the ones you happen to like. It's no good just
picking and choosing. You must try at everything, do you hear,
everything. Every subject on the curriculum is useful, you'll
need it. You wouldn't be learning it otherwise."

I thought about the algebra that he hadn't done for forty
years.

"No university will take you without a Science subject, let
alone Oxford or Cambridge. You could get into Oxford if you
put your whole mind to it. Your *whole* mind and nothing less."

That pulled me up with a jerk. Suddenly I understood. Ever
since I had come top in five subjects I had been labelled
"Oxford possible." Oh, no, oh, no. Not that again, I thought
miserably.

I was in there with the headmaster for three-quarters of an
hour. It was a real genuine Miss Mackintosh. I must try at
maths, what's more I must come top in it, and in physics, and
in chemistry. After forty-five minutes' hard hammering I was
reduced to tears. As a matter of fact I owed my life to that.
When I started snivelling and looking for a handkerchief the
headmaster said, "Well, I don't want to draw this out. In future
I am going to instruct the staff to punish you if you continue
to slack," and dismissed me.

I stumbled out. He doesn't believe me, I thought, he thinks
I'm lying. He thinks I can do maths perfectly well if I want to.
He thinks I just enjoy being bottom. It's going to be detention,
detention, all the way, a whole nightmare year of it. Why on
earth did I bother to leave St. Rhadigond's?

I found my class in the passage between the geography room
and our form-room. I joined on to the end of the line, still
feeling dazed.

"Oh, hullo, Birdie! He had you in there long enough, didn't
he?"

"What was he on about?"

"Oh, blah blah blah," I said. "He'd just got round to signing
my exam results, and noticed my maths. It wasn't so bad,
actually, because he had his fire on and it was lovely and warm
in there. Tell me what vile homework we've got for English."

I went over and over the interview in my mind all day. I could
still feel the headmaster's eyes boring through me. He had thick
dark hair that half-hid his eyes so that you might if you were in

favour get away with the impression that he was an amiable looking man. But, if he stared straight at you, it was enough to give you nightmares ever after. I really did go cold all over when I remembered him saying, "So you spend roughly an hour and a half on your homework? *How roughly?*"—at the same time paralysing me with that awful stare.

When I had finished describing the interview to Daddy, he just looked as if he felt sick and said, "Schoolteachers! Ugh!"

"But he's such a nice man," said Mummy. "Sort of nondescript but quite pleasant."

"Pleasant! Nondescript!" I gasped.

"What a mug you were to come top in five subjects in the exams," said Daddy crossly.

"Yes, that was silly of you, wasn't it," Mummy said.

"Oh, I'm sorry!" I said, hiding my face with my napkin. "I thought everyone would be so pleased."

"Poor Child, and instead we're all angry," laughed Mummy. "And now what? I suppose they'll kill you to get you up to Oxford standard."

It certainly looked as if they had every intention of doing so. About a week after the interview the headmaster transferred me to the A stream, the clever stream. It was rather like changing schools. I had to get used to a whole lot of new girls. But that didn't worry me. It was the lessons. I was frightened of the maths and science and tried like anything, but we had suddenly leapt miles ahead, and as I was shockingly behind anyway I didn't have a hope. I began to get extra work detentions, here and there.

The A stream had a different English teacher, the senior master for maths and physics, the other history teacher and another mistress for geography and scripture. I didn't know any of them. They seemed somehow distant, but I thought it was only because they were strange to me and trying to keep me up to the mark, and that it would soon be all right. But it wasn't, somehow. I could never seem to get more than six or seven out of ten, even in English. Once I spent the whole evening, absurdly, killing myself to write what I thought was a brilliant essay. I handed it in and waited in suspense to see what the master would say. About a week later it came back marked "6 minus 3 for untidy handwriting$=\frac{3}{10}$."

"I think it would be best if in future you wrote much less and concentrated more on your writing, Antonia," said the master. "Meanwhile would you re-write it really neatly in the lunch hour? Can't you manage to write italic, or Irene Wellington, or something? I've never seen a writing like yours before. I'm sure you can't have learnt it at school." He was right, I hadn't. Mummy had taught it to me.

Maths was trigonometry now, a desperate mixture of algebra and geometry of a queer kind. There were all sorts of funny tables and signs that I simply couldn't fathom. Once Mr. Rogers explained in great detail a sum to me, about finding angles of triangles when you were allowed to use books of tables but not a protractor (why one more than the other?) and for homework he set me specially a sum which he said was identical. I slaved away for hours at it. I had no difficulty at all in imagining myself back at St. Rhadigond's. It was just the same nowadays. As I worked, the lecture the headmaster had given me at that interview went round and round inside my head. "If I were you, I'd say to myself : 'I'll master this if it kills me.' I'd sit down and I'd work and work at that maths if it took me all night every night, until I understood it. That's what you ought to do. A girl of your ability has no right to slack. You should go flat out at everything all the time, particularly at subjects you don't like. In future I'm going to see that you do." I remembered that apart from the first interview when I changed schools this was the first time he had ever spoken to me. I was getting the idea about schoolteachers now. They were only there to scold you, and they scolded you if you did well and they scolded you if you did badly and the only way to escape was to pretend to be stupid and come in the middle.

It was the square root tables that put everything wrong. I'd almost hoped I was getting that sum right until then. After that it was minuses all the way, right up to the answer, when it finished up "Angle CBR $= -36°$." I thought hard, and finally decided that if there hadn't previously been such a thing as a minus angle there was now, and I wasn't going to settle in to another hour's work redoing the sum just for the sake of a silly little dash. I felt tired and depressed and fed up, and at that moment I simply didn't care if I did get detention next day.

I did, of course, and just as at St. Rhadigond's, it led on to a whole long incessant chain of detentions, extra work, staying in at break, in every subject. I had to give up painting, except on Sundays, because there wasn't time for that and for homework. Mummy said, "Well, if it's either or, I know which I'd choose," and always seemed quite cross when I did the homework.

Meanwhile Daddy was getting Christmassy, at the same time as being Parisian, so that he was going about wearing bohemian artists' bows with bits of tinsel stuck in them, and wearing his Damuels ski-ing beanie with his artist's smock, which he really did wear for painting and managed to get covered in paint. Christmas cards were coming in by every post, from either Mummy or me. Daddy went about chuckling and singing Christmas carols or else sitting in front of our yuley loggy fire shrugging his shoulders and saying, "Non. Ce n'est pas vrai. Tu le crois, hein, chérisette?" which meant he was thinking about rickety attics and *La Bohème*.

When I went back to school after the Christmas holidays I somehow hoped that all the rows would have blown over and it would all be back to normal, and I would be able to run about looking for new grass and opening buds in the lunch hour instead of doing extra chemistry, and gossip with Baggles and Peacock as I used. But it wasn't, of course. In fact the tension and pressure were worse than ever. Only a term and a half left, and I was no further on in my bad subjects. I still couldn't even understand basic things in maths like what an equation actually meant. Mr. Rogers wasn't much help there. He only said silly things like "It doesn't *mean* anything," which in fact I had gathered long ago.

By March, Daddy's wanderlust was so bad that he was quite pathetic. He said, "Why did I have to send you to school? Why should some niggling schoolmaster stop me from going to Paris when I want to? Why have you got to have your Easter holidays so late? Why don't you do something about it? Move Easter, or get ill, or something."

One evening, as I was slaving away at my biology, dreadfully behind because of my physics calculations taking so long (even then I hadn't got them right) Daddy suddenly looked up and demanded, "What are you doing, Antonina-Selina?"

"Well, just now," I said, "I'm writing notes about the life history of the tapeworm."

"The *tapeworm*?"

"Yes, Daddy, how it pushes through the pig's intestine and embeds itself in the flesh—and then I'm going to draw a diagram—"

"Well, why are you? Why don't you stop and go to Paris? When can you leave school?"

"I don't know, Daddy. Not in my lifetime, anyway."

"No, that's what I think. What's school-leaving age? Sixteen? Seventeen?"

"Fifteen, I think, isn't it?" said Mummy.

"Fifteen, is it? How old are you?" Daddy asked me.

"I'm fifteen, Daddy," I said, smiling, as I remembered how he had stuck my fifteen candles into my cake and had painted me a birthday card of an upside down 15. Then suddenly I realized what Daddy was getting at, and forgot all that.

"You're fifteen? You mean to say you've been going to school for months when you needn't have been? Oh, Totty!"

I gaped at him.

"And you can leave tomorrow, and we can be in Paris by Thursday—and we can drink absinthe in the Deux Magots—and paint abstracts—and live in a studio—" He was chattering with excitement. "You must paint too. We'll all paint. And you shall have that term at the Sorbonne I've always promised you, and wear black jeans and be a student, hein chérisette?"

"Oh, Daddy!" I gasped. "Oh Man! But—but what about my G.C.E.? I can't leave in the middle of studying for that. I'm taking it in June."

"Oh, never mind that." Daddy waved it aside. "You can study for it by correspondence in Paris, and fly home for a week in June to sit for it, and have the autumn term at the Sorbonne."

"Yes! Yes!" Mummy shouted. "Oh Child, you're liberated!"

"No more school? No more school?" I felt dazed. "No more school!" I jumped up, kicking over my desk. "No more rows and bullyings and headmasters and maths and physics—and the Sorbonne instead of sixth form—and art school instead of Oxford—Oh, do you really mean it?"

"Now, Tot, you can't say we're trippers now," Mummy said. "Queuing for chewing-gum soup with all the most penniless poets in Paris, and you almost a student, and certainly looking like one."

252

"No, we're not trippers now," I laughed. "And Daddy's a real bearded bohemian artist, and you're a real Parisian goldfish-breeder." Daddy was shrugging and muttering into his beard, probably something about "Tu n'as pas raison, chérisette."

We hadn't been able to get a studio, of course. We kept seeing them advertised and got very excited, but it turned out that "studio" in French only means "bedsitter." But we squeezed into a pension in the Rue Jacob.

"How does that young man manage to look so thin?"

"Well, you'd look thin if you lived on black coffee."

"He isn't living on black coffee. He's just going to have chewing-gum soup. And that's the most filling thing I've ever eaten. He ought to be fat."

"He must be a poet then, and depending for his reputation on looking starved and romantic."

"How tiresome of him. It makes him look just like every other young man in Paris. I meant to make a huge collection of sketches of Parisian faces, but they're all exactly alike."

"Never mind, I think the pictures you've done of the American tourists are awfully good."

"Oh, yes, they are, aren't they?" said Daddy suddenly.

"And I simply love all yours," I said to him. "They're all peculiar. You could tell they were Paris anywhere."

"I was just thinking," said Daddy, "of one of that street, with the awning stretched across the picture like that, you see, and all the rest sort of chimney-pots and paving-stones, semi-abstract, you know."

"It does sound gorgeous," I said. "Do you think, Daddy, that I could knock off my American tourists for a while and paint that picture I was telling you about, the street next to ours through the bottom of a wine glass?"

Our turn for a table came round, and we went in and began our soup. It was supposed to be onion soup, with melted cheese on top. The cheese was chewing-gum, pure and simple. It even tasted of chewing-gum. Underneath was a most extraordinary mixture of lumps of bread and thick tangles of stringy vegetably stuff, which might or might not be onion, depending on how you were feeling. There was no question of being starved and poetic afterwards. We couldn't have eaten any more lunch if we had tried. We had it as an occasional treat. Usually we had a vile thing called *assiette allemande* at another restaurant, and there the queues were even longer and the people even younger and more haggard. It was the cheapest place we could find, and even then our *assiette* cost as much as steak and two veg. in England.

But today was my last lunch before I started on the special Sorbonne students' canteen meals. So we were having chewing-gum soup to celebrate. Though I wouldn't have dreamt of telling Mummy so, I was secretly looking forward to getting away from her and Daddy for a bit.

I got all the G.C.E. passes I needed, without having to bother with any of the subjects I couldn't do. I took English, language and literature, French, history, scripture, art and biology, which I had never found very difficult as it wasn't mathematical. That gave me seven passes and I only needed five.

I took all the exams in London, in a great room entirely filled with nuns and negroes, all taking G.C.E. too. The nuns were very calm and self-controlled, but the negroes all went on writing frantically long after we were told to stop. In my history exam I sat next to an albino negro, and all the time I was trying to make myself concentrate on Metternich I kept finding myself thinking about the albino and wondering whether he called him-self a black man. All the same, I managed to pass. Mummy had put me in for seven subjects on the automatic assumption that I would fail in at least two. I just had to pass in them all, after that.

31

I STARTED AT THE art school near Bennington at the beginning of the spring term. I went through the hall, looking for somewhere to put my stuff, and suddenly emerged into a small yard full of beefy-looking girls shovelling clay about. I retreated hastily, and stood looking round. I had felt so jubilant, coming home from France, but now I felt depressed and miserable. I thought about St. Rhadigond's and Bennington, and how I had started so confidently and then finished by running away from both of them, with everything gone wrong and a lot of new enemies. True, it had been maths in both cases that had sent everything wrong, and there wasn't any maths here. But I still wouldn't fit in, suddenly I realized that. Maths apart, I hadn't fitted in anywhere. I thought about all my friends who had turned out not to be friends—Tatley, Barker, Lynda, Fishscale, Bobbles—the list went on and on. I just wasn't the sort who made friends.

"Hullo, are you new? You look lost," said a boy, coming up.

"You're right, I am new and I am lost," I said.

"Well, all the other new people came last term you see, so we haven't got the welcome mats out for any more," the boy explained.

"I couldn't come last term, though. I was in Paris—at the Sorbonne."

"The Sorbonne!" He stared at me. "Well, you should brighten us all up a lot, then. I went through Paris when some of us went camping in Portugal last summer, but I never managed the Sorbonne."

His name turned out to be David, and he was in textile printing, which the principal had written to say I was to go into myself, straight away, omitting the usual preliminaries as I had missed the first term. David took me up to show me round before classes started. I was expecting him to order me about. Everyone always did. But he didn't. I was amazed.

The walls were covered with the most wonderful designs, squirls and shapes and squiggles, the sort of thing I had always longed to be able to do. I felt inspired even to see them. David showed me his. I particularly liked one, a pattern of broad intertwining loops and bands in different shades of blue.

"This is all cushy stuff," David said. "You wait till you get on to picking the fleas out of sheep in woven textiles!"

I laughed.

When we came out at the end of the afternoon I had half an hour to wait for my bus back to Tedford, and so I went across the road for some coffee with David.

"Who's your favourite artist?" he asked.

I began to tell him. Feininger, early Mondrian, Kokoschka.

"What about the old masters?" he interrupted. "Breughel for instance."

"Oh, I can't bear him," I said. "He was a caricaturist."

"A caricaturist! Oh, no. He just painted people as he saw them."

"I bet he didn't. All his people are alike, and they're all animals. They look exaggerated to me. Rembrandt, now . . ."

"Well, yes. Rembrandt had a different philosophy," he admitted.

I turned my cup round in my hands, mentally comparing Rembrandt and Breughel. It suddenly occurred to me that I was enjoying myself. Talking to a boy and enjoying it. It would have been fantastic, out of the question, with any other boy I had met before. It's all right, I thought. I do fit in. Art students still have their corners on. They've escaped. I've escaped. Everything's going to be all right after all.